THE PROFESSOR OF TRUTH

ames Robertson is the author of the novels *And the Land Lay Still*, *The Testament of Gideon Mack*, *Joseph Knight* and *The Fanatic*. *The Testament of Gideon Mack* was longlisted for the 2006 Man Booker Prize, picked by Richard and Judy's Book Club, and shortlisted for the Saltire Book of the Year Award. *And the Land Lay Still* was the winner of the Saltire Society Scottish Book of the Year Award 2010. James Robertson is also the author of *365*, a collection of 365-word short stories. A new story is being posted online on each day of 2014 at www.fivedials.com/365, and the complete collection will also be published in book form by Hamish Hamilton.

If

THE PROFESSOR
OF TRUTH

James Robertson

PENGUIN BOOKS

PENGUIN BOOKS

Published by the Penguin Group
Penguin Books Ltd, 80 Strand, London WC2R ORL, England
Penguin Group (USA) Inc., 375 Hudson Street, New York 10014, USA
Penguin Group (Canada), 90 Eglinton Avenue East, Suite 700, Toronto, Ontario, Canada M4P 2Y3
(a division of Pearson Penguin Canada Inc.)
Penguin Ireland, 25 St Stephen's Green, Dublin 2, Ireland
(a division of Penguin Books Ltd)
Penguin Group (Australia), 707 Collins Street, Melbourne, Victoria 3008, Australia
(a division of Pearson Australia Group Pty Ltd)
Penguin Books India Pvt Ltd, 11 Community Centre, Panchsheel Park, New Delhi – 110 017, India
Penguin Group (NZ), 67 Apollo Drive, Rosedale, Auckland 0632, New Zealand
(a division of Pearson New Zealand Ltd)
Penguin Books (South Africa) (Pty) Ltd, Block D, Rosebank Office Park, 181 Jan Smuts Avenue,
Parktown North, Gauteng 2193, South Africa

Penguin Books Ltd, Registered Offices: 80 Strand, London WC2R ORL, England

www.penguin.com

First published by Hamish Hamilton 2013
Published in Penguin Books 2014
001

Copyright © James Robertson, 2013
All rights reserved

The moral right of the author has been asserted

This is a work of fiction. Although the author has drawn on the Lockerbie bombing and
conviction of Abdelbaset al-Megrahi as inspiration, the characters in this work are entirely fictional
as is all dialogue and interaction between characters. Businesses, places, events and incidents are
either the products of the author's imagination or are used in a fictitious manner

Set in Fournier MT Std
Typeset by Palimpsest Book Production Limited, Falkirk, Stirlingshire
Printed in Great Britain by Clays Ltd, St Ives plc

ISBN: 978-0-241-14534-0

www.greenpenguin.co.uk

MIX
Paper from
responsible sources
FSC   FSC™ C018179
www.fsc.org

Penguin Books is committed to a sustainable
future for our business, our readers and our planet.
This book is made from Forest Stewardship
Council™ certified paper.

For Marianne, again, with love

The distance that the dead have gone
Does not at first appear;
Their coming back seems possible
For many an ardent year.

And then, that we have followed them
We more than half suspect,
So intimate have we become
With their dear retrospect.

Emily Dickinson

PROLOGUE

When I think of Nilsen now, how he came and vanished again in the one day, I don't feel any warmer towards him in the remembering than I did when he was here. I don't even feel grateful for what he gave me, because he and his kind kept it from me for so long. But I do think of the difficult journey he made, and why he made it. What set him off, he told me, was seeing me being interviewed on television, after Khalil Khazar's death. He said he'd watched the interview over and over. He'd wanted to feel what I felt. But you cannot feel what another person feels. You cannot even imagine it, however hard you try. This I know.

When Khalil Khazar died, the news went round the world in minutes – in text messages, in emails, through social networks, on radio and television, via websites and by telephone. I got the call at home from Patrick Bridger, a BBC journalist I knew and trusted. We'd talked, a week or so before the end, about what we would do and where we would film, knowing that it could not be long. 'Alan, I'm on my way with a cameraman and a soundman,' Patrick said. 'We'll pick you up and head straight to the location.' I didn't take any more calls. I was giving Patrick an exclusive. It was a way of controlling things.

While I waited for their car I thought about how the news would be received in different parts of the globe. There would be tears, I knew, but also there would be laughter. There would be grief and jubilation, clasped hands and clenched fists, loud dismay and quiet satisfaction. There would be one family mourning, other families celebrating. Some people would feel a sense of resolution, of justice having been done. Others would feel, as I did, a sense of things unresolved, of justice having not been done. A guilty man or an innocent man had gone to his grave: it depended on your perspective. Soon enough, politicians would be making statements; mere citizens such as myself would be making statements. Others, politicians and mere citizens alike, would be keeping their mouths closed. There would be headlines in the papers, archive footage on the news channels. Opinions would be voiced, opinions withheld. And through all the noise and all the silence, one thing and one thing only would be certain: Khalil Khazar was dead.

I knew what I was going to say in front of the camera. I had a good idea of the kind of questions Patrick would be asking. *What happens next? With Khazar's passing, will new information come to light? Do you think there is any previously unseen evidence that might prove his innocence? Or do we already know everything there is to be known about these events?* Would his guilt still stand, in other words, and was there nothing more to do but watch as more hatred was heaped on his departed soul?

Last night I replayed the clip of that interview and tried to see it from Nilsen's point of view. I found myself wondering about his life – where he had come from to reach me. I had no knowledge of him except what I'd gathered from those few hours we spent together. I watched myself speaking against a backdrop of old grey stone and grass so green with life it must have hurt him to look at it. The camera pulled back to reveal the castle, panned to show the town spreading down the hill, the farmland and hills in the distance. It looked like a good old country, Nilsen had told me, and it did. Scotland, at the end of a Scottish summer. I looked tired, he'd also said, and he was right about that too.

'I do not believe his death changes anything,' I said to the camera. 'I do not believe anything will happen as a result. I am sorry that he is dead, because he was a human being, like me. He had nothing to do with the bombing. He has died because of his illness, but still suffering a terrible injury, an injury that our justice system inflicted on him. I wish I could say that his death makes things different, or better, or that it closes a chapter, but none of that is true. Everything is still as it was, and we are no closer to finding out the truth about who really killed all those people twenty-one years ago, who killed my wife and daughter. There is nothing to celebrate today. I am sorry that Khalil Khazar is dead.'

Then Patrick asked his questions, and I answered them. While the clip was still playing, my phone rang. I paused the film and picked up the phone on the third ring. It was Carol.

'How are you doing?' she said.

'I'm fine,' I said. 'And you?'

'Fine. I've just finished writing that paper on Muriel Stuart.'

'Well done. Can I read it?'

'I was hoping you would. How have you got on today?'

'Not too badly,' I said. 'A bit of writing, a bit of thinking. I'll tell you when you come over.'

'Is that all right? If I come?'

'Yes. There's a bottle of wine in the fridge.'

'I'll be with you soon, then.'

'Good. Remember to bring your paper.'

She hung up, and I went back to my face, freeze-framed on the screen, older-looking than its years. I searched for my father in that face, but I did not see him. It was more like seeing a stranger, some grey visitant from the future peering in through a window. But it was myself, looking out from the past. I closed the thing down.

I thought of Nilsen deciding to make the journey, and me at the other end of it. He came with a purpose because, he'd said, it turned out that I was right in that interview. Khalil Khazar had died, and the world had waited – or it had not – for something to happen, and nothing had. One death – three hundred deaths – did not stop the world from turning.

Many things, of course, had happened. A tornado had left a trail of destruction. A civil war had raged. A famine had grown. A government had fallen. A sportsman had failed a drugs test. A film star had been exposed in some scandal. Weeks had become a month, two, three months. Snow had fallen. But Khalil Khazar had not spoken from the far side of his death.

So Nilsen decided to come and find me, and to make something happen before he ran out of time. He came because he could. He had knowledge, and it was in his power to give it to me.

I

ICE

I needed a break. I had been working for hours – or so I could just about persuade myself, since I'd been sitting at the computer all morning. Through the window I could see the sky still heavy with cloud, but the snow had stopped falling for the time being. I felt half-asleep: some fresh air might not be a bad thing.

I put on a jacket, gloves and thick socks. I was just lacing up my boots when the telephone rang. It was set to ring eight times before the answer-machine kicked in. I reached it on the fourth ring. I said, simply, 'Hello?' because I had learned that it was sometimes better to retain the option of not being myself, and a male voice said, 'Dr Tealing?' 'Who is this?' I asked, and the line went dead. I dialled 1471 and the familiar automated, polite, female voice intoned, *A caller who withheld their number rang, today, at 1227 hours. Thank you for calling. Please hang up.*

It was not so unusual. I didn't think much about it. I finished tying my boots, went outside, fetched the snow shovel from the garden shed, and started to dig a path from there to the back door of the house.

There had been quite a fall, three or four inches. Each shovelful lengthened the path I was making by less than a foot. The snow was dense and weighty. After a few minutes, despite the cold, I was sweating. Muscles in my back and shoulders began to protest, but I liked the feel of the effort. I worked like a machine, with regular, repetitive movements, and with the mindlessness of a machine. This, too, I liked. When I reached the back door I paused, stretched, then bent to the task again, this time going round the house to the street.

It is an ordinary suburban street, one of a number of drives, crescents and avenues that form a little residential district where once was rough pasture. The houses, most of them built in the 1960s, are modest in size and of no great character. When new, they were doubtless called contemporary. Now, surrounded by mature trees and hedges and having borne the effects of half a century of Scottish weather, they are all a little tired and dated. Some are doing better than others. Mine has not had the care and attention it might have received from someone else, or from myself in different circumstances.

I was – I am – a lecturer in English Literature. The University where I work is an institution of no great age located in a part of Scotland that positively groans under the accumulation of history. I am fifty-five as I write this, not much older than the University, yet I too feel the burden of past events upon me.

I am the PhD kind of doctor. Some of my colleagues are disdainful of other academics who do not have these letters after their names. I, obviously, do not attract such disdain. Instead I receive sympathy, or a kind of hushed reverence which has nothing to do with the power of my intellect and which I do not find flattering. There are occasions when I would much prefer their disdain. I am, after all, like most of them, only a lecturer. But I am special, because unlike any of them I lost my wife and daughter when the aeroplane in which they were travelling was blown out of the sky by a bomb.

I never wanted to be special, not for this or any other reason. Nevertheless, I am.

I could once have been a professor – *the* Professor – of English Literature. Important people in the University invited me to apply for the then vacant Chair, and I was advised that it was as good as mine if I wanted it. Yes, I could have been a real professor, and who

8

knows, somewhere in a storeroom there might even be a real chair, commissioned in the 1960s. That was eighteen years ago, when the code of governance concerning appointments was less rigorous, and to be told such a thing, and told it not all that discreetly, was not uncommon. Perhaps the people who suggested it (the Principal of the University and the Dean of Faculty) thought that being a professor would take my mind off the bombing, which had happened three years earlier. Perhaps it was a suggestion born, at least partially, of kindness: they felt it would be good for me as well as for the University. And perhaps it would have been, but nobody can now say, because I declined the invitation and did not apply.

I *am* a professor, but only an imagined one. No one knows this but myself and my colleague Dr Carol Pritchley. It is our secret – our secret joke really. It is what this is all about and why I am writing it down.

I have plenty of space in this house that was built, and bought, for a family to live in. I have two rooms for work, and two computers. One room – the study – is for university work. It was where I had been that morning. The other – the old dining room – is where my special work goes on. The Case, I call it. The two rooms and what they contain are as separate and different as day from night.

It was late January. The days were short, meagre of light. A sense of confinement had pressed on me all winter. I'd seen no one for weeks, not even Carol. She was not just my colleague but also my friend. My occasional sexual partner, to be specific. Our relationship was an on-off one, and it was off at that time. We'd had a couple of ill-tempered days together at New Year, nothing serious, just enough irritation to make it seem like a good idea to give each other some space, and this was my space, closed-in and solitary. The snow added to the oppressiveness, yet there was also comfort in the way it deadened everything. To be half-asleep, or feel only half-alive, is sometimes a relief.

Carol and I would meet soon, say little, possibly nothing, about our fractious New Year, and resume our relations. That was how we conducted ourselves. It seemed to suit both of us pretty well, although a greater degree of emotional commitment might have suited Carol better. But, to be frank, the way we were was about as much as I could cope with.

When the new path was complete I fetched the grey bin from beside the shed and wheeled it out to the pavement. There was a grey bin for general rubbish and a green bin for compostable matter, and they were emptied on alternate Fridays. That week it was the turn of the grey bin. But maybe the bin men wouldn't come. In a country of unpredictable winters you never know whether snow will bring everything to a standstill or people will soldier on stoically, even when it is futile to do so. So it was from force of habit rather than in faith that I brought the grey bin to the kerbside, ready for emptying in the morning. Others, I noticed, had done the same.

Actually I didn't give a damn about grey bins and green bins, not when I thought about it. That was the point: not to think about it. Just to do things, to get through the waking hours and the hours that were supposed to be for sleep, was all, at that juncture of my life, that concerned me.

That 'juncture' of my life had been going on for twenty-one years.

There hadn't been a snowplough along the street all day. Presumably the priority was to clear the main roads. The street was churned and criss-crossed by tyre marks where some residents had managed to get their cars out. The parked cars were covered in smooth, thick, white mattresses.

My driveway was empty. No car had sat in it for twenty years, except when my parents came to stay, which had not happened in a long while and was unlikely to happen again. (I don't drive, never have.) If anyone had been going to attempt a journey that day it would have been Emily, but she wouldn't have wanted to drive any-where. She'd have gone sledging with Alice.

For a moment they flashed before me, Emily and Alice, packed together on a sledge, whooping with delight, rushing down a white slope in bobble hats and with stripy scarves flying. They were the ages they always were. Then they were gone.

I gave Emily's car to my sister, or she took it away, I don't remember which. I just wanted it out of my sight. And indeed my sister obliged and I never saw it again.

I was alone in the street. I pulled back a glove to look at my watch: one o'clock. It occurred to me that the schools might have closed because of the weather. I had no memory of having heard children passing the house earlier. But if there was no school, why weren't there children outside now, building snowmen, throwing snowballs, taking sledges to the park? Didn't children enjoy snow any more? Did they spend all their free time in their bedrooms, insulated from the real world, watching TV or playing computer games? *All* of them?

I thought these thoughts, then chided myself for having them. It served no purpose to resent children for being what and who they were, for not being Alice. But again, that was the point: there *was* no purpose to my resentment. It was simply there.

My neighbour Brian Hewat had not only put out his grey bin and made a path to his front door, but had also cleared the snow from the stretch of pavement in front of his house. Seeing this, I felt an obligation to do the same, and set to work again. The red plastic shovel scraped less easily and more raucously over the surface of the pavement than it had over the smooth stone slabs around the house. I was slightly ashamed of the noise. It was as if I were boasting about my sense of civic responsibility, even if only to the deserted, smothered street.

Which, however, wasn't quite as empty as I'd thought. As I finished, and was shouldering the shovel to return it to the shed, I became aware of someone standing a few yards away. A man in a long black coat, hands in pockets, and with a black woollen hat pulled down over his brow and ears. I had no idea how long he'd been there. He must have walked up the street when I was busy digging, and the snow had muffled his approach.

'You're being a good citizen,' the man said.

Even in those few words, the American accent was unmistakable, although I could not have identified the region to which it belonged. I was surprised, and then, almost immediately, not surprised. The voice of the man on the phone half an hour earlier, and that of this man standing in the snow, telling me I was a good citizen, were one and the same.

'People don't clear the sidewalks any more,' the man said. 'They don't even consider it. "That's somebody else's job, what do I pay my taxes for?" You know what I'm saying? But I come along here and I find not one but two of you, right alongside of one another.'

I nodded in the direction of Brian's house. 'He beat me to it,' I said. Brian was retired, he had more time on his hands, theoretically.

'Good citizens, all the same, both of you,' the American said.

'It doesn't take much.'

'It takes more than some people are prepared to give.'

I was not happy to be having this conversation. I felt it as an intrusion, that it in some way threatened my privacy, even though anybody looking at us would have assumed we were neighbours exchanging a few superficial words about the weather. The American, however, was not a neighbour. He was unknown to me, yet I was already sure that I was not unknown to him, and that our words carried some meaning to which I was not yet privy. A low anger began to simmer inside me.

'Can I help you in some way?'

'Yes, I think you can,' he said. 'And maybe I can help you.'

'Who are you?'

Slowly he took his right hand from the pocket of his coat. It was

as if his brain had consciously to instruct the arm to withdraw, bringing the hand with it. The hand was gloveless. It pointed behind me,
at the house.

'I think we should go inside.'

Of course I could have said no. I could have said, not until you tell
me who you are and what you want. But I saw that this would be
pointless. There was an order in which things would happen, or they
would not happen at all. For me to find out who this man was, I
would have to allow him into my home. I did not want this, but it was
necessary. Already I knew that it was essential to continue the conversation.

'This is about the bombing, isn't it?' I said.

'Let's go in,' the American said, and without waiting for a reply,
because he knew that he was not going to be refused, he started to
move, heading towards the back door, along the path that I had made
for him through the snow.

2

So many years had passed, yet I would still always try to reach the phone whenever it rang. Missing a call when I was out, that was one thing: it was what the answer-machine was for. But I never could get out of my head the notion that the one call I ignored when I was in would be the one that counted, the one that, if only I'd picked up the phone, I might later have thought of as 'the breakthrough'. There *had* been breakthroughs of various sorts, but each one had only ever been from one locked room into another. The years had been like a succession of cells in a vast old prison that refused to release me. Time was my Château d'If. I would scratch away at one wall with the blunt knife of hope, the ragged nails of despair, and then one day the stone would crumble and there'd be enough space to scramble through, so through I'd go, only to be confronted by another wall. Yet still I clutched the blunt knife, and sucked the ragged nails. Even after all the disappointments, I refused to abandon the possibility that I might find out who had murdered my wife and daughter; who had *really* murdered them. This was why I followed the American inside.

He sat at the kitchen table. I made coffee, not because I was feeling hospitable but because some kind of preparatory ritual seemed necessary before we got down to whatever business it was that had brought him to me. After the nipping cold, the kitchen felt as hot as a laundry. It even looked a little like one as I had clothes drying on the pulley above our heads. I had taken off my gloves and jacket, but left

him. He did not drink from the cup. He said, 'Are you ready to meet your maker?'

Whatever I was expecting, it was not this. The simmering anger I'd felt outside rose to the boil. I stood up.

'I don't know who you are,' I said, 'but I seem to have mistaken you for someone else. If all you're here for is to try to convert me or save me or whatever it is you people do, then you needn't bother finishing your coffee.'

Nilsen was not in the least perturbed. 'I'm not a missionary,' he said.

'You can get the hell out, in fact.'

'It was a question, that's all. Just give me an answer.'

The dark eyes stared. It was possible that I had let a madman into my kitchen. I wanted Nilsen to leave. I certainly did not intend to humour him. Yet I found I could not deny him what he wanted.

'I don't believe I have a maker,' I said. 'But if I'm wrong and there is one, then, yes, I'm ready. There are a few things I'd have to say to him.' And, thinking it would annoy him, I added, 'Or her.'

'Sit down,' Nilsen said. He made me feel like a fractious guest in my own house. 'I'm trying to give you some context,' he said. 'The thing is, I *am* ready for my maker. We've got a contract, him and me. He's going to take me to him, but first I've got to straighten a few things out.'

'Oh for God's sake!' I said. If he heard this as a profanity, if it offended him, he didn't show it. That face didn't show much in the way of emotion. For a man who'd found Jesus – I presumed that was the particular maker to whom he referred – he didn't seem filled with joy and gratitude.

'I'm dying,' he said.

'We're all dying,' I retorted. I was still standing. Out of nowhere a wave of something – not sympathy but perhaps grief or bitterness or exhaustion – washed through me. This happened, still, after twenty-one years. To cover myself I went to the window, as if to check the weather. Snow was falling again, lightly whitening the cleared path. 'Tell me something I don't know,' I said.

'I have cancer,' Nilsen said. 'So I am dying in a certain way and at a certain rate.'

I turned to face him. 'That has nothing to do with me.'

'Yes it does,' he said, and with a skeletal index finger he pointed very firmly at the other chair. Again I could not resist. I sat down. Nilsen had my attention. I thought, I'll give him five minutes.

'It doesn't make me unique,' Nilsen said. 'I know that. There are millions of us. But when some doctor tells you your days are, literally, numbered, you start counting. And you weigh up a lot of stuff. First off you weigh up the chances. Maybe you bitch about the bad hand you've been dealt. Me, I never smoked, never drank to excess, ate well, kept fit – so why me? You chase that one around for a day or two, and then you quit. That's all past, and there's no profit in it. Then you think about the time you have left. You make a list of things you want to do while you still can. I started to do that and then I threw the list away. I didn't need a list. Anything I could put on it would be nothing to what I'm going to experience. I've got the keys to the kingdom. But like I said, God has a contract with me, so I need to make everything straight before I stand before him. I need to settle my debts. I've been doing my rounds.'

'Then you do have a list,' I said. 'A different one.'

Nilsen sipped from his cup. 'Good coffee,' he said. It sounded genuine. That a man in Nilsen's situation should still appreciate the insignificant things of life did not surprise me. I had my own 'situation', took my own momentary pleasure in tastes, smells, sounds. Maybe that is the most delight there can be – swift, sensual, small – when the roof of your world has fallen in. The difference with Nilsen was that he saw a ladder to some other place ascending from the wreckage, and from the way he was talking celestial light was shining down through the hole. Whereas when I tasted good coffee, that was all I experienced.

'What kind of cancer?' I asked.

'Does it matter?' There was a brief defensiveness in his voice, then it resumed its controlled calmness. 'Let's say it's the kind that kills you.'

This sounded evasive and I did not like it. I had had my fill of evasion over the years.

'Maybe your maker will pull off a miracle,' I said.

'He already has,' Nilsen said, 'but not in the way you mean. I've had the treatment, the chemo, all of that. That's over. The miracle is that he has promised to save me in the next life.'

The flat, matter-of-fact way he made this statement was striking. In it was neither sanctimonious whine nor eager, preacherly insistence that I join him on the salvation road. He seemed entirely rational about something entirely irrational.

'This,' he said, glancing around the room, 'all this, is just a prelude.'

I picked my next words with care. 'I've been told a lot of things,' I said, 'which turned out not to be true.'

'It's why I'm here.'

'That were downright lies, in fact.'

'I understand.'

'Would you take off your hat, please?'

He frowned. 'Would I what?'

'Listen to me,' I said. 'A total stranger appears. He may have some information for me, or he may not. How would I know? He tells me he's dying. How would I know? I'm asking you to take off your hat.'

'That won't prove anything.'

'Perhaps not,' I said. 'Nevertheless . . .'

Nilsen sighed, then bared his head with a single sweep of one hand. Soft white hair sprouted in uneven patches from his pitted scalp. Until that moment I had not noticed how sparse the eyebrows were. 'Satisfied?' Nilsen said, and replaced the hat. He sounded almost hurt that I had doubted him. For a moment I felt that I had the advantage.

'I don't recall your name,' I said. 'I sat through the trial, I've read the documents, the newspaper articles, the books — thousands of pages — but I've never seen your name in them. Now you turn up, after all this time, and the only reason you can be here is because you have something to tell me about the bombing. That is the reason, isn't it?'

Nilsen inclined his head about a millimetre.

'Why should I believe you know any more about it than I do?'

'You don't recall my name because it isn't there,' he said. 'If you mean "Ted Nilsen", that is. Even if you don't . . .'

Perhaps I was in the presence of a phantom. People see something and then, afterwards, they are not quite sure what. Maybe they haven't seen anything. When he was gone and I had washed up his coffee cup, maybe I too would wonder if I'd imagined him. But it also occurred to me that a man who went unrecorded in his line of work — I had no doubt that he worked in intelligence — might be one in possession of the facts that had eluded me for so long, facts that had never been in the rooms I had been in, or not at the same time anyway.

I waited for Nilsen to continue. He was staring at me but not really *at* me, and just as I realised that his voice hadn't so much trailed off as ground to a halt he emitted a small sound, neither a grunt nor a squeak but somewhere in between, and seemed to freeze up entirely. Shock was on his face and I wondered if that was how someone looked just after they'd been shot but before they knew what had happened.

'Are you in pain?'

He gasped. 'I have something to take,' he said. 'Some water . . .' He was not able to complete the sentence.

I went to the sink and filled a glass from the cold tap. The snow was thick again, piling up on the outside sill. I took the water to him, and he reached for his coat, brought a foil pack from one of its pockets and broke out a capsule. He swallowed. We let some minutes pass, and the muscles around his mouth began to relax.

'Prayer is good,' he said, 'but the drugs are sometimes better. Quicker, anyway. Prayer takes a little time.'

He wiped his mouth with the back of his hand. If the pain was still there he seemed to have control of it. 'You know what defines us?' he said. 'Extremes. Not daily normality. What is that? It's nothing. What defines us is the edge. Extreme pain. Extreme weather. Floods and fires and hurricanes.' He nodded at the window. 'Snow and ice. Acts of extreme violence. These things make you conscious of yourself. You only realise what it is to be alive when death is howling at you.'

There was more urgency in his voice, and less of a drawl. Maybe it was the drug kicking in.

'Then God takes you home,' I said, 'and all is well. Is he one of your extremes?'

'God? Aha.' Nilsen said this as if I'd been trying to catch him out and might have succeeded had he not been cleverer than I. He drank some coffee. 'Tell me, were you even alive before the bomb went off?' he said. 'I mean, really alive?'

The anger surged again inside me. 'Yes I was,' I said. 'You can keep death and pain. I was alive every day and I knew it. I was in love with my wife and I adored my beautiful daughter.'

'Extreme love,' he said. 'That's another one. And before that?'

'You don't give up, do you?'

'Haven't yet. Never gave up on nothing yet.'

His five minutes were over. Not that he knew it.

'What about you?' he said. 'You don't give up either, do you?' And, after a pause, 'I have brought you something.'

I thought I would give him another five.

*

'You've always interested me,' Nilsen said. 'You were an awkward fit. You were assessed as not having any allegiance.'

'Allegiance?' I could equally well have challenged the word 'interested' or the word 'assessed', but they surprised me less.

'Don't get me wrong,' he went on. 'Your first allegiance was to your loved ones, we all understood that. But beyond that. Beyond country, even. What was your philosophy, your world view? When you started making a fuss' – he saw me bridle again and made a small concessionary gesture with the palm of one hand – 'when you gave us trouble with your questions, it wasn't clear what boundaries you recognised, or if you recognised any. It wasn't clear where you would stop. You could have been a unifying force, someone who spoke for all the victims' families. You bridged the Atlantic with your loss. But you were obstinate. You weren't prepared to shut up. Not so long ago that enraged me. Who was this guy? Did he think he was smarter than we were? But now, you know what, I respect it. I admire you. In your shoes I would have been the same. I see that now.'

I did not want his respect or his admiration.

'The only thing I've ever felt an allegiance to,' I said, 'is the truth.'

'That's a slippery substance, truth,' Nilsen said.

'Not where you're going.'

For the first time since he'd appeared in the street, for all I knew for the first time that day, he smiled, his lips pulling back like a dog's. He had bad, uneven, un-American teeth; discoloured, as though he'd once smoked heavily. But he'd said he never had. Maybe it was the disease, eating at his gums, leaving his teeth like a rickety picket fence in need of paint. The smile lasted only a second or two. Then he laughed, a short hacking rasp.

'Not where I'm going,' he repeated. 'You're right. Only one truth where I'm going.'

He added, as if he'd had to be reminded, 'That's why I'm here.'

I waited. What were a few more seconds after twenty-one years?

'I've been carrying this stuff around a while,' he said. 'As long as you have, although not in the same way, I admit. But you know, for a lot of us this wasn't just about finding out who planted the bomb. Maybe it was to begin with, but then it became something else. More than just the job. We didn't just *want* to solve the case. We *needed* to solve it. There's an investment. I'm not talking budgets here, I'm talking emotional capital, mental capital. The bigger the crime, the bigger the investment. And they don't come any bigger than this one.' He paused. 'Well, not until 9:11 they didn't. 9:11 put everything else in the shade. But I was out by then. Retired. I was sitting on the porch sucking cocktails with little umbrellas in them when those planes came in out of that blue sky.'

There was a strange mix of naivety and cynicism, softness and hardness, in the way he spoke. I am innocent, it seemed to suggest, but don't even think of messing with me. *Out of that blue sky*. I watched him watching it all again, the first impact and explosion, the billowing black plume, the second plane roaring in, angled, slamming through the second tower. How would such a man react? The detail of the little umbrellas must surely be false. I couldn't picture Nilsen half-cut and helpless in a deckchair. Stunned, maybe; shocked, yes – how could you not be shocked? But already, before the mighty pillars crashed, he'd be starting to calculate who could have done this thing and how, he'd be unpacking the sharp-edged possibilities and likely responses even as he wondered perhaps – with beguiling innocence – 'Why do they hate us so much?'

I thought of my colleague Jim Collins – an unpretentious Welshman who couldn't care less if you had a PhD or not – and how he'd once answered a visiting professor from Virginia who had posed that question, some months into the occupation of Iraq. 'Why does half the world hate us so much?' 'Because you have to ask,' Jim Collins had said, and the visiting professor had looked puzzled, thinking maybe Jim was making some kind of joke, but he wasn't.

Nilsen was retired by 9:11, he'd said. Out. But did you ever really get out?

I thought, when did we give up saying 11:9? Was it out of courtesy – it was their atrocity, after all – or carelessness? Or was it envy?

And Jim Collins had followed up, 'But look on the bright side, the other half wants to *be* you.' And this time everybody, including – a little nervously – our visitor, had laughed.

'They say everything changed that day,' Nilsen said. 'Well, in a way I can buy that. But all that really changed was the scale. We were already at war, had been for years. Most people didn't know it. But I did, and you did. Didn't we?'

'I never thought I was at war with anyone,' I said. 'I don't *buy* that, as a matter of fact. If I buy that it means I've bought a lot of other crap from your easy-fit good-and-evil T-shirt store. Which I haven't.'

It didn't sound as cutting as I intended. It sounded a little childish. Nilsen, expressionless, said, 'Didn't I say you were obstinate?'

'I am what I am,' I said. 'I don't care what you call it.'

'Call it a compliment.'

Silence fell between us for a few seconds. Then Nilsen spoke again.

'Twenty-one years ago. You went down there almost at once. How long were you there?'

'Seven days,' I said, 'or eight. I have never been quite sure.'

'You got there when?'

'The day after it happened.' I didn't intend to elaborate, but what was to be gained by holding back? 'I spent the first days talking to people, being talked to, not really believing any of it even though it was right there in front of me. The waiting was terrible. I was waiting to be summoned, to be told they'd found my family. Then I was summoned, and there had been nothing to wait for after all, and I had to leave.'

'I remember an overwhelming need for action,' Nilsen said. 'Physical exertion. Thinking came later. There was a bunch of us. We were desperate to make sense of what had happened but that was going to take time and care and procedure and before we could get to that there was this other thing. I arrived the third day. So I was with you in a way, alongside of you, though back then I had no idea who you were, didn't know your name as yet. Maybe we went past each other. I was there for a purpose – a different purpose from yours – but for an hour, maybe two, all I could do was go from one piece of wreckage to the next, one dead person to the next. I was pumped. Everything in my training told me to slow down, to assess methodically, but I couldn't. I was striding, not pausing at all. It was all I could do not to break into a run. I needed to sweat. Now what was that about?'

'What was your purpose?' I asked.

'My view, it was the body telling the mind, you're not ready to deal with this yet, let me take over for a while.' He spoke as if he had not heard my question, but I knew he had. 'They already had great areas of the countryside cordoned off. Obviously they were trying to keep people out, minimise contamination of the evidence, but it made things difficult. You know this. There were journalists, relatives like you – people with legitimate reasons for being there, but who might step in the wrong places, compromise the scene. We didn't know what kind of scene, crime or accident. There were hundreds of police, soldiers, volunteers, sweeping and tagging. And then there were the others, the trophy hunters, who had nothing to do with it except they wanted to grab themselves a piece of the fuselage, somebody's shirt or sock or something. So later they could say, "Guess what this is." Ghouls. It still makes me mad to think of them.'

I wondered if they trained people like Nilsen to use phrases like 'minimise contamination' and 'compromise the scene', or if it just came naturally after a while. And I was thinking that much of what he said could be heard two ways. 'Made things difficult', for example. 'Step in the wrong places': what exactly did that mean? And the word 'ghouls' raised in my mind an image of old hags in shawls cutting the buttons off dead soldiers on Napoleonic battlefields: did it generate something similar for Nilsen? And would it madden him further if he knew of the small thing I had done on one of those days, I did not know which, before I left?

'What was your purpose?' I asked again.

Again he ignored me. He seemed very sure that he could. 'But they couldn't contain all that vast space,' he said. 'A space the size of London. The debris was spread over many, many square miles. You know this. There was the main impact and then there was the rest of it. Bodies and baggage and chunks of airplane scattered across fields and forests and parks and streets. I remember a woman caught in a tree, still in her seat. A boy, eleven, twelve maybe, who looked like he'd just fallen asleep where he lay, next to somebody's car. How much of all that did you see?'

'Enough.'

'The smell of aviation fuel. I thought I'd never get it out of my mouth. They were tagging the victims, doctors were checking the injuries, certifying the deaths, the police were marking the exact locations where the victims were found. They stuck markers in the ground with labels on them that fluttered in the breeze like little flags. A lot of bodies fell on the golf course. It was like someone had picked up all the holes from three courses and scattered them over the fairway, a body beside each pin. There were craters where the bodies hit. You wouldn't think a human body could make such a deep imprint in the earth. Broken, half-naked. I've heard a lot lately about dying with dignity. Counsellor talk. Those people weren't left with any dignity. Then the teams with the body bags moved in.'

He stopped speaking and I thought maybe the pain had come back but he seemed only to be remembering. The way the brain runs silent footage that can never be cut or wiped. Recollection – an apposite word in the context. In this, at least, Nilsen was as haunted as I was.

And, like me, he didn't seem to have had much patience with counselling.

'I have to tell you,' he said, 'that great respect was shown. There was a deep sorrow in those workers, and they did what they had to do with gentleness and care.'

'No, you don't have to tell me,' I replied. 'My difficulties were never with the people on the ground, the ones clearing up. Never. That was the worst job in the world. My difficulties have always been with people like you.'

He gave the faintest of nods, an acknowledgement of some kind. Then he went on.

'From the passenger manifest they had the names of the dead, but the bodies still had to be identified. You know how it was. They moved them to the temporary mortuary in that high-school gym. It depended on the condition of the victim – whether a relative would be asked to do the identification. If the injuries were too severe, identification was done by other means, dental or medical records. None of this could happen quickly. Thankfully the weather was cold. Your case turned out to be different of course.'

'Yes.'

'I remember you saying once it was like losing them twice, and not being able to say goodbye either time. Isn't that what you said?'

'You seem to know.'

'You wrote about it later, or were interviewed, one or the other. You were quoted anyway. And you said for a long time you were numb and then the numbness went and you felt the loss all over again. It was important to feel it, you said. It was what drove you on. I understood that when I read it. All of us on the investigation, we were in the biggest event of our professional lives, and we had to get a result. Accumulating facts wasn't going to be enough. We had to get inside what had happened. I recognised you. You were a kindred spirit.'

'That was before I gave you any trouble,' I said, wanting to quash any notion of kinship between us.

'I used to like trouble,' he said. 'Life didn't seem much without it.'

3

I'd gone by train and then by bus and was there twenty hours after it happened. I could not have stayed away. Outside the bus station I asked someone where the local tourist office was, and was told that if it was a room I was looking for, I was out of luck. All accommodation for miles around was already booked out by journalists and film crews. I stood in the middle of the pavement clutching my overnight bag, and did not know what to do next.

The faces of everybody going by looked like the faces of people one might see leaving or entering a hospital. An old woman with white hair passed me, glancing at me as if I too were a hospital visitor or patient, dreading disaster or having had it confirmed. I saw a café and managed to find a seat and order a coffee.

A few minutes later I became conscious of someone sitting across the table from me – the woman with the white hair. She was small and bright-eyed, in a hefty tweed coat.

'What are you doing here?' she asked. It was not an accusation. 'Have you lost someone?' Her hand shook my arm gently as if to waken me.

'I don't know,' I replied. 'Yes, I think so. My wife and child.'

'And you're waiting for news,' the woman said. She might have been sixty or eighty, my mother or my grandmother.

'I've had the news,' I said. 'I'm just waiting.'

The import of those three words struck home. That was exactly what I was doing. I was a man waiting at some gate for two people who were never going to come through it. I already understood this. I was a man in arrivals holding up their names or their photos but they would not arrive and eventually there would be nobody else coming through and I would have to go away alone. The brutality of this realisation brought a sob from my throat and tears from my eyes. I did not expect the sob, nor could I stop the tears. This would be the pattern for months to come but I was not yet prepared for these moments, let alone used to the pattern, which anyway would never be so regular that it could be called a pattern.

The old woman wiped her own eyes. I saw her hand on my arm.

'I don't know what to do,' I said. 'I have nowhere to stay.'

She said, 'Finish your coffee and come with me.' I did as I was told, and allowed her to lead me, away from the town centre, up a hill of old stone cottages and through an iron gate into her own home. There was a spare bedroom. In the tiny sitting room she lit the gas fire. She made tea and I drank it but couldn't face anything to eat. Her name was Mrs Hastie.

'You stay here as long as you need to,' she said. 'Come in and go out whenever you like. I never lock the door.'

'Thank you,' I said.

'It's a dreadful business,' she said. 'A dreadful business.' The way she said it, did she know, before the thing was a day old, did she know in her old bones, despite the caveats and cautions on the news bulletins, that the crash had not been caused by bad weather or mechanical failure but by some calculated, deliberate act of human hand? Of course she did. I did. We all did.

I was exhausted from lack of sleep the night before, but now at least I had somewhere to collapse when I could no longer stand. I went back into the town. It was crowded with people, many of them in some uniform or other if they were not from the media. Everywhere I met shock, sympathy and offers of help. Anger, too, though the anger was not directed at me. The police had set up an emergency information centre and I went there, registering my name and other details, such as they were (this was long before the ubiquity of mobile phones, emails and laptops), but not gaining much new information. Relatives of other passengers arrived. Some of them wanted to share their grief and frustration and fear but I couldn't do any sharing. I returned to Mrs Hastie's, fell asleep, woke to watch the news on her television. I ate but did not taste the food she prepared. She was a kindly woman, with an instinct for knowing when to speak, when to stay silent. She did not ask questions, and I was grateful for that.

Over the next few days I read every newspaper I could find; sat for hours in the café; stood on the edge of the field where the nose of the aircraft lay like a fish head with men crawling over it like yellow flies; looked into one half-vanished street and then turned away, because there was the greatest devastation, a deep blackened trench where the main part of the plane had hit and gone up in a fireball, taking several houses with it. I did not then know, but suspected, that I was looking into the extinguished funeral pyre of my family. I went back to Mrs Hastie's to sleep for a fitful hour, returned to the café, read the same news in different shapes. I used Mrs Hastie's phone to make calls to my parents and sister, to Emily's parents in America, to Jim Collins. I tried to give Mrs Hastie money for the calls but she refused, with something close to violence, to take so much as a penny. I checked in regularly with the police, anxious for the moment when I would be called to the school gymnasium. But the call did not come. I was drowning in the intense activity going on all around me, in my own inability to act, in the huge media presence, in the kindness of the local people. Everything smelled and tasted of burning. I retreated again to Mrs Hastie's but her gas fire began to nauseate me. Her spare bedroom was a kind of sanctuary but it too became oppressive. I thought, I will go mad if I stay in. But if I go out, I go out into another madness.

I went out.

*

When air traffic control lost contact with the plane it was flying in a north by north-westerly direction at 31,000 feet. A lot of experts had been found and placed in front of TV cameras to give their opinions on what had happened. There had been no Mayday call, nothing at all from the pilots. One second the aircraft was there, the next it was gone, its single radar echo multiplying, scattering and fading on the monitors. The wide dispersal of wreckage on the ground indicated that the plane had come apart at a great height. The general consensus was that, whatever had caused the catastrophe, it would have taken about a minute for the largest pieces of the plane to reach the ground. Passengers and crew, if not strapped in seats or otherwise attached to the fuselage, might have plummeted through the night for two minutes, perhaps a little longer. They would have fallen with everything else, suitcases, handbags, blankets, the paraphernalia of air travel, a precipitation of human lives and possessions. That terrible downpour filled my head. Day and night, it never ceased.

In a newsagent's I found a battered Ordnance Survey map of the area, missing half its cover, and bought it. Then I went back to the field where the dead nose lay. I had been told that the bodies of the pilots had remained in the cockpit for two days, while men peered in and gingerly worked around them, assessing their last actions – what switches they had switched, whether they had had time to fit oxygen masks. I had also heard that the cockpit voice recorder had been discovered in a nearby field. Official-looking people came and went. I watched, and whenever I got the opportunity I asked – could I speak to someone who knew about the physics of trajectory and descent? I didn't put it like that. I said, 'Is there someone who can tell me how an aeroplane falls out of the sky?' Eventually a man with little round glasses, curly hair and a beard was pointed out to me. 'He's your man.'

He was writing on a clipboard. He looked up as I approached and immediately saw the map in my hand. He said, 'Oh, these are like gold dust, where did you find it?'

I said, 'In a shop. It was their last one.'

'We need all the maps we can get,' he said, reaching for it.

I did not let it go. 'You can have it when I'm done with it.'

The man stared at me and seemed about to lose his temper. It was only then that I saw how tired and distressed he looked. I wondered how I looked to him.

'My wife and child were on the flight,' I said. 'I need your help.'

I unfolded the map and asked where on it – above what point on it – the disintegration had most likely happened.

He scowled through his round lenses. 'Impossible. I couldn't be that precise.'

'Be as precise as you can be.'

'It's not that simple.'

'I'm not asking for it to be simple. I want you to make an informed guess.'

'How can I? We don't even know the cause yet. I mean, if it was structural failure or something else. We just don't know.'

'It must have been very sudden,' I said. 'Mustn't it?'

'Yes, very sudden.'

'You can't rule out an explosion, can you?'

'I'm not ruling anything out.'

'Suppose it was an explosion?'

'I'm not saying it was an explosion.'

'I'm not either. But if it was? Where above this map would that have been?'

'It's just not possible to say,' he said, so aggressively that I took a step back. He saw this, and added, more gently, 'I wish I could be more definite.'

'Please help me,' I said. I did not recognise my own voice.

The man looked at me afresh but could not hold the look. He took a pencil from his pocket and held it over the map, shook his head as though about to give up, then rapidly drew a circle.

'Don't hold me to this,' he said. 'There are so many variables. But if. Roughly. Roughly here.'

He stabbed the map with the pencil. 'I'm sorry,' he said. I folded the map, thanked him, walked away. He called after me, 'Wait!' but when I turned he only said again, 'It's not possible to say,' as if I were blaming him for the crash. Later, the next day, I would seek him out and give him the map. But for now, roughly, I knew what I was going to do next in this place and time of madness.

I boarded a local bus heading south on a route that went to various tiny settlements and villages, but I was not going to any of these. There were only two other passengers, both women, sitting silent and apart. The driver, a fat man, greeted them by name when they got on. He would be cheery and loud in normal circumstances, I guessed, but his hellos were quiet and brief and so were their replies, and he looked at me with a knowing deference – an expression I would recognise only too often in the years to come – when he saw me board.

'Where to, sir?' he said. I told him I wanted to go only a few miles, and he said that the minimum fare was to the first village on the route. I paid him and received my ticket. The bus set off. My finger traced the journey on the map. I watched it doing so, as if it did not belong to me, and when after several minutes it approached and entered the pencilled circle, I called to the driver to put me down at the next stop. The bus pulled in a hundred yards later beside a wooden shelter opposite some farm buildings. Next to the shelter a broad track led into a dense plantation of conifers.

'Are you sure this is where you want off?' the driver said. Yes, I said, I was going to walk back into town, but not on the road, I wanted to stretch my legs and get some fresh air. I pointed up the track. 'Up there.' The driver leaned from his seat to see where. 'You'll be one of the relatives,' he said. Suddenly unable to speak, I acknowledged this with a nod.

He tugged on the handbrake, switched off the engine and hauled himself out of his cabin. He stepped from the bus and gestured for me to follow.

'You'll get fresh air up there all right,' he said. 'Follow the track for half a mile and where it splits go left. It'll take you to the top of that hill, see? You get a good view, even on a day like this. It's a long time since I was there but you can see for miles.'

'Thank you,' I said.

A few spots of rain fell. The driver glanced at my shoes, already scuffed and filthy from walking among the ash and debris of the town. 'Sure now? You can stay on board if you like. I end up back in town. No extra charge.'

'I'm sure,' I said. He seemed to want more. 'You're very kind.'

'What else can we be?' The words burst from him. 'What sort of people would we be if we weren't kind?' Then he got back in the bus, started the engine and drove off. He gave me a wave, or perhaps it was more a kind of salute. The faces of the two women stared as they went by, their mouths moving as though trying to whisper something to me. I set off up the track.

I had not gone a quarter of a mile when I came upon a white van parked across the track. The van was unmarked but, as I approached, the driver and passenger doors opened and two men in police uniform got out. One was wearing a radio and it was he who spoke first.

'Afternoon, sir. I'm afraid access to the hill is closed.'

'I'm only going for a walk,' I said.

'Sorry, sir. Access is closed.'

'Because of the crash?'

'That's right, sir.'

'They're searching for wreckage,' the second policeman said. 'Nobody's allowed up there unless they're authorised. Are you authorised?'

'No,' I said. 'No, I'm not authorised.'

They both shrugged. They might have been choreographed.

'I'm not going to touch anything,' I said. 'I just want to walk.'

'Sorry, sir,' the first one said. 'We can't let you beyond this point.'

I thought about arguing, and I thought about telling them who I was, using the instrument of my loss to break open their compassion as I had with the bearded, spectacled man. But I could see that this would not work on these men. I saw that if they knew I was a relative they would be even less likely to let me past. So I shrugged too, turned and headed down the track, until I was out of sight round a corner. There I paused until I heard the van doors slamming shut again. Then I stepped across the drainage ditch and pushed off into the trees, taking an angle that I thought would cut well below the van but bring me out, eventually, far beyond it.

It was tough going through those whippy, spiky, close-set trees, but the climb and the stings and scratches of the branches were a distraction from the endless rain of death in my head. After a while I emerged into a firebreak, and tramped up a steep, grassy slope, protected from view by the tall trees on either side, slipping occasionally in my un-sensible shoes. I came to a deer fence at the upper edge of the plantation, walked along it till I reached a corner post that I could get some purchase on, and hauled myself up and over the wire. A few hundred feet below lay the road where the bus driver had set me down. Ahead lay the grassland and heather of the hillside. My socks were already soaking, the shoes ruined. The sky was full of cloud.

I put back my head and looked skywards. Up there somewhere was where it had happened. The bomb, if it was a bomb, exploded. Then what? The plane coming to bits like a balsawood model of itself, the cockpit, the front part of the cabin, the wings, the engines, the rest of the fuselage – all separating. No time for brace positions, oxygen or prayers. The aircraft was no longer an aircraft, contact between crew and passengers over – no time for responsibility, no time for reassurance or warning from flight deck to cabin. The ruthlessness of the moment was also its only grace: there was hardly time, perhaps none, for fear or pain or thought of what was coming.

So I fervently hoped as I stood on the hillside below, roughly, where it had happened.

I imagined a gale-force wind howling through the main part of the plane. The experts in the media – but could you have expertise without experiencing what it was like? – had painted their pictures well. I felt intense chest pain, a desperate struggle for breath. I thought I would pass out. I saw the wind ripping clothes, jewellery, headphones from unconscious people; a storm of personal possessions – books, papers, toys – roaring in the broken tube that was all the cabin now was; people not wearing their seat belts, or who were standing in the aisles, becoming part of this storm. Some would be sucked out into the ice-cold night – as cold as Antarctica in winter at that height – and some seats too would become detached and would fall with their occupants still in them.

I pushed on a few hundred yards, then stopped to get my breath back. How carelessly we use such phrases. To get my breath back! I looked up again. It was still early afternoon, but the light was poor and the sky loomed with dull menace. It was impossible *not* to think of those terrible things happening above the clouds, not to see a plane full of people breaking into many pieces. I stared, searching for the first drops of human rain. I thought of the two minutes of falling, that long, brief, breathless tumble, as of parachutists without chutes, the blacking-out, the faint, feeble grapple for consciousness, the agony of cold, the bursting lungs, the rush of the air and the distortion of vision, the stars spinning and mixing with the lights of earth, that infinite, aching two minutes in which your brain is too scrambled to say no, or call for help, or reach for the child who so recently, so long ago, was beside you, or say goodbye to the man who loved you. I stood staring to heaven and nothing came from there, no mercy or redemption. Whatever had come had come already and it was not sent by God. I stood, arms outstretched and empty, like a man praying but I was not praying, I was crying, because it had come to this and I had come to this place, and they were not with me, Emily and Alice, they were gone for ever.

I lurched forward through grass and heather. Then I stumbled and went down, clutching at a thick clump of grass to stop myself sliding. I wiped my face with a muddy sleeve. I wiped the hand that had clutched the grass, and got off my knees. As I pulled myself upright I saw something resting on the heather. I reached, lifted it, turned it over between my fingers. It was nothing, yet it was something, a man-made thing in this inhuman expanse. A kind of peg, plastic, greyish, with a hole on one side into which something else had fitted or by which it had fitted on to something. It had been dropped or had fallen there. I looked up at the sky again, then back at the object. It was the colour of the cloud. A piece of cloud.

Whatever had come had come already. I recognised the thing. It was the rotating clip with which, on an aeroplane, you secure your table to the seat in front of you. It was not cloud, it was aeroplane.

I looked around more closely. Could it have fallen there alone? Surely there must be other debris near by. But I could see nothing else. I held the clip tight in my fist. It was so light. Perhaps that was why it was where it was. The chaotic confusion of shockwaves and winds had conspired to send this tiny, almost weightless thing tumbling and jerking five miles to land there, at my feet.

I heard a shout and looked up. A line of men in visibility jackets had appeared on the crest of the hill above me. I thought one of them had called to me and I nearly called back but then realised that they had not seen me, that the shout had been among themselves. They were walking slowly, methodically, four, five, six of them. There would be more beyond my vision. If they did see me they would challenge me. They would want to know where I had come from, who I was, what – if anything – I had found. And I knew at once that I was not going to hand over the clip, not to these men nor to anybody else. Nor was I going to leave it where I had found it. Would anyone else find it if I did? What possible use could it be to them? What value could it have for anyone but myself? It was mine. It was what I had come there for. I felt its smooth, already familiar shape in my hand, then slipped it into my trouser pocket. I turned and made my way back to the fence, and from there to the road, and in the gathering darkness of the afternoon began to walk back into town the way I had come by bus.

When I finally arrived at Mrs Hastie's house, she had a message for me. I was to go to the police information centre. 'Have they found them?' I asked. 'They didn't say,' Mrs Hastie said. What else could they want me for? I went, trembling with tiredness and cold and fear. But as I learned soon enough, there was nothing left to fear.

I keep the grey plastic clip on my desk, in a little wooden bowl; the kind of container that one might fill with rubber bands or drawing pins, but nothing else sits in that bowl except the clip. Sometimes days pass without me noticing it, but then I do. A memory occurs, or perhaps there is something on the news, and it is there for me to pick up and hold. To recollect. It never wears out, it never changes. It has a kind of permanently renewable energy. It warms quickly to my touch and that is all it does. I like its banality, its uselessness, the way its utility was removed for ever by the destruction of the aircraft. It became something different then, something useful only to me. This is why it landed at my feet, or rather why I landed beside it. In that moment it became mine, and my only regret about removing it from the scene is that I didn't find a second one to go with it.

Emily and Alice had been sitting in row 25, from which they could look out over the port wing. The main fuel tank was directly beneath them. It transpired that my imagining of them falling like parachutists without chutes was false. You could not call it wishful thinking – I never, of course, wished it on them – yet there was a kind of angelic possibility in such a descent, some birdlike moment when they, in my mind's eye, swooped up and glided away, and did not touch earth. Behind this image, which for a while was often with me, lay a reason: their total disappearance. The reality was that they must have been together in their seats until the main section of the plane crashed into the ground. The fuel went up in a fireball at such a temperature that flesh and bone were instantly incinerated. Identification of most of the people in the central rows of the aircraft was down to tiny surviving scraps. For a few, it proved impossible. No trace of Emily or Alice Tealing was ever found.

Later, much of the clothing contained in their luggage was returned to me, but of them or what they were wearing that night there was nothing. They fell to earth not in two minutes but in barely one, travelling, at the moment of impact, at more than 120 mph. They were almost certainly not conscious. I like to believe this, and also that, conscious or not, they were holding each other. Holding hands, at least. Sometimes, even now, I wake in the night and I am leaning over the backs of their seats, checking that simple act of union like a solicitous steward, and someone else, whom I ignore, is screaming at me to sit back down.

For a while, although it went against all my principles, I liked to think something else: that just as the bomb made a sudden and permanent separation between my own two lives — life before, life after — so had it done for Emily and Alice; that, since they vanished so completely, they had indeed swooped out of this life into another. I knew this to be nonsense, and not even comforting or purposeful nonsense, as I could not picture any paradise into which they might have flown, where they might still be holding hands and alive. Yet for a while, until I began to question the whole mechanism of the thing that had happened and brought me to my lonely knees, I really wanted to believe it.

4

'What was your purpose?' I asked for the third time. 'What brought so many of you there so quickly? You say you got there on day three but you weren't the first. Nobody knew for sure it was a bomb at that point. It was what we feared, it was what we *felt*, but nobody knew.'

For a second – no longer or shorter than any other second – Nilsen's face changed. It happened and was over. I couldn't even say what the change was, but I saw it, and I realised we had entered a new zone.

'*We* knew,' Nilsen said. 'That's why we came. We knew because of the flight time. Air traffic control lost the signal thirty-eight minutes in. As soon as we had that information we knew, in all probability, it was a bomb.'

He put his hand to his mouth, as if he'd let something slip out by accident. But by now I was pretty sure that nothing he did was by accident. He was signalling to me. Just the two of us in that kitchen in the middle of a snowstorm, and the intelligence part of him still found some things impossible to say out loud.

He said, 'What is your view on coincidences, Dr Tealing?'

I said, 'I don't give them much thought.'

'I do. I don't believe in them, but I think about them a lot. Chance is a big brush. When you get down to fine detail, it's too clumsy. In my experience coincidences are ways of avoiding explanations.'

'But you believe in miracles?'

'They're not down to chance. What I'm saying, thirty-eight

minutes was too precise to be a coincidence. It had to be a part of the explanation. We recognised that.'

What this implied was only what I had worked out for myself over the years. Nevertheless, to hear it from this spectral, fading man chilled me despite the heat of the room.

'That's always been denied,' I said. 'You're telling me the direct opposite of what's been the official line for years.'

'You asked about purpose,' Nilsen said. '*That* was our purpose. To establish a line. First to ascertain what had happened, then to gather evidence.'

'That way round,' I said.

'There's an overlap. The order isn't fixed.'

'You're admitting this? Now?'

'That is my purpose *here*, Dr Tealing. To set the record straight. With you.'

I had my elbows on the table. I felt very tired suddenly. I leaned my head into my palms, closed my eyes. At last, I thought. Some abusive language rose to my lips but went no further. Insults would neither help me nor hurt Nilsen.

A hundred thousand pinpricks of light were flashing behind my eyelids. I would have preferred it if he had patronised me by calling me Alan. Maybe then I could have shouted at him. I felt repulsed, relieved. *Ted* Nilsen. I wanted him out of the house. I wanted him to say more.

'The irony is,' I heard Nilsen say, 'if the flight path had been different – if the plane had headed west a little sooner – we wouldn't be having this conversation. If it had gone down over the Atlantic.'

'Don't talk to me about irony,' I said.

'What I'm saying, we wouldn't have had a trail. But that's academic. We dealt with what we did have. Complex evidence gathering. The police did pretty well in the circumstances. They combed all that farmland, all those moors and forests, and they got almost everything. Fragments of engine, spoons, razor blades, headphones. It's astonishing what they got. The sheer impossibility of gathering it all together and rebuilding it. You hear what I'm saying? The *impossibility*. But it was done. It had to be done, so we could work out the narrative. You know what I mean by the narrative?'

I opened my eyes. First irony, now this. 'I teach literature,' I said. 'I should know.'

He did that concessionary thing again with his hand. He was going to explain anyway.

'The log of the journey. You start an investigation and you're starting a journey. Sometimes you set off and you draw the map as you go. You're looking for some end point but you don't know what or where it is. And other times you do know, and it's just a question of how you get there. The narrative is how you get to the right destination.'

For twenty-one years only one narrative, and a broken one at that, mattered to me. The fracture occurred when Emily and Alice were murdered. Everything in my life before that moment stopped, and everything after it began, right then. I too was a victim of their murders. This, of course, is why I have been in regular receipt of the awed sympathy of my colleagues.

I don't mean to be cynical. But one can absorb only so much.

Nilsen professed faith in an afterlife. I don't know how that kind of faith works – whether Nilsen had it before and lost it, or picked it up off the street one day, or whether it was always a vague thing inside him that came into focus only when he discovered he was terminally ill – but I have no interest in it. I have an interest in truth – the hoped-for destination at the end of *my* narrative – and truth and faith are related only occasionally, but then merely by chance. Did Nilsen consider himself 'born again'? Do I care? No. I do, however, know that such a thing as rebirth can happen – that a man can be transformed, joyfully reconfigured. I know this because it happened to me.

Once, in another life, in another world, a quiet, polite boy was growing up in a quiet, polite street in a small town on the south coast of England. Alan Jonathan Tealing. I was bright, what they call 'academically inclined'. At school I excelled at English. I wrote near-perfect essays that greatly satisfied my teachers – partly, I see in retrospect, because my balanced paragraphs, good syntax and well-regulated imagination gave back to them, ripe and unbruised, the fruits of their own fundamentally conventional wisdoms. I could sit exams without fear or panic and I did so, passing them with ease. There was talk of Oxford or Cambridge but I came from a family uncomfortable with any ambition that might seem immodest, and so the talk came to nothing. Instead, without quite understanding how or why, I found I had applied to, and been accepted to read English Literature at, a young university in an old northern English town sufficiently distant from home to make it seem, when I got on the train, as if I were embarking on a great adventure.

I arrived: the local accents and beers were different, but not much else. I settled in and continued in my unassuming ways, an assiduous taker of notes at lectures, a well-read contributor to tutorials. The university library was a vast brutalist block of six storeys, which I inhabited daily and for a while thought the only necessary place on earth. My tutors, like my schoolteachers, praised my written work. I passed – again without trouble – all my exams. Yet, deep down, I felt fraudulent. This was for two reasons. First, for all that I absorbed the literature I was studying, for all that I could discourse on it with great seriousness, in speech and on paper, I could not clear from my head a small but irreducible conviction that it was *not* necessary, that it was neither important nor useful. Second, I knew I was not as clever as my tutors seemed to think. My mind was not agile and athletic: it merely strolled. It absorbed everything, retained what was needed, could reshape and regurgitate on demand, but where was the spark of original thought, the sharp points to my questions, the precipice of an idea that I might fearfully or excitedly look over before jumping? They were nowhere. 'Have you thought of a career in the Foreign Office?' one lecturer asked. 'You'd make a fine diplomat.' She meant it as a compliment but I was dismayed. Diplomacy implied constant compromise: was that what I was best at? I worried that I might saunter through the rest of life and never know what it was to feel anger, or pain, or triumph, or despair, or love.

I went to classical concerts and the film club in winter, and in summer rowed clumsily on the river or took long walks through the soft, buzzing countryside. I had friends – and they had me – just conventionally unconventional enough to perpetuate the belief that our existence might actually be exciting. We smoked some pot. We drank fine ales in old country pubs. Sometimes – we were students, after all, with the obligations of students – we drank too much and behaved badly. I had a girlfriend in first year, but we parted at the end of it; I had another, and we parted at the end of second year. Both times I was sorry but not hurt. After a while I wasn't even sorry, and neither, I am sure, were they.

I sat my final exams, passed them, and graduated summa cum laude. Ah, now, my lecturers said, spreading their hands, the limitless possibilities! Research, a PhD, an academic career – the path of my future was laid out before me. I could become one of them! They used the word 'limitless' without irony. I listened and understood. The ease with which they spoke made me uneasy. Despite my success I still felt, only now not so far below the surface, a fraud. I was twenty-one, but feared I might wake any morning and find myself fifty. This did not stop me applying, successfully, to return in the autumn as a postgraduate. I did wonder if this was really what I wanted to do with my life, but, unable to think of an alternative, I did not hesitate for long. The man who agreed to be my supervisor made helpful suggestions as to what areas of research I might find interesting. 'Don't narrow your options too soon,' he said. 'You can specialise later.' It seems that I have, consciously or not, followed that advice ever since.

I went home for the summer. My parents were proud of my achievements. My sister, Karen, three years younger, had steadily and carelessly underachieved at school, left at sixteen and got a job as a checkout girl in a supermarket. Sometimes I felt I was achieving for two. This did not make me dislike Karen, or even feel superior to her. Despite having only our parents in common, she and I got on pretty well. Neither of us, I think, felt threatened by the other.

Our parents didn't seem disappointed in Karen: she went out at weekends, she had a boyfriend, she was happy, and they were happy that she was happy. Dad worked in pensions and life assurance; Mum in the county council's finance department. They left the house together at eight o' clock, she came back at five, and he came back at six. They had been doing this for years. I didn't know, really, what they did in their jobs. In the evenings and at weekends they cooked, cleaned, gardened, did the shopping, went for walks, read the papers and watched television. Life was one routine task or leisure activity after another. As a family we did our best, in the best tradition of middle-class England, not to upset one another, and for the most part we succeeded.

It could not be said, at that point in my life, that there was anything at which I had totally *not* succeeded. And then, that summer, there was. My parents bought me a dozen driving lessons – a present in honour of my first-class degree – and a week before returning to university I took the driving test. The instructor advised against it: he said I wasn't good enough, but I wanted it out of the way. I booked one last lesson immediately before taking the test in the instructor's car. 'Good luck,' the instructor said without a smile. He handed over the keys and went off to buy himself a coffee, leaving me vaguely amused by his pessimism. I shouldn't have been. I failed. Not marginally; not because I nudged the kerb or miscalculated my stopping distances or forgot to indicate while turning left. No, I failed spectacularly, stalling the car half a dozen times, kangarooing down the street in first gear, nearly bumping the car in front of me at a junction, then narrowly missing a cyclist when I pulled out without checking my mirrors. This was when the examiner ordered me to park and switch off the engine. The test was over. I didn't argue. I moved to the passenger seat, stunned and humiliated by defeat. The examiner drove back to the test centre, and handed the keys to the instructor. 'I did warn you,' the instructor said. 'Never mind. We can try again.' I said I would phone him to arrange more lessons the next time I was home. I had no intention of doing so.

Mum and Dad, separately and together, tried to persuade me back behind the wheel. I would regret it if I didn't master this particular skill, they said, not to mention – although, delicately, they did – the waste of money if I gave up. But the experience had shaken me. I couldn't face the thought of a second failure. Only Karen, who didn't then show any interest in driving but would later learn with no difficulty at all, offered comfort. 'You think about things too much,' she said. 'What does it matter if you can drive or not?' Her question lodged. I began to construct a defence: just why *did* I need to be able to drive? There were buses, trains, bicycles. I was an accomplished pedestrian. Anyway, I couldn't afford a car and wouldn't know what model to buy even if I could. Cars were antisocial, dangerous, polluting. I made a badge of honour out of my inability. Who needed a car? Alan Tealing didn't.

Two years into my postgraduate study, the condition of being carless seemed simply to reinforce the idea that being an academic, pursuing knowledge of no practical purpose in an out-of-the-way place, was my natural state: I could barely imagine myself as anything else. I led some tutorials; gave presentations at seminars; buried myself in research for my PhD. I read and read and read. I absorbed a lot of literary theory and forgot most of it. I understood what the theorists were saying but they were saying very little. What the writers they were writing about said was much more interesting. But would I be able to survive in this world if I didn't speak the language of theory? I would find out, no doubt.

Seeing a notice about an international conference on late-nineteenth- and early-twentieth-century fiction, the very period of my research, I brought it to the attention of my supervisor, who urged me to submit a proposal for a paper. It was accepted. The conference was to take place in Philadelphia. I had never been to the USA before – had never been further than France and Spain on family holidays – but, with the assistance of the department, I raised the funds to go. And it was in Philadelphia that I met Emily.

She was at the registration desk, handing out welcome packs, when I arrived on the first morning of the conference. I can still picture her, her shape in the plum-coloured sweater, her smile, her efficiency, the way her black hair fell across her face when she bent to find my lapel badge. This, I now know, was the moment of rebirth. This was the moment of love at first sight – a concept detestable in fiction (too clichéd, too random, too unreconstructed) but which, on the basis of my own experience, I have to accept is possible in real life.

'Wow, haven't you come a long way?' she said.

'I'm giving a paper,' I said, thinking that this easily justified the distance.

'Isn't everybody?' she said.

I felt foolish, but she said it so pleasantly that I didn't care. 'Are you?' I asked.

'Me?' She laughed, and smiled again, and I forgot that anyone else was in the queue behind me. 'I'm not even majoring in Literature. I'm just here to earn some money to pay my school fees.'

'But you could sit in on some of the sessions?'

'I have to sit out here,' she said. 'But even if I could, wouldn't they bore the pants off me?'

'No, I don't think so. Well, not all of them.'

She looked at me sceptically. 'Which ones would you recommend?'

'Well . . .' She confused me. I waved the welcome pack at her. 'I'd need to show you in the programme.'

'How about yours?' she asked, and when I started to make some excuse she interrupted me. 'You surely haven't come all this way to give a *boring* paper?'

Someone shuffled impatiently behind me and I took flight. 'I'd better go,' I said. 'I'm holding everybody up.'

'See you later, Mr Tealing,' she said.

'See you later,' I replied.

And I did. Every time I came out of the conference theatre or one of the nearby seminar rooms that day, which I did as often as I could, Emily was there at the desk. Nearly all of the name badges were gone, and she was seated, somehow looking relaxed on the hard, small, black chair, reading a paperback. I went over to her. I had nothing particular to say, I just wanted to talk to her, be around her. She had folded her book back on itself, something that I with my reverence for books never did, yet somehow it seemed fine that she should. I asked what she was reading and she showed me the cover. It was a detective novel, by an author I'd never heard of. This was fine too. Her irreverence in the context of the conference, with its distinguished speakers and erudite themes, made me want to laugh.

'What does "epistemological relativism" mean?' she asked.

'I'm sorry?'

'Don't apologise,' she said. 'It's not one of yours.' I reached for her novel and she batted my hand away. 'Don't be silly, it's not in there either. How about "textual reflexivity"?'

'Well –' I began, but she cut me off, and read from the conference programme.

'The paper right before yours tomorrow is called "Manifestations of Epistemological Relativism and Textual Reflexivity in the Narrative Structures of Three Novels by Conrad". I just wondered what the heck it meant.'

I had wondered too. I thought about trying to explain it to her, but then saw that she didn't want it explained. Anyway, I couldn't. 'I don't know,' I said. 'Maybe you have to turn up to find out.'

'Don't know or don't care?' she said. It must have shown on my face. 'Oh, I see, both. Will you have to turn up?'

'I think it would be rude not to,' I said, 'since I'm on straight after.'

'I think I'll skip it but creep into yours,' Emily said. 'At least I understand your title. Tomorrow at eleven, then. Look, I have it marked.' And she showed me her copy of the programme, and there was my name, Alan Tealing, circled. I felt famous, and rich beyond measure.

'What about tonight?' I asked. 'There's a reception. Are you going to be there?'

'No way,' she said. 'I'm out of here at five. Somebody else is doing the waitressing. Good luck to them.'

'I thought you might be hosting it.'

'God, no! What an idea!'

'What are you doing instead, then?'

'I'm not doing anything instead. I'm going home.'

'Well, would you let me buy you a drink before you do?' I couldn't believe I'd asked her. I couldn't believe I sounded so confident either, because inside I was terrified she'd say no.

'What about the reception? Shouldn't you network?'

'Shouldn't I what?'

'Circulate. You know, like blood.'

'I'd rather go for a drink with you.'

'Well,' she said, 'that would be very nice. There's a crummy little bar I know where *nobody* else from here will go.'

'That sounds perfect,' I said.

That was it, then: Alan and Emily. I can still recite that exchange word for word, as it happened. Or I believe I can, which is almost the same thing. I can't, however, remember what we discussed over several drinks in the crummy little bar that evening. We could have talked until dawn, but I had to get up early to rehearse my paper. And she did creep in, telling me later that she'd enjoyed it and that I was a natural lecturer. Other speakers simply read their papers out, often very badly, then sat down again. What was the point of that, she demanded. They might as well have mailed them. But I had only glanced at my text, and had spoken with passion, and she'd felt that what I had to say was important.

'Really?'

'Yes, really.'

'But you said you didn't sit in on any of the sessions, so how do you know about the other speakers?'

'I lied,' she said, and she showed me her programme again. 'See, you weren't the only one I marked. But you're the best – so far.'

I always knew what attracted me to Emily – her smile, her eyes, her face, her figure, her warmth, her openness, her vivacity, her American can-do attitude, her not caring what other people thought. I was attracted by her name too, Emily. She was named after the poet Emily Dickinson, and that was fine, she said, because she happened to like Emily Dickinson's poems. 'Presumably your parents do, too?' I'd asked. She seemed less sure of this. 'You know what, I think they liked the *idea* of her. Mom kind of admired her isolation. And her poems are very short, mostly. I think that helped.' 'Do you have a favourite?' I asked. 'I have lots of favourites,' she replied, and would not be forced to choose one above the rest – which endeared her to me still more. I can think of a thousand other reasons, but what attracted Emily to me?

Perhaps my quietness, my politeness, my diffidence, even my accent. Like our voices, our humours – in the medieval sense – were different but complementary, I thought. She was sanguine, I phlegmatic; she was spring to my winter, air to my water. I put this to her and she said, 'In the medieval sense! What about in the twentieth-century sense? You like my jokes and I like yours.' It was true. When we quarrelled, which was seldom, it blew up in a moment and then was gone. Sometimes, I know, I irritated her with my cautiousness, but with one exception I never found her enthusiasm anything but inspiring. She thought I was passionate, brilliant, funny. And I was, or I could be with her urging me on.

The exception was the business of my not driving. She was incredulous that at the age of twenty-three I couldn't drive, and even more so that I had no intention of retaking the test. But I had made a virtue out of failure, and would not be budged, and Emily, rather than be defeated, came to see my refusal as a kind of charming old-world quirk. Later, when Alice was on the way, she nagged me to take lessons again – it would make life with a child so much easier if both of us could drive – but I wouldn't do it, and after a while she ceased trying to persuade me. As Karen had asked long before, what did it matter? Emily drove, I didn't. It wasn't, after all, necessary for me to drive. We were together, and we had Alice. That was all that was necessary.

A few weeks after the conference, following a flurry of letters, and a couple of phone calls neither of us could afford, Emily came to visit. A few weeks after that, I returned to America to see her. It was on this trip that I first met her parents, Alfred and Rachel. Before I went home I asked Emily to marry me, and she said she would.

5

When, all those years ago, the Dean of Faculty suggested that I apply for the Chair, he said that the University was keen to have a generalist 'at the helm of the good ship English Literature'. He actually came out with that absurd phrase. He himself was a generalist, he said, a historian equally at home in the seventeenth as in the nineteenth century. The man who had just vacated the Chair, Harold Pritchley, was a specialist (Modernism). He was also (the Dean did not say this but we both knew it to be true) a mean, vindictive, arrogant dipsomaniac. Specialists were all very well, the Dean said, and of course from the point of view of research they were essential, but the University felt that somebody with a broad yet convincing knowledge of the whole range of English Literature should now head up the department. If a person of my qualities were appointed it would send out a message.

'And what would that be?'

The Dean looked perplexed, as if I'd asked an unfair question.

'Well, that we espouse excellence in all things. That we value breadth as well as depth. That we are not a den of obscurity.'

'I see.'

'That we are connected to the real world.'

Maybe it wasn't kindness after all. Maybe it was opportunism. What the Dean said next seemed to suggest the latter.

'Not everybody was enamoured of Harold Pritchley. His way of conducting business.'

'I didn't think anybody was.'

'A brilliant mind, of course. But he rather polarised opinion. And alienated potential friends and sponsors.'

'He certainly alienated me,' I said.

'So I gather. Be that as it may. You'd be an excellent successor to Professor Pritchley, Alan, not least because you are so unlike him.'

What they wanted, obviously, was not a brilliant mind but a safe pair of hands. How Harold Pritchley would have sneered.

'You are greatly respected, you know,' the Dean said, somewhat too late.

I wasn't interested. I wasn't even flattered to be asked. I could see why the Dean's words fitted me and why the Dean thought I would fit the job. A generalist: that was me all right. Most of my colleagues specialised. Some of them had areas of special interest so special that nobody else was allowed in. I, too, had once specialised, that is to say I had written my PhD thesis, but since then I had dabbled in and hovered over several centuries of great and mediocre writing, with the result that I knew more about everything but less about anything than anybody else in the department. My knowledge of literature *was* convincing, but also – that old feeling again – fraudulent. There is a famous campus novel in which literature academics play a game called 'Humiliation', the winner being whoever admits to the most shameful omission in their reading. An American professor wins by confessing to having not read *Hamlet*. I am not like that – I am the opposite. I *have* read everything, from Shakespeare to the Modernists and beyond. Fiction, plays, poetry – I can't, now, quite imagine the *years* of reading this has entailed, but I know they have happened – yet I remember very little about any of it. Perhaps the detail was overwhelmed by the sheer volume. Nevertheless, I can when required comfortably sustain a long conversation about most authors and their works, whether in a professional or social setting (the two usually overlap). And I can, in my lectures to first-year students, express an opinion on just about any literary work without betraying the overwhelming blankness of my memory of it. This, it seems to me, is a worse crime than not having read it in the first place, a far worse form of obscurity than possessing knowledge so profound that nobody else can understand you. Without Emily to embolden me, I would never have taken the Chair, even if I had wanted it, for fear of being found out.

Since the bombing, people have seldom challenged either my opinions or my ignorance: they are anxious not to hurt my feelings. Nobody, as far as I am aware, dislikes me. Harold Pritchley disliked me, but then he disliked everybody and everybody disliked him, and anyway he is long gone now, supercilious and drunk in Cambridge. There are two other people in our department who are generally disliked. They either offend their colleagues' political or gender-related sensibilities or simply have unprepossessing personal habits. They are probably the cleverest of us all – another reason for their unpopularity. Neither of them, I am sure, was invited to apply for the Chair vacated by Professor Pritchley, which was in the end filled by an outsider, bland and bureaucratic, who is still in it eighteen years later.

Sometimes it takes me a minute or two to remember what my own PhD was actually about. Very occasionally I open my bound copy at random, and it is like reading something written by someone else. There it is, 65,000 words, typed and bound, and a sentence or a paragraph may come back to me, more or less intact, but the actual writing of it is a lost mystery. True to the advice of my supervisor, I took a broad theme and applied it to a number of works by different authors (I played safe – Conrad, Kipling and Buchan are all in there) and everybody was happy with that. If my arguments had gaps, I wrote with sufficient confidence and wit to cover them. As Emily found when I gave my paper in Philadelphia, if you stand back a bit I can be rather impressive. Later I rehashed and expanded the thesis and published it as *Romance and Cynicism at the Height of Empire*. For a while it was an Open University text.

My forte is the sweeping statement, the summarising paragraph suggestive of much learning, the conclusion that looks like a distillation of years of accumulated knowledge. I am perfect for delivering the lectures in the first- and second-year survey courses. These lectures are popular because they are entertaining and fast-moving, and name-check so many writers, famous and obscure, that everyone's favourite author is guaranteed a mention. In order to refresh my lecture notes I have made occasional investigative forays which might lead to more serious research, but have usually become bored before any detailed study is underway. Sometimes as a result I have had a paper accepted by some journal or other, so my publications record is quite respectable. I am a kind of authority, if anyone needs one, on semi-neglected, unfashionable Edwardian writers such as Chesterton and Galsworthy.

My task on sabbatical was to write a monograph on a little-known novelist, David Dibald. Although Dibald lived almost all of his life in Sussex and is regarded (insofar as he is regarded at all) as an English writer, he was born in this town, and for this reason his papers were gifted to the University's library by his daughter in the 1970s. Perhaps she felt that this would be good for the University, in the same way that the Dean of Faculty felt a Professor Tealing would be good for it. Apart from by myself, however, the papers do not seem ever to have been looked at.

Dibald wrote four moderately successful novels between 1906 and 1914 and was killed at Ypres the following year. I find the books quietly moving. Dibald was concerned with continuity in life, with patterns, with those things of the world that may be described as 'recurring' or 'unchanging': the annual cycle of birth, death and rebirth in nature is often referred to, plants and animals are carefully observed, as too is the work of humans that goes with the turn of the seasons – ploughing, planting, reaping. Another theme focuses on the way men and women of his time were of the land while the land, at least in its wilder aspects, retained its independence from them and kept its own timescale, dwarfing the timescale of a human life. Each of his novels suggests that knowledge is gathered only slowly, with the passing of years, and that even then no single person, not even if he or she should live to a great age, can ever acquire complete knowledge. Dibald, ironically, tried to articulate this when very young, between the ages of twenty-two and thirty, and then the war came.

There are obvious reasons why all this, from a completely forgotten writer, might appeal to a man like myself, a man in my position. I do not need to rehearse them, but in addition I like the fact that Dibald expressed no interest in literary movements or theories, but wrote in a consistently unpretentious style about unremarkable lives, before his own (for the time) unremarkable death. He was one of the also-rans of that generation, or of any generation. 'Showed promise, largely unfulfilled,' his literary obituary might have read.

Too many people write books, in my view. Far, far too many people write novels. Libraries and second-hand bookshops are stuffed with their outpourings. What I find attractive about Dibald is the total absence of signs of arrogance or ambition. He seems just to be having a stab at writing down his take on life, disguising it as fiction. All novelists do that of course – do it bravely, or arrogantly or stupidly, or well or badly – and in most cases within a few months of publication, or five years later, or perhaps five years after death, nobody gives a damn what their 'take' was and nobody is reading their books. But here was I, nearly a century on, reading David Dibald, reading him and liking him and thinking that he was pretty good, and that if he hadn't been killed so young he might well have become famous.

Fame isn't the point, though. Survival, is that it? No, because none of what anyone writes or thinks or feels or believes, none of it survives for long. You survive only through your children, and I have no child and Dibald's daughter donated her father's papers to the University probably knowing that if she didn't they'd be chucked on a bonfire or into a skip when *she* died. She saved her father, but for what? To be read by a lecturer who doesn't think literature has anything to say, but who nevertheless goes on, year after year, telling his students that it does.

And now I am supposed to be writing a book about Dibald. A publisher has expressed interest – more interest, in fact, than I have in my subject. I know, at bottom, that I don't want to tell the world about David Dibald. Dibald is mine, a calm, solitary backwater in which I can drift undisturbed. If I actually write the monograph, I will only have to find somewhere else to drift. I might even have to confront that feeling which increasingly threatens to overwhelm me, that my work, my life as an academic, the very stuff of my learning, all those hours and days and years of reading, the thousands of books I have devoured – literature, in its entirety – all of it is utter futility and a complete waste of time.

Perhaps one day I will have the courage to say that, out loud or in black and white on paper, and have done with the whole bloody charade.

6

'You think you know what happened,' Nilsen said. 'Sure you do. You've been outspoken about it. It's your honestly held, reasonably argued opinion that there was a miscarriage of justice. That a man was found guilty of something he didn't do. And behind that, you've said, there was subterfuge, suppressed evidence, political pressure, conspiracy . . .'

'I've never used that word,' I said. 'I've always been careful to avoid it.'

'Nevertheless . . .' Nilsen answered, baring his teeth in the unlovely smile. He was echoing me from some distance back in the conversation, and we both caught the echo but only he smiled. 'That's what your theory of events amounts to, a conspiracy. In the absence of proof, that is.'

'The absence of proof isn't my responsibility,' I said.

'Well, let's not go there. Let's, as you requested, get to the point. You think a whole lot of things happened. I'll tell you what *I* think. Let me go through it, and you listen. You don't have to agree with me. Just listen till I'm done.'

'If you imagine I'm going to sit here nodding like a poodle –' I began, but Nilsen stopped me with a completely different word and a different tone.

'Please,' he said. And then again, more quietly, 'Please.'

I'm not sure I knew how I'd been going to finish my sentence, but I didn't finish it.

'I'm going to level with you,' Nilsen said. 'That's why I'm here, to take a load off of my conscience. I told you outside, you can help me and I can help you. So please, listen to what I have to say.'

'What is it I'm about to hear?' I said. 'What you *think* happened, or what you *know* happened, or what happened? Because I really don't need any more theories.'

'Just listen,' he said.

I thought of the work I'd been doing before I went out to clear snow, the work I should be doing now, the pointless, impractical work on David Dibald that was the reason for my being on sabbatical and that I wasn't really getting done and that was of no importance. Literature makes nothing happen, I thought. Auden said that, or something very like it. In my other life, when Emily was with me, I would have contested it. She certainly would have. She'd crushed that niggling insecurity in the old, young Alan Tealing so that I'd hardly felt it, and then she had died and it had come back, stronger than ever. So now there wasn't anything I would rather be occupied with than listening to Nilsen. I didn't doubt that I would have heard before whatever he had to say, but what was to be lost by hearing it again? There wasn't anyone in my life as it was that I'd rather have seen sitting where Nilsen was. Not Carol, not Jim Collins, nobody. So I emptied the last of the coffee from the cafetière into our cups, and put the kettle on to make more, and I let him talk.

'In the days immediately after the event,' Nilsen said, 'various claims of responsibility were made, some of them plausible, some not. Within a week we knew for sure what we'd believed from the start, that it was a bomb. The wreckage confirmed it. Very soon we had some pretty strong theories as to who had done it. British intelligence were thinking along the same lines. The police were doing their thing too, progressing the investigation.' He weighted that last phrase with something that might have been contempt. 'We were all sharing information, and we were coming to the same conclusions. After about three months we knew a lot, and after six we knew so much you could say we were certain. One theory was so far in front of all the others it stopped being a theory. It became what we knew.

'The police had identified the suitcase that contained the device. We knew where it had been located in the aircraft hold. We had fragments of clothing, recovered at the crash site, which had been in that suitcase. The clothing had most likely been packed round the bomb. We knew the item the bomb had been loaded into, a radio cassette player, we knew the make and model. We knew that the bomb had detonated thirty-eight minutes after take-off and that pointed to a particular type of timer, and when we put that together with the cassette player we got scared because we recognised the combination. There was a Palestinian group based in Germany. The German police, with our assistance, had broken it up a month before the bombing. That group had been making devices designed to bring down airplanes just the way this one had been brought down. Maybe there was a connection. We didn't know how the bomb had been ingested into the baggage system but we were working on it. So we had all this. What else did we need?'

In detective novels of the kind Emily had loved, the detective or someone else at this point says 'a motive'. And sure enough Nilsen said it, or came close.

'We needed motivation. You know what the motivation was. Revenge, retaliation, call it what you will. We were at war with another country, a Middle East state with ideological, political and religious aims diametrically opposed to ours. And that war isn't over yet. It isn't open warfare. Some of it makes the news, most of it doesn't. There's a lot of rhetoric, a lot of bluster. Back then there was hostage-taking, hostage-trading, military and naval stand-offs, and behind that another level of conflict. Assassinations and arms deals, negotiations that never officially took place, all of that.

'But then something happened that was so big it couldn't be hidden. One of our warships shot down one of their aircraft. A civilian aircraft. It was a mistake, a terrible one. Three hundred lives wiped out. Yet we didn't admit responsibility. We said the action was justifiable, because the ship's commander thought he was under attack. We regretted what had been done, but we defended it. We even gave the guy a medal. Eventually we paid some compensation, but that was years later. Six months after that warship fired off its missile, the flight your wife and daughter were on goes down. So, sure, there was motivation.

'Motivation, suspects, method. We had two out of three. A hostile government that had commissioned a revenge attack, and a group prepared to do the job with the expertise to do it. It was the method, how the bomb had been ingested into the system, that we didn't have. And we still lacked a lot of detail. Without the detail there were too many gaps. The narrative wouldn't hold together. We had to firm it up, then we could do something with it. Make the accusation, take out the offenders, bring vengeance down on the heads of the avengers – whatever we wanted to do. But we couldn't do it until we had fully constructed the narrative.'

'You keep saying "we",' I said.

Nilsen looked quizzical.

'Like you were running the investigation. You, the Americans.'

He seemed to think about that for a few seconds. 'The police were running the investigation,' he said, 'but we were right alongside of them. These were our people who'd been hit. We had an interest, I think.'

So far nothing was new. I'd been over this territory thousands of times, worked out or guessed it all. I remembered the word 'ingestion' from the trial. It made it sound as if the aeroplane had swallowed the bomb. Nilsen wasn't being specific. He didn't need to be. We both knew exactly what he was saying, who he was talking about. We were way beyond the specifics. What I didn't know was where he was going next, and for a moment even he looked a little lost. Maybe my intervention had thrown him. I wished I hadn't said anything, willed myself not to speak again. Not to nod or shake my head either: I didn't want Nilsen thinking I was with him or against him. I just wanted him to continue.

'Trouble was, the narrative we had, we didn't like it,' he said. 'Not at all, but the politicians wanted something from us. The usual thing. They were under pressure to deliver to the media, to the people.' Again, I detected a note of contempt. 'Who had done this? Who was responsible? People always want to know the end of a story. So we told the politicians some of what we had but we kept the worst back and they didn't like even what we did tell them, but for different reasons. When we laid out what we had for them, what they saw was the finger of accusation pointing at the wrong country. How could that be? Its people hated us, we hated them. How could it be the wrong country?'

I kept my mouth shut.

'Time,' Nilsen said. 'A couple of years earlier and it would have been the right country, but time passes and things change. The power balance shifts. Your enemy becomes your enemy's enemy and that makes him your friend. Or your friend becomes ambitious, threatens your other friends, and that makes him your enemy. New alliances are required, new understandings. Realignments. That's what time does. And then there's place. No, not place. Context. The Middle East isn't a place. It's a cauldron of oil and creeds.'

That watchtower look was on me again. Nilsen seemed now, with that last flourish, to be inviting some response. I heard the subtleties in his sentences, the considered grammar. I thought, I could be marking a student's clever essay; or I could be the student, being patronised. I declined, at this stage, to comment.

'There was a war coming,' Nilsen said. 'A real, open, hot war. We knew it was coming, and that we would be in it. Staying out wasn't an option. Maybe we could live without the creeds but we couldn't live without the oil. But if we were going in there with force, into that context, that cauldron, we needed to neutralise some of the countries we usually regarded as hostile. Not just neutralise. Some of them we needed on our side. So we couldn't go accusing them of having commissioned or paid or in some way facilitated a bunch of terrorists to bring this airplane down. Whether they'd done it or not, making that accusation wasn't going to help bring about the realignment.'

I pushed the plunger down on the fresh jug of coffee, thinking of old war movies and men behind enemy lines blowing up bridges, and refilled our cups.

'So the politicians wanted a different narrative,' Nilsen said. 'That was something of a relief to us. The one we had didn't make us look good. It made us look – incompetent at best. We'd been watching the group in Germany a long time. A situation like that, you try to leave things undisturbed if you can. Then suddenly it's time to move, you go in and make the arrests, break the thing up. You hope you haven't cut it too fine. When you're working with other agencies co-ordination is always an issue. We were working with the Germans, plus some others. We cut it very fine.

'You know this,' he said again. And he was correct, but it was as necessary for me to hear it now as it seemed to be for him to let it out. 'There was somebody inside that cell. Someone who'd switched loyalties. That's how we were so well informed. When there's someone in deep there is one priority and that's to keep him there. He's an investment, a lot of time and effort has been spent on him. You expect payback. Someone in that position, he's living on the edge. If his cover goes, he's dead. So he has to be authentic. This man was authentic. He was part of the factory. He had a history as a bomb-maker. Ten years earlier, we'd have happily seen him dead. But he'd changed sides. He was our early-warning system.'

'What was he supposed to warn you about?'

'About the bombs. Their state of readiness. He was supposed to build them so they were inoperable but he couldn't do that and remain authentic. What he could do was give us updates, so we could move in time. Because obviously we couldn't have a scenario with a device he'd been instrumental in preparing. If one got away, if a device like that was ever used, even if there had been good reason for our involvement, it wouldn't be forgiven. Wouldn't really be forgivable.'

'No,' I said. 'It wouldn't.'

'So we had to make sure that scenario never arose.'

A little pulse of excitement ran through me. Sit tight, I told myself, let him talk. I'd felt that pulse too often before not to repress it now, but Nilsen was circling round something. I was sure his words were edging towards some kind of admission or confirmation.

'What I'm saying,' he said, 'is we had motivation too. Everyone had motivation.'

I inspected my fingernails. Give me it, I begged him silently. I can't make you but you've come here with something. Give me it.

But already he was veering away. 'It became in our interest to make the narrative fit the destination,' he said. 'There had to be another way that the bombing could have happened.' I tried to keep listening, but had I missed something? 'We unpacked everything we had, and we ditched what was now irrelevant and re-used what couldn't be retracted and we built the narrative back up again. You have to understand something: we weren't lying to ourselves, or to anybody.' He raised his hand to stop whatever I might have to say about that. 'We were coming at it from another place. Who could be in the frame? It had to be a hostile regime or organisation but one with no current strategic importance. A regime we didn't need any favours from but which had plenty of reasons for wanting to hurt us. We had a fat file full of outfits like that. Any one of them could have the motivation to do this thing. But *how* did they do it? Not the way we'd thought. The methodology had to change.Same explosive, different timer, different bomb-maker. Same suitcase, different location for ingestion. We looked again at the flight schedules, the feeder flights, how unaccompanied baggage was transferred. None of this was easy. Some of the evidence didn't fit. We downgraded it and we searched for new evidence to put in its place. We had people in research who knew what we needed. I'm not saying evidence was fabricated. It's what I said before – we didn't just want to solve the crime, we needed to solve it. So much was riding on achieving an outcome. You could say we were desperate.'

Another pause. His coffee was untouched. An oily sheen lay on its surface. I could see that he was struggling with something. He looked even greyer than when he had first come in.

'No,' he said. 'No, you see that's not good enough. *That's* why I'm here.'

Just for a minute it was as if he were alone in the room, arguing with himself. His hand went to his head and off came the woollen hat again, and he hit his knuckles against the threadbare dome. Then he sat, eyes down, with his elbow on the table and his hand covering his brow. I heard sharp little breathing noises coming from him and thought perhaps he was crying. Then the noises stopped and he looked up, first to the ceiling, then back to me. He hadn't been crying. He'd been praying.

'Thank you for your patience,' he said, and I might have said something about that, about just how long I'd been waiting, but he went straight on. 'What I said then. We were desperate but that's no excuse. There *was* fabrication. There *was* tampering. It wasn't just that we dropped irrelevant evidence, we suppressed things that were relevant but disruptive. Maybe the first time you do that it's some tiny, insignificant detail. Everything else fits but this one piece won't click home. You try it every which way. It just won't go, but if you trim it a little it will. Or maybe you don't trim it, you find something else that doesn't belong but fits better in the space. You put it in and it looks perfect and after a while you don't want to take it out. Then you have to get rid of the awkward non-fitting piece. You go through that process once, and the second time it doesn't seem such a big deal, and then you remind yourself that what you're trying to do is reach a destination and it doesn't matter so much how you get there, just get there. And there is urgency, pressure from above. So you keep going.'

I felt an unearthly dislocation from everything, there, in my own home, hearing this. I was not recording it, it was not being written down, there was no one to hear it but me. It was worthless. I could not imagine myself beyond the confines of the room. I guessed it was still snowing but could not bring myself to look. The kitchen was a capsule floating in space. Time was frozen, suspended. Only, of course, for Nilsen it wasn't, not if he was telling the truth about his cancer. But was he telling the truth about anything?

'It is despicable, what you're saying,' I said.

'I'm not excusing it.' He fitted the hat back on his head. 'I'm telling you how it happens. I said I would level with you and that's what I'm doing.'

'You're too late,' I said.

'No, I'm not too late,' he said. 'I can't be.'

This was a man whose whole life had been about getting results: a man of certainties faced with one looming certainty, one last result. But the conviction in the way he insisted he was not too late, that it was not *possible* that he was too late – it struck me that this was not a conviction based on his own abilities. It came from somewhere else, from his God, and I realised that I did not trust this source any less than if he had been feeding me the other, more worldly, harder-edged certainties I'd been getting from people like him for twenty years. On the contrary, and much to my astonishment, I trusted it more. Nilsen's faith was *more* credible than all of the rational bullshit.

'Forensics,' he said, as though somehow tapping into my thoughts. 'Don't you love the clinical precision of that word? How can such a word lie? How can that science be wrong? But it's never the science. It's the application, the people doing the science. They weren't immune to hubris, or the need for self-protection, or career enhancement, any more than the rest of us. Some of them weren't even real scientists, they'd moved sideways from other careers and picked up their knowledge as they went along. They'd messed up in other cases, both sides of the pond, but we didn't want to hear that, not then. Sure, they're discredited now. A man who's never going to work for the FBI again, washed up in some dirty little laboratory in California, a mile from the Mexican border. Another over here — what does he do for a living? He's a chiropractor. This is his daily job. He analyses your spine and tells you that if he can straighten it out all your other health problems will disappear too.'

He shook his head, the belief of a minute earlier now replaced by disbelief, or so it seemed. It occurred to me that there were less useful occupations than easing people's back pain.

'Let me tell you the rest,' he said.

'I know the rest,' I said. And yes, I could have picked up his story and gone with it to the end, and it wouldn't have been so very different. The difference lay in who was telling it. This stranger — this man I had never before seen from a world that I could, in my previous life, never for a moment have imagined would touch me — was telling it. To hear him was an experience both dreamlike and real. Like a dream, because he went on talking in a kind of coded, non-specific language, as if he were trying to ward off the bogeyman of betrayal, of broken confidences, the possibility of another listener outside in the snow. He spoke of this regime or that regime, of 'the island', 'the airport', not naming names, or inventing new names for old familiar characters. I understood what he was saying, inferred everything I was supposed to infer, but the words were cloudy, the room as thick with them as the air outside was thick with snowflakes. Yes, it was like a dream, but it was also real because it was happening in my own kitchen, across my own kitchen table, and on the wall behind Nilsen the second hand of the kitchen clock ticked its relentless way round and round the dial. And as he talked, something changed between us. We became – I hesitate to use this word but can think of no other – more intimate. Something intense, almost tangible, stretched between us, and this is the strongest sensation of memory I retain of the hour that thus passed. That, and the admonishing wag of the clock's second hand. These things might, of course, not have happened, Nilsen might never have said what he said, and the memory could be the memory of a dream. But then, everything could be the memory of a dream.

You rearrange the pieces of the narrative. Some things become simpler, others more complicated. That chain of client, procurer, perpetrator can be dispensed with. Now there is a hostile regime – 'rogue state' is another favoured term – with agents of its own who could have constructed and placed the bomb. It has been sponsoring or carrying out acts of terrorism for years. There is every possibility that it was involved in this one.

You start a trail from your regime. Your *new*, hostile, rogue regime. There is a man who works for you, a junior operative in their intelligence service. Very junior – he services their cars. Let's call him Ali. You don't know how good a mechanic Ali is but he's a lousy informer. For months he gives you nothing of any value. Then one day he does. He gives you a name. He knows you have been looking for someone – let's say someone whose life is open to interpretation – and he finds someone, a security officer for the national airline. Ali knows this person. You check him out. Yes, you reckon, this could be the one you have been seeking.

His name is Khalil Khazar.

You are perfectly aware that Ali is not reliable. He wants money. He wants protection. He wants a new life in the USA, a better life for his wife and child. (Yes, and who can blame him for that?) He will tell you anything. Nothing he tells you should be taken at face value. You understand. It's okay. The more you pay Ali, the more he tells you. The more you like what he tells you, the more he earns. He tells you a great deal about Khalil Khazar, and some of it is useful to your restructuring of the narrative.

Because of his job, Khazar travels. He spends a lot of time in hotels, in meetings in anonymous breeze-block buildings on industrial estates on the outer edges of city sprawl. Airports are a second home to him. Lagos, Zurich, Riyadh, Prague, Cyprus, Malta. Sometimes he travels under his own name, sometimes he uses a coded passport with another name, issued at the request of the regime's intelligence service. Why does he have such a passport? Why do such people, of any state, have multiple identities? Well, it doesn't matter. The point is how you interpret such movements. It doesn't look good for Khalil Khazar, but it looks better for you. You build up a picture of who he is, where he has been. Where he was on a particular day. On the morning of the day in question he was on a Mediterranean island. He'd arrived the day before, stayed the night, then flew home again, on a flight that left the island around the time that another flight took off for Germany. That second flight connected with a flight to London, a feeder flight to the transatlantic flight that was destroyed by a bomb that evening.

So now you have one trail leading from the hostile regime to an island, and another trail leading from the wreckage of the aircraft to London. And they are connected – tenuously, but connected nevertheless – by two flights, one from the island to Germany, and one from Germany to London.

You go through it a hundred times. You examine it from every angle. The bomb exploded on a plane that took off from Heathrow, London. Was the bomb loaded, *ingested*, at Heathrow? If it was, then Khalil Khazar can't have been involved. He hasn't been in London for years. Travel there is restricted for him because there are no diplomatic relations between the UK and his country. If Khazar isn't involved, then neither is his country. Think again. You have two trails that almost meet. To make them meet, the bomb must *not* have been ingested at Heathrow. It must have come in from somewhere else, on another flight, on a feeder flight, and been transferred to the New York flight. Okay, this makes more sense. The two trails don't come together in London. They come together on the island. You follow the bomb back to Germany, back to the island's airport, and you try to work out how Khazar could have put the suitcase containing the bomb into the system there.

But it would make so much more sense to load the bomb at Heathrow.

Not for Khalil Khazar. Impossible for him, because he was never in London. On the day of the bombing he was on the island, at the airport, catching a flight home. And also it would depend on the type of bomb. If the bomb was detonated by a barometric timer, of the type built by the terror group based in Germany, then yes, logically Heathrow makes more sense. The way it works . . .

But you know the way it works. You are angry and frustrated now. You are going round in circles. You do not need this. You know how a barometric timer works.

How it works: it lies dormant so long as it is on the ground. Doesn't matter where it is, in the boot of a car or the hold of an aircraft, it is asleep. The timer is activated only when the plane is airborne, the mechanism reacting to the drop in air pressure as the plane gains height. Activation usually occurs seven or eight minutes after take-off depending on the rate of climb. The way the group in Germany set their devices, the timer would then run for thirty minutes before triggering the bomb. If it was that kind of bomb, you'd expect it to have detonated thirty-seven or thirty-eight minutes after take-off.

Which is what happened.

But you're on a different trail now, so it *couldn't* have been like that. You go through it once more, voicing your hypotheses, scribbling down timings, working it out all over again. You've missed something, perhaps something obvious. If Khazar planted the bomb, he could *not* have introduced it at Heathrow. But if it came in on another flight it would have blown up before it even got to Heathrow, *if* it was triggered by a barometric timer. So – of course – it had to be another kind of timer. The bomb *had* to be triggered not by barometric pressure change but by ticking time. You set the timer running, you get the suitcase into the system, and when the time runs out the bomb goes off.

It's so simple when you say it. But how does the bomber know how long to set the timer for? He puts the suitcase on one flight, it's to be transferred at another airport to a second flight, then in London transferred on to the target flight, and then it's to blow up over the Atlantic. One unaccompanied suitcase going through all those airports, all those security systems, with all the possibility of detection, baggage mix-ups, delayed departures and arrivals – how long does the bomber give it? Maybe it doesn't matter where or when or on which plane it blows up. Maybe if he's an inefficient bomber it can blow up on the ground with no one on board for all he cares. But he isn't inefficient. He has a job to do, and he cares a great deal about getting it right. There is money in it, and vengeance, even a cruel, barren kind of justice. The trouble with your simple explanation is that it isn't simple at all. It's ludicrously complex and has a huge likelihood of failure. If the bomber wants to bring down a particular plane he's going to put the bomb on to that plane, not any other, and he's going to use a device that detonates only when that plane is well into its flight.

Then that bomber must be the wrong bomber.

The right bomber used a different kind of timer.

You talk to your forensics experts again – your future lab technician and chiropractor – and they go back to the fragments of clothing from the primary suitcase and have another look. And they find

72

something, a tiny fragment of circuit board embedded in a shirt collar. So tiny it might almost have been missed. In fact it *was* missed first time round; well, not missed but overlooked, there's some confusion over when and where it was found and how it was catalogued or not catalogued, which would explain why nobody thought there was anything special about it back then, but now they do. Now it is very special. It is the key to everything. It comes from a timer, the right kind of timer, the kind of timer that will fit with the narrative that has a bomb in a radio cassette player in a suitcase going on its merry undetected way from one airport to another even though a warning was circulated to look out for bombs in radio cassette players because you and the Germans and God knows who else *knew* there was at least one of the damn things out there. But that was before, that was the old narrative, and now you have turned the page, and there you find that a batch of these other, non-barometric timers was once supplied by the manufacturer to the hostile regime and that Khalil Khazar, travelling the world under his own name or another, *could* have had a role in acquiring them.

And then Ali gives you another name. He understands, as you do, or *because* you do, that the bombing wasn't an act of individual insanity but one of shared ideology. If Khazar was involved, he can't have acted alone. So Ali gives you Waleed Mahmed, also employed by the national airline, its station manager at the island's airport. As with Khazar, the suggestion is that there is more to him than appears on the surface, that his work for the regime goes far beyond what is given in his job description. Whenever Khazar is on the island he spends time with Waleed Mahmed. Waleed Mahmed is a well-known face around the airport, especially at the check-in and information desks. This is not to say that he is free to wander wherever he likes, but he does have detailed knowledge of the airport and its security procedures – which, as it happens, are very thorough and very thoroughly adhered to. Anybody wishing to circumvent those procedures would find such knowledge useful. Khalil Khazar and Waleed Mahmed together make an interesting team.

But Waleed Mahmed's whereabouts on the day in question are not known. It cannot be established if he was at the airport, or even on the island. Nobody can be found to verify where he was. If he had been at the airport, where his face was so familiar, somebody, surely, would have remembered. This does not rule him out as a suspect, but it makes it all the more important to concentrate on Khazar, who, carrying a false passport, went through the airport that day.

Ali the car mechanic has done well for you, done well for himself, earned himself and his family a new start in America, but his paid-for testimony won't stand up under legal scrutiny in a courtroom. Which is where, sometime, somewhere, this is all heading. You need to press and bend one more piece into place in the jigsaw, so that you can pin this crime on Khazar and Mahmed, one or the other or both, and, through them, on your hostile, strategically unimportant, wickedly motivated rogue state.

One more piece. You need an eyewitness.

I was staring at the window. A constantly shifting curtain of white flickered outside. The snow was now so thick that it made the daylight sickly and feeble, and it was not even three o'clock. I wondered how I was going to get Nilsen out of the house if the weather did not improve.

'We are almost there, Dr Tealing,' he said. 'We are almost at the end.'

I said again, 'You are too late.'

He shook his head.

I said, 'Do you really think I will join in this ridiculous game of yours, after all these years?'

'A witness,' he said. 'Someone who saw Khalil Khazar handle the suitcase on the island. He was at the airport, on the day of the bombing, in order to fly home. What else was he there for? It's too much of a coincidence, and you know what we think of coincidences. Surely we can find someone who saw him. Join in, Dr Tealing? Yes, of course you will. You already have. You can't help yourself. As I was saying. We need a witness.'

He was right. I could not help myself.

'Parroulet,' I said.

7

After the bombing, once the shock diminished and I began to accept that what had happened really had happened, I found myself having dreams about Alice, myself and Alice, night after night. Had I gone for counselling, no doubt I would have learned that this was normal, part of a process. But I chose to be my own counsellor, standing outside and apart from myself sometimes as I grieved, and I worked it out unaided. She was my daughter, but she could not be with me in the new reality I inhabited; reasonable, then, that she should walk and run and laugh instead through my shallow sleep. She was always happy in these dreams, never fearful or hurt or anxious. Sometimes we were at home, watching television together, or out in the garden. Often we were on a beach, kicking at the frothy ends of waves. I would pick her up and carry her deeper, threatening to launch her into the sea. She'd be screaming and laughing, knowing – absolutely trusting – that I would never ever let her go no matter how very nearly she might seem about to leave my grasp. And someone – I wanted it to be Emily but I never got to see who it was – was taking pictures of us. Alan and Alice posed for the camera: hunter with seal under arm, ogre with captive princess, man with daughter clinging to neck. But it wasn't Alan, it was me, and the dreams were more wonderful, more intense and pure, than the experiences on which they were loosely based. I wished I could have stayed in them for ever, those happy-ever-after dreams, but of course I couldn't. I would wake from them with tears pouring from my eyes, and lie in the darkness a few steps from the empty bedroom where she had once slept. After a while I would get up, and go downstairs to try to read. This was years before I got involved with the Case. No wonder I cannot remember all the literature I have read: great chunks of it passed before my eyes in those dead nights. I took it in but where it went after that I do not know.

And then a time came when she no longer came to me in dreams. And a while after that I found, to my horror, that she had faded a little in my mind, and I would catch up a photograph of her and Emily, terrified that I would not recognise them. And yes, there they were behind the glass, but I saw also that they had gone, or perhaps that I had gone. I was looking at a photograph in which they were still six and twenty-eight, while I was racing towards middle age, and on beyond that to decrepitude.

Had I gone for counselling, I might have asked the counsellor, how is it that I hardly ever dream of Emily? I asked it of myself, but I didn't come up with any answers.

Once, when I was coming home from work on the bus, earlier than usual, a man and a little girl got on, two or three stops after I had, and sat across the aisle from me. She was six, seven at most – Alice's age – and in school uniform. The man was probably ten years younger than I, tall and thin, with untidy curly hair, and there was a boyish, gently ribbing tone to his voice when he spoke to the girl, his daughter. He'd just picked her up from school. I had a vague sense of having seen him before. Maybe he taught at the University. As soon as they were seated the girl made him open the free newspaper he'd picked up on entering the bus, a copy of which I'd been idly, blindly leafing through, and they began what was evidently a regular game. He took the left-hand page and she the right-hand one of each spread, and as they turned them they counted the pictures of different items on each side. The winner was the one with the highest number by the time they got to the end of the paper. The first time through it was houses, then it was animals. She won both times. 'You're much too good at this,' he said, as she called out a dog and two horses to his solitary fish. 'Oh, that's so unfair!' he groaned, a minute later. 'Look at all those cows! That's, uh, 98–3 to you.' She giggled at his plucked-from-the-air number but kept concentrating. She didn't miss a trick, with her heart-shaped, pixie face and shining blue eyes and the same out-of-control curly hair as her dad's. I couldn't keep my eyes off her. It wasn't clear who was more snuggled into whom. I knew how she would smell to him: not *what* she would smell like, but *how*, to *him*, her father. 'Let's play again,' she said. 'But I always lose,' he said. She insisted. This time they were car-spotters. For a few pages it was close, and he kept up a running commentary – 'One to me, two to you, oh, another to me, we're both winning, oh, now I'm ahead, I'll beat you this time, I'm winning 3–2.' Her legs kicked up with pleasure. I forced myself to sit back. I could see what page they were on, and began turning my own paper in time with theirs. Together we turned, and again, and then there came a story about floods in Italy, and a photograph of a car park full of floating cars, dozens of them, on the right-hand page. 'I give up,' the father said. 'Why are they swimming?' the daughter asked. My eyes stung, my tongue was suddenly choking me. Her wonderful, innocent question ached in my ears. I stood up and pressed the bell, and lurched from the bus a mile short of my usual stop. I thought I was going to be sick with jealousy.

I walked the rest of the way home in tears, remembering Alice's first day at school. Emily hadn't wanted to upset her by crying when she had to let her go, and so we'd agreed that I would take her. It was a ten-minute walk to the school. Alice chatted all the way, telling me the exact contents of her school bag, which we'd packed together the night before and repacked in the morning; and then, as the school building loomed and she saw all the other children in their new blue shirts, and the other fathers and mothers, converging on the gate, she fell silent and clutched my hand more tightly, and I felt my own pulse quicken and my throat tighten. But she was brave, we were both brave. She said, 'Will it be all right?' I said, 'It'll be fantastic, just you see.' And she said, 'Are you coming with me?' 'No,' I said, 'but I'll get you to the door, and make sure somebody is there to show you where to go, and then you'll be fine.' 'But where will I go?' she asked. 'You'll see when you get inside,' I told her. And she accepted that, because it came from me, and said, 'Okay,' quite casually, as a girl ten years older might have said it.

So we came to the door and I said, 'Now give me a kiss and a hug,' and she did, and her teacher was there, who recognised her from the visit we'd made at the end of the previous term. 'Hello, Alice,' she said. 'Do you remember me?' 'I think so,' Alice said, and she took the teacher's hand and in she went. I let go of her, and she of me, so easily that I hardly realised we had done it. She didn't look back, and it was over, not such an ordeal for either of us, but at the end of that first day, and all the too few schooldays that followed, either Emily or I would be there to greet her and take her home, and that was the thing, that was the joy and the pain of the man and his little girl on the bus, the thing that could never happen for me and Alice again. And I hoped that Emily had been able to keep holding her hand all the way, and that if there was a door maybe they had gone through it together.

Emily had wanted Alice to experience Thanksgiving. Rachel wasn't keeping well again so she and Alfred couldn't – wouldn't – come to Scotland. 'But it would mean taking Alice out of school,' Emily said.

'So, take her out of school,' I said.

'The school disapproves. *I* disapprove. I don't want to get into that habit.'

'Once won't matter. She's only six.'

'If we go, will you come? It would be lovely if we could all go.'

'I can't,' I said. 'The University . . .'

'. . . would disapprove.'

'To put it mildly. I'd be breaking my contract. Sorry.'

'I kind of figured that. Would you mind very much if we went without you?'

'Yes,' I said, 'but I'll get by. It'll be good for Alice. She should see your folks more often. And they'll love you both being there for Thanksgiving.'

'We'll only be gone a week,' Emily said. 'And we'll be together here at Christmas, just the three of us.'

'I can hardly wait,' I said, and I meant it, not a trace of irony in there.

Before the sweeter, kinder dreams came the one from which, for a long time, I thought I would never escape, the dream that toppled my world, that stifled the born-again Alan and left the dead me in his place. It was my dream, but it was about Alan.

He was in his office at the University, with a stack of essays waiting to be read. A long evening lay ahead. The weather was grey and drizzly. He drank black coffee from a flask, marked a couple of essays. Outside it grew dark. He drank more coffee, looked at his watch. Six o'clock. They'd flown to London from Edinburgh that afternoon. He thought of them queuing at the gate, boarding the plane, waiting for take-off. He marked a few more essays. Some rain splatted on the window. He looked at his watch again. Just after seven. They would be airborne. He thought of them up there above the rain. Then what, in this dream? A jolt, a strange rearrangement of the air, some paranormal flicker? He poured the last of the coffee, turned to the next essay. Very bad handwriting (I can see it still): good student, bad writing. He began to decipher it. The phone rang. He reached across the desk and picked it up.

'Alan? It's Jim.' Jim Collins, his Welsh realist colleague, analyst of male anger and angst in post-war working-class fiction, Barstow, Sillitoe, Storey, Hines, all that. Jim was Alan's senior by a few years, not that they noticed the difference. He had a daughter, Lisa, the same age as Alice; they were at the same school. He had two sons as well, older, and an ex-wife on the other side of town, and they all seemed to get on fine between the two households. Jim had a cool, commanding way of speaking. He said, 'Alan, didn't you tell me the other day that Emily and Alice were going to be flying to the States?'

'Yes,' he said. 'They've gone already.'

'They've gone? Good. Thank God for that.'

'Actually, they should be in the air right now. They were flying this evening from Heathrow.'

In the dream the words 'they should be in the air right now' repeated several times, the emphasis shifting along the line like a crow hopping along a wall. The crow bounced up and down on 'right now'.

'Heathrow?' Jim's voice had suddenly lost its authority. 'Shit.'

'What?' Alan said. In the dream he wasn't perturbed. Why would he have been? 'Shit' was such a small, unimportant word. 'Shit happens', and similar phrases. He said, 'What's up?'

'There's been a report on the radio. A plane crash in the Borders. They're saying it's a transatlantic flight from Heathrow. I don't know if that's right, but that's what they're saying.'

'On the radio?' Alan said. 'Where are you?'

'I'm at home. I'm going to put the TV on. I'll phone you back.'

In the dream Jim Collins hung up. In the dream Alan Tealing paused, wondering what to do. Even then he wasn't really worried. A plane crash in the Borders had nothing to do with him. Emily and Alice had *left* Scotland, to go to America. There was no radio or TV in his office. He was half an hour from home if he walked, ten minutes by bus if there was a bus. He wasn't thinking of taxis, not yet. He looked at the essay again, deciphered a few more lines of the dreadful scrawl in which were hidden some good ideas about *Wuthering Heights*.

The phone rang. In the dream he heard it ring and the air seemed to crumble between his hand and the phone. The hand picked up the receiver.

Jim said, 'The plane was flying from Heathrow to New York. It was scheduled to take off at six o'clock.'

Something lurched in Alan's heart, like a mad dog throwing itself against a door when the bell is rung.

'I've written down the flight number,' Jim said, and he read it out.

Alan heard himself say, 'That's their flight.'

The next thing was someone calling from a distance, as if through a dense fog or in the blackest of starless nights. 'Alan!' the voice called. 'Alan!' He tried to make the voice wake him. He tried to make it sound feminine, Emily's voice, and he tried to hear Alice's voice alongside it, or beyond it, 'Daddy!' but they wouldn't come. 'Alan!' the voice called. 'Are you there?' and he was, the receiver still pressed to his ear, and Jim was saying, 'You'd better go home, Alan. You need to go home. I'll meet you there.'

He left everything as it was, the essays in two piles, the flask, the mug, the scattering of pens and books on the desk. He went out of his office and down the stairs into the drizzling dark. He found a taxi or got on a bus or walked home but I have no knowledge of how he made that journey. He came round, or out of whatever state he was in, when he heard Jim Collins's voice again.

'Alan,' Jim said.

Jim was standing under the street lamp outside the house, in a raincoat with the collar turned up. Alan stopped in front of him. In the dream, he did not seem able to speak. 'You're getting wet,' Jim said. Alan looked down at the lapels of his jacket and saw that it was so. He had come away without his coat. How stupid, to have done that in such weather.

After a few more moments Jim said gently, as if to somebody elderly and forgetful, 'Do you have your key?' Alan looked down again, beyond the soaking jacket, and his two clenched hands were there. He raised them, turned them over. Perhaps he pushed the right one forward a little, I cannot say, but Jim grasped it and opened out the fingers. The key lay in the palm. Jim took it, and Alan saw the outline of the key like a ghost on the skin, apart from where the notched part of its blade had dug in so deep that it had drawn blood. 'Come in out of this,' Jim said, and he unlocked the front door and Alan followed him into the empty house. Jim switched on lights, and the television, and Alan sat down and sitting there he found out what he already knew, that the dream was not a dream, it was real and happening before his eyes. Jim watched with him, then he said, 'Here,' and helped him shrug off the jacket and took it away somewhere. There was a noise of glasses in the kitchen, cupboard doors, and then Jim was back in the room saying, 'Where do you keep your drink?' And right after that the telephone started ringing.

When Emily traded her country for mine, I thought she was making a great sacrifice, but she always denied it. It was an adventure – as almost everything, however mundane, was an adventure for her – and anyway it made sense, because shortly before the wedding took place I had completed my PhD and successfully applied for a lectureship in Scotland. Emily had urged me to apply: she didn't have a career path like me, she said, she just had a life path, and she'd go wherever it took her. And it was true that Scotland was a new country for both of us: I'd never crossed the border with England before I went for the job interview.

How different, though, was the old Scottish town with its newish university from the kind of place I'd once imagined us living in: some pretty New England haven with its 'Little Ivy' college shining in the bright glories of the fall, and white clapboard houses basking in the regular heat of summer. Everything in Scotland was grubbier, rougher at the edges, colder. The town did have its share of leafy walks, parks, quiet streets, abundant big-treed gardens and solid Victorian villas; and there was the history, the old churches and cobbled streets, and the castle; but it had quarters, too, of deprivation, waste and ruin. Yet on the whole Emily liked it, even our unremarkable house in its unremarkable suburban crescent. When I apologised for taking her away from her homeland she said I was trying to saddle her with my own disappointment. 'You're the one who lost out,' she said. 'You got a real taste for it when we got married, didn't you?'

She was right. We'd honeymooned in Cape Cod, gone to Boston and on up to Maine, and I had loved it, feeling as if I were on a movie set of an earlier America. Later, when Alice had arrived and I worried again that Emily might be homesick, she breezily denied it. 'You just want all those clichés,' she said. 'Dodging squirrels as you bicycle to class, you and Alice at the soda fountain in some old-time diner – I can read you like a book. America's not like that.' But it had seemed so to me. 'Anyway,' she always said, 'we can do the States later. You get a job at Harvard, and then we'll all go home.' It was probably never going to happen, but it was pleasant to think it might, and Emily even had her parents keep an eye out for possibilities for me – a year or two on some exchange if such a thing could be arranged. And when she went with Alice for Thanksgiving on that last journey she'd said, half-seriously, that she was going to do some scouting for me. Afterwards, I considered whether going to America might be the best thing I could do, to get away from all that was familiar, but I had neither the heart nor the energy to attempt to organise it. The only place I went after their deaths was into myself.

Emily's parents, Alfred and Rachel, were both academics. Alfred was an economist and Rachel a sociologist. They were steady, competent, conservative people who worked in different parts of the vast further education network of the state of Pennsylvania. It seemed that they spent far more time on administration than they did teaching. If their jobs excited them intellectually, they never revealed it to me. They were learned but not imaginative. Maybe this was why their daughter wasn't interested in research or teaching herself. Alfred and Rachel had provided a safe, conventional upbringing for Emily and her two older brothers, and by the time she was in her twenties she had had enough of it.

Then why, I sometimes asked myself, did she choose to be with me? However much her love had changed me, made me bolder, warmer, wittier, I was still the same polite English boy underneath. The question – and the further question it provoked – disturbed me deeply, and disturbs me still now, long after she is gone. Was I – am I? – merely Alfred in disguise?

8

'You say his name with something like disgust,' Nilsen said. 'And yet all Parroulet did was identify the suspect.'

'Wrongly identify him,' I said.

'He was asked questions by the police and he gave answers. That's what he did. It was a year after the bombing, the rethink had happened, the island was now the likely point of ingestion, so the police investigation went there. Khazar had stayed in the Central Hotel the night before the bombing and he'd gone to the airport that morning, so what do the police do? They speak to taxi drivers. Are they going to *not* speak to taxi drivers? So they speak to Parroulet, and he remembers the passenger he drove to the airport that day. It's how investigations happen, Dr Tealing.'

'He was wrong,' I said.

'He picked out Khazar's face from a bunch of photographs, and later he picked him out in person in an identity parade. The prosecution had a case against Khazar and Parroulet made it better. That's all he did. He didn't find Khazar guilty. He didn't send him to prison. But the main thing he didn't do, he didn't put a bomb on an airplane and blow it out of the sky. He didn't kill anybody.'

'No, he just delivered his lines,' I said. 'First the police coached him, then your people. Or maybe your people first. That's what you said, isn't it? "The order isn't fixed." Maybe it was you who coached him. Is that where you fit in all this?'

Nilsen shook his head. I didn't read it as a denial, and pushed again.

'At what point did he know that there was money on the table?' I was playing the game now, just as Nilsen had said I would. 'That if he said what you wanted him to say, in court, he'd never have to work again? New life, new identity, because of something that happened thousands of miles away and had nothing to do with him. When did that piece of providential bounty become clear to him? He was never going to get it in writing. Not like your car mechanic, your Ali. You couldn't put Ali in the witness box because there was a paper trail of payments there and the defence lawyers would destroy him as a witness. So how did Parroulet know he was going to be thanked? Was it like this, now – all nods and silent signals? Was it?'

Nilsen said nothing, did nothing.

'You got what you needed from him anyway,' I said.

'He gave evidence that the court decided was credible. Sometimes, the way you've attacked his testimony, you and others, sometimes it's like you thought he was the terrorist, he was the one who should be rotting in jail.'

'I just wanted the truth,' I said. 'He didn't give me it. None of you did.'

'I'm saying a little perspective is required. That's all I'm saying.'

'I went to that trial thinking that Khalil Khazar was the murderer of my family. I went there to hear the evidence that would convict him. I went to get justice. And what I got was Parroulet and a whole new barrow-load of injustice. How much perspective would you like me to have?'

'Parroulet said what he said in court. It was thirteen years after the event. Nobody can remember everything clearly after all that time. But he'd given statements to the police before that, he'd picked Khazar out before that, and when he was asked if he'd changed his mind on anything he said no. And the court decided that what he remembered was good enough. You can't blame Parroulet for what the court decided.'

'He was supposed to tell the truth. He didn't. And incidentally, I remember plenty with absolute clarity. There are some things you don't forget. They're etched into your mind.'

'Some things,' Nilsen said. 'You're very sure of yourself. But have you never been mistaken? Never smudged the edges of a fact? Never been economical with the truth? You said you spent seven or eight days down at the crash site. So was it seven or eight? And what happened on day seven, if it was day seven? You saw stuff, things happened, but on which day? Day three? Day five? And what did you really see? Is what you remember what you saw? How accurate does a memory need to be before it's deemed to be genuine?'

'That is different,' I said, 'and you know it.'

'I don't know as much as I used to,' Nilsen said.

Perspective. Evidence. Testimony. I had heard these words, and others like them, so often that they had become almost meaningless. The game of words – of building, destroying and reconstructing scenarios – that I played inside the snowstorm with Nilsen was a version of the game that had been played all down the years from the moment of the bomb's explosion: by the police and the intelligence services of several countries, by scientists, security experts, explosives experts, terrorism experts, Middle East experts – experts in everything, some of whom had been summoned eight years before to appear in court as expert witnesses; and by the massed ranks of politicians, lawyers, journalists and judges. You could have filled a sports stadium with the players of the game.

There had been key moments: when, for example, the police liaison people told relatives on both sides of the Atlantic that they had identified the type of timer and who had supplied it and to whom; when the indictments against Khalil Khazar and Waleed Mahmed were issued; when, after years of stand-off followed by years of negotiation, the regime agreed to let them stand trial, and they agreed to go; when, at last, thirteen years after the event, the trial began (a special trial in a special court convened in a foreign city, a neutral place, a court without a jury but with international observers and officials to monitor the process and judge the judges); when Mahmed was acquitted for lack of evidence, but Khazar pronounced guilty; when Khazar's appeal failed; when he began his life sentence in jail; when he was pronounced to be dying of cancer; when he was pronounced dead. Key moments, yet none of them, the last least of all, really was a key, not the one that I had for so long hoped to find.

This is what we were told had happened. This is the story, or the bones of the story, that the court heard and that the judges apparently believed. There was more, of course, much more. Weeks and weeks of evidence, some of which looked firm and some of which looked unstable. But what it came down to, when you boiled and scraped all that mass of written and verbal fat away, what it came down to was what Martin Parroulet said he had seen.

Parroulet was, to look at, a man of no great distinction. Of average height and build, a little plump, he had a slumped, round-shouldered carriage that spoke of far too many days behind the wheel of a car. He was balding but he tried to disguise it (ineffectually, of course) with a comb-over. His teeth were yellow from smoking, and his eyes narrow, suggesting shortsightedness although I never saw him wear glasses other than sunglasses. He looked like a man who had always been middle-aged. It was hard to imagine him as a boy, although his lower lip sometimes protruded, especially when he was being closely questioned, as if it might not take too much to make him cry.

At eight o'clock on the morning in question – the morning of the day of the bomb – Parroulet was, as usual, waiting at the taxi rank on the street opposite the Central Hotel. His car was at the head of the rank. There were five or six taxis behind his, and he and the other drivers were standing on the pavement, smoking and talking, as was their custom. The doorman from the hotel whistled, again as was usual practice, and signalled that a taxi was required. Parroulet drove to the end of the street, U-turned and arrived at the hotel entrance. The guest was already on the pavement. 'Going to the airport,' the door-man told Parroulet, who, having first released the lid of the boot, got out to open the door for his passenger and help with his luggage. This, according to Parroulet, consisted of a medium-sized hard grey suitcase and a small black attaché case. The passenger resisted Parroulet's attempts to load both items into the boot of the car. He insisted on putting the suitcase in himself, laying it flat in the other-wise empty boot, and kept the attaché case with him when he got into the back of the car.

Parroulet was shown a suitcase, previously identified to the court as being of the same make and model as the primary suitcase, the one that had contained the bomb. He was asked if he recognised it. Yes, he did. Had he ever seen a similar suitcase? Yes, he had. Where had he seen it? In the boot of his car. It had been placed there by the pas-senger he took to the airport that morning. And it was similar to the one now presented to the court? It was identical. Was he absolutely positive about that? He was.

The drive to the airport took twenty-five minutes. In that time Parroulet tried to engage his passenger in conversation. He asked him when his flight was, and was told that they had plenty of time, two hours or so. He asked where he was flying to, and was told, 'I am going home.' Parroulet asked where home was but received no answer. The man in the back seat opened his attaché case and appeared to busy himself with papers inside it, although Parroulet could not see what these were. It appeared to Parroulet that his passenger did not wish to engage in conversation. In the rear-view mirror he had a reasonably clear sight of the man. He described him as dark-complexioned, Arabic-looking, of average weight, a little under six feet tall, with thick black hair. It was a sunny morning and he was wearing sun-glasses, which he pushed up on to his forehead when reading the papers, but lowered again when he stopped. He spoke in French, which Parroulet spoke, but said so little that Parroulet was unable to identify which country he might be from.

The prosecution asked Parroulet if he had ever been asked by the police investigating the bombing to identify the man he had driven to the airport that morning. Yes, he had. When was this? About a year later. About a year after the bombing? Yes. The police had visited him on several occasions and shown him photographs of various men, and asked him if any of them looked like his passenger. And had any of them? Yes. On the first police visit, he had thought that two or three of the photographs looked a little bit like the man, but he could not be positive. The police had returned two days later with more photographs. How many? Eight or ten. And had he thought any of these looked like the man? Yes, this time he'd thought that one of them was probably a picture of him, although it wasn't a very clear image. And did he now see, in the courtroom, anyone resembling the man from that picture? Yes, he did. Would he point to that person? Parroulet pointed at Khalil Khazar. Did the police show him more photographs after that? Yes. And did he positively identify his passenger from any of these? Yes, several times. And did he see that man in the courtroom? Yes (pointing at Khalil Khazar again). More recently, did the police arrange an identity parade to see if he could pick out the man whom he had driven to the airport that day? Yes, they did. When was that? Last year. And did he pick anybody from that parade? Yes, the same man. Could he point him out? Parroulet pointed at Khalil Khazar. 'That is the man.'

At the airport Parroulet had pulled into the drop-off lane and stopped. The passenger had got out of the car immediately and was waiting, with his attaché case, beside the boot by the time Parroulet had released the catch and got there himself. The passenger retrieved the suitcase himself. He had money ready for the fare, and did not wait for any change. Parroulet was surprised because he had not appeared very friendly and yet left quite a substantial tip. Parroulet said goodbye and the man muttered a reply, then turned and walked through the doors into the departures hall. It was about 8.30 a.m.

Parroulet drove away from the drop-off lane, intending to return to the taxi rank opposite the Central Hotel. However, as he sat waiting for traffic lights to change at the airport exit he glanced behind him and saw a silver pen lying on the back seat. He leaned back and retrieved it. It looked expensive to him. He was sure that it had not been there at the start of the day, and as he had only had the one fare he assumed that the pen must belong to the man he had just dropped off. As the lights changed to green, he was able to turn left and rejoin the road back to the terminal building. He said that if the lights had not changed at that moment, and if he had not been thinking of the large tip left by his passenger, he might not have taken that decision.

Arriving back at the drop-off zone, he parked his taxi and hurried in to the departures hall. He knew he should not leave his vehicle unattended but as it was a registered taxi he believed he could do so for a short while without getting into trouble. The airport was quiet, there were only a few people checking in, and he reckoned he could easily spot his passenger, return the pen and be back in his car within two minutes. In fact he saw the man at once, walking across the concourse towards the check-in area. He appeared to be coming from the vicinity of a desk where unusually bulky, heavy, fragile or otherwise special items were deposited and processed before being taken by trolley through to the airside baggage-loading area. Parroulet hurried towards him, and when a few yards away called out, in French, 'Wait, sir.' The man looked startled, even frightened, and began to retreat. Then, recognising Parroulet and seeing the pen held out towards him, he came to a halt. 'Your pen,' Parroulet said. 'You dropped it.' 'Thank you,' the man replied. 'It was not important, but thank you.' He took the pen and said 'thank you' a third time, then continued on his way to the check-in desks. Parroulet watched him take his place in a short queue, then returned to his car and drove away. It was only later that he thought it odd that, although the man had evidently not yet checked in, he was carrying only the attaché case. Of the grey suitcase there was no sign.

The prosecution made much of this incident. 'You said the man looked frightened. Could you think of any reason why he should be frightened?' 'Maybe because I am coming at him quite fast. Maybe he think am I going to attack him.' 'Why would he think that?' 'Maybe if he has done something bad, if he think am I airport security.' 'Again, I ask, why would he think that?' 'I don't know, he look nervous, afraid. Also he is sweating a little much.' 'And this man, could you confirm, was the same man that you had driven to the airport?' 'Yes.' 'The same man that you see here in this court?' 'Yes.' 'Yet he was no longer in possession of the grey suitcase even though he had not yet checked in?' 'That is what I think, yes.'

The defence lawyers, cross-examining Parroulet, also had plenty of questions. 'You were first interviewed by the police, you said, a year after the bombing?' 'Yes, about a year.' 'The police record confirms this. It confirms the date on which you were first interviewed and shown photographs. The police record also shows that you were interviewed and asked about the identity of the man you drove to the airport on many more occasions. Nineteen times over the course of twelve months. Do you remember these interviews?' 'They were very many, yes. I don't remember everything that happen all those times.' 'But do you remember when, from a photograph shown to you by the police, you first identified this man here as your passenger?' 'I don't remember exactly.' 'It was not during the first interview, Mr Parroulet.' 'I don't think so.' 'In the first interview you picked out three pictures that you said might be of your passenger. None of them was of the accused.' 'Maybe. It is a long time before.' 'It wasn't until the second interview, according to the police record, that you said you thought a photograph of the accused might be of your passenger.' 'Okay, if that is what police record says.' 'That is what the police record says. Even then, though, you were doubtful. You said that the photograph was not very clear.' 'Well, but later they show me a better one.' 'A different photograph?' 'Yes, and better.' 'This was, in fact, Mr Parroulet, during the fifth interview you had with the police. And later they showed you yet another photograph of the accused, by which time you were much more certain that it was of your passenger, even though more time had passed.' 'Yes, I see it more clear.' 'But a great deal of time had passed since you had seen the man. And when he was in your taxi, you only saw him in the rear-view mirror, and you said he was wearing sunglasses most of the time, so how can you be so sure that the photograph was of the same man?' 'I remember him. He take off the glasses sometime.' 'He pushed them on to his forehead?' 'Yes. And also in the terminal, when I give him pen. I see him more clear then.' 'But even then he had his sunglasses on.' 'Yes but he is not difficult to see. I see him right away.' 'I don't dispute that you recognised him at the time, Mr Parroulet. But I question whether, a year, fifteen months, two years later, you could positively and definitely identify the man in these different, sometimes not very clear, photographs, as the passenger wearing sunglasses, of whom you had only occasional and brief views while you were driving, who hardly spoke to you, and whom you never saw again.' 'I only tell you what I tell police. It is the same man.' 'And do you see that man today?' 'Yes,' pointing at Khazar, 'that is the man.' 'When you saw the identity parade of suspects, nearly a year ago, you identified the accused as the man who was in your taxi.' 'Yes.' 'You were, and are now, quite sure about that identification?' 'Quite . . . sure.' 'You seem to hesitate, Mr Parroulet. Do you mean absolutely sure or partially sure?' 'I am sure, yes, very sure.' 'Do you think that, after being shown so many photographs of one man over a long period of time, you may have identified that man as your passenger, not because he actually was your passenger but because you recognised him from the earlier photographs?' 'No, it is him. It *was* him.' 'Did the police encourage you to pick that man by repeatedly showing you his picture?' 'No, he is in my car that day.' 'But they did repeatedly show you his picture?' 'Yes, I see it many times.' 'Do you not think it possible that you may have been mistaken, and that you are mistaken today, all these years later?' 'No, I am not mistaking. It is him.'

And more and more and more. The minutes that had passed between Parroulet's dropping off his passenger and returning to give him the pen were crucial. How many minutes? How long does it take to walk across the terminal concourse? When did Khalil Khazar check in? Did he check in anything at the oversized luggage desk? No. Did he have only one item of luggage, the attaché case, when he checked in? Yes. Could he have disposed of another item during those minutes? Yes, but nobody could say how he could have done so. Surely this had to be demonstrated? Not if Parroulet's sightings of the grey suitcase were correct. Back and forth it went across the courtroom, the two sides challenging each other's questions and conclusions, Parroulet looking bewildered at the detail he was being asked to recall after he had given so many statements to the police, and after all those years had gone by. I don't blame him for being bewildered – I would have been – but he stuck to his story with a doggedness of which I was not initially suspicious. Indeed, at first I was willing him to be consistent, to be strong, because I wanted to see 'the accused' found guilty. I believed Khazar was the bomber. I never *wanted* to think of him as innocent. But the longer I watched and listened, the greater the doubts that began to cloud my mind, the less I believed the evidence against Khazar, and the more I thought that something was seriously wrong with the trial.

I watched and listened along with the other families, those who could bear to be there. Day after day we went to court, and sometimes in the evenings we talked, but at other times I wanted to be alone. As the days turned into weeks, I wanted my own company more, the space to think by and for myself – because, when we talked, I saw a gap opening up between myself and most of the others, especially the American relatives. We saw and heard it all together, the same words and images, the same productions of evidence, the same arguments and counter-arguments, but we drew different conclusions. It seemed to me that regardless of the flaws and inconsistencies in the case being built against him, regardless of the lack of credibility of some of the witnesses, including Parroulet, the other relatives were determined that Khalil Khazar must have done what he was accused of having done. It would have taken something huge and incontrovertible – a watertight alibi, for example – to dissuade them of his guilt. There was nothing like that to clear him. He had been at the airport on the right day and at the right time. He had a life that was in partial shadow. He had been seen – by Parroulet – in possession of a suitcase identical to that which had contained the bomb. He had been seen – by Parroulet and others – *not* in possession of this suitcase when he should still have had it with him. Like the others, I began by wanting his guilt to be beyond doubt. I also wanted him to speak for himself, but he never did. Either this was by his own choice or on his counsel's advice, but he remained silent. That might have been seen – *was* seen – as an admission of guilt, but not by me. As the trial went on, I felt more uneasy, then more despairing, then unwell. Sometimes the body knows better than the mind when something is wrong. Several times when the court rose I had to hurry away to be sick.

The indictment against Waleed Mahmed turned out to be based on nothing more than the dubious words of the car mechanic Ali. Khazar and he were supposed to have acted in concert, and the inference to be drawn from the indictment was that Mahmed, with his inside knowledge of the workings of the island's airport security systems, had taken the primary suitcase from Khazar that morning and somehow circumvented those systems and infiltrated it on to the flight to Germany. From there it had gone on its way, tagged to be transferred to London and thence to New York. But during the trial no explanation was ever given as to how this amazing act of subterfuge was carried out. Nor was it demonstrable, according to all the records of the airport authorities and the different airlines operating there, that an unaccompanied suitcase had been loaded on to the original flight. In their summation, the judges acknowledged that this was a major difficulty for the prosecution. There was no evidence that Waleed Mahmed had been at the airport that day, no evidence that he had taken the suitcase from Khazar, no evidence that he had managed to get it on to the plane bound for Germany. The case against Mahmed was accordingly dismissed.

Yet the inference lingered. Somehow Khazar had got that suitcase, laden with its deadly contents, through the security system and on to the plane. The judges' view was that no record of that suitcase existed precisely *because* it had bypassed the airport's rigorous baggage reconciliation procedures. And so, taking all the other evidence and weighing it up, the court concluded – although it could not say how he had done it – that Khalil Khazar had indeed achieved his aim, and was therefore responsible for the murder of Emily, Alice and two hundred and seventy other people.

I used to think that the only question I wanted answered was, who killed my wife and daughter? I used to think that nothing else mattered, and indeed for a long time nothing else did. Nor did I care about why, or even how – only about who. The motivation of the killer or killers was of no interest to me, their religious or political grievances, the rights and wrongs of their cause, whatever it was, utterly irrelevant. I felt that if I allowed myself to consider such issues I would be distracted from the only item of any consequence, the need to identify the murderers and put them behind bars for the rest of their lives. And when Khalil Khazar and Waleed Mahmed were accused, and later arrested, and finally brought to trial, I thought that the beginning of the end was in sight, that my single desire might actually be realised. But then the trial went wrong. The case against Mahmed was quickly shown to be built on sand, and I dismissed him long before the court did. That left Khazar. Slowly yet remorselessly, the proceedings ate away at my confidence in his guilt too. With each new day I was forced to be dissatisfied with some of what was presented as proof. My mind could not accept what my heart wanted to. I found myself asking new questions in my head. I wanted to stand up and shout, 'This is wrong, you have the wrong man, how can you have the wrong man?' but I did not because I still hoped that as the trial reached its conclusion some overwhelmingly convincing piece of evidence would eradicate all my doubts and I would be able to go home knowing that justice had been done. Instead I went home fearing the very opposite.

I left the trial with my grief renewed and doubled. There were news teams from around the world outside the building, reporting on the verdict, and of course they wanted to know what we, the victims' families, felt. I could not speak to them. I should have been able to stand in front of the cameras and say that the long chapter was over, the nightmare was at some kind of end. Others were doing just that. There were people making statements on behalf of families, governments, the police. I recognised three policemen, senior officers who had all been working on the case from the start, smiling and laughing together. I had spoken to them all over the years, when they had given us updates and briefings, cautioned us against hope, guided us from despair. One of them broke away to go to talk to some reporters, to express what would presumably be some degree of satisfaction. They'd finally got one of the accused. Disappointing in some respects, but . . . a bird in the hand and all that. The other two watched him go. I noticed they stopped laughing, and one of them, catching my eye, turned his back on me.

I pushed through the crowds and hurried away. I walked as far and as fast as I could, until I found myself in a park. People were exercising their dogs in the distance, a couple of ragamuffin pigeons pecked at the grass, a feeble fountain was gurgling, as it seemed to me, its last gurgles. A few wooden benches were stationed around the fountain, one of them occupied by a sleeping vagrant, the others empty. I sat down and watched and listened to the expiring fountain. I put my head in my hands. I wanted a beer, gin, whisky. I wanted to be drunk. No. The last thing I wanted was alcohol. No. The last thing I wanted was this.

A man had been found guilty of killing Emily and Alice, a man who, I feared, was either entirely innocent or, if involved at all, was only a minor character in the plot. (I can use the language of literary analysis as well as Nilsen or anyone. It's my job.) My loved ones, all those loved men and women and children, had been murdered, and now, was a possibly innocent man to rot out his life in jail while the real killers remained at large? As I sat on that park bench and the fountain spluttered and the pigeons coughed and the tramp on the bench snored I realised that I was nowhere near the end of the nightmare. A new nightmare was beginning, and this was the one in which I would spend days and nights and years in my own Château d'If, my fingernails broken and my forehead resting against the cold dampness of stone walls. This was the fate that now awaited me, although I did not know it at the time: to be imprisoned like Dumas's old priest, imprisoned too like Khalil Khazar, imprisoned for the crime of not being able to believe.

I was dimly aware of a man in a light raincoat sitting down at the other end of my bench. I hardly glanced at him. Instead I stared at the shabby pigeons and the tramp, and the new arrival sat staring at whatever he was staring at. After a while, feeling an aching weariness creep up my legs and into my back, I gathered myself to leave.

The man said, quietly enough but I didn't miss a word,

'Something's very wrong, Dr Tealing. Don't look at me. The court hasn't heard the half of it. Don't look at me. I'll be in touch.'

I raised myself. The pigeons poked the air, the tramp snored on. I walked away. But of course when I was at a distance I did look, and he was still sitting there, the policeman who had turned his back on me.

9

George Braithwaite was a lecturer in Jurisprudence in the Faculty of Law. Before the trial I knew him only by sight, a small, neat man of about sixty, with a round pink face and a hurried walk that suggested he was on the hunt for truffles. He had been a solicitor for ten years, working in criminal defence, before entering academe – a career move that made me wonder if he was any good at law in either practice or theory. But Jim Collins knew him well, and thought him both intelligent and decent. 'A little cold,' he said, 'but you'll get no nonsense from him.' A week after the trial, I contacted Braithwaite through Jim, and requested a meeting. I had said, when asked by journalists for my reaction to the verdict, that I was confused by the fact that Mahmed had gone free while Khazar had been convicted, but I had not gone into further details. It was generally assumed that I, and the other relatives, were disappointed that Mahmed had 'got away with it'. I had told Jim Collins that I had misgivings about the trial, but again had not discussed them in any depth. This was why I wanted to talk to his cold but decent, no-nonsense legal acquaintance.

George Braithwaite suggested we go for a drink somewhere after work. 'Nowhere too public,' I said. 'Come to my flat, then,' he said. He lived near the castle, in what was left of the old medieval quarter. He showed me into a room with commanding views over the whole town, and went to fetch some wine. The room was full of dark antique furniture, two deep-red leather armchairs and a sofa, heavy Victorian oil paintings and bookcases containing large volumes on art, architecture, photography and design. The room was uncompromisingly masculine. I had not speculated whether there was a Mrs Braithwaite, but it seemed there was not. Not, of course, that that meant anything.

He returned with two glasses and a decanter of red wine on a silver tray. 'Do you drink claret?' he asked. 'I bought a couple of cases of this a few years ago and it's just coming into its own.'

I said that sounded fine. I indicated the bookcases. 'You don't seem to have any books on law,' I said.

'Oh, I have, but not here,' he said, pouring the wine. 'I have all the law I need at the University. This is my home.' He gestured towards one of the leather chairs. 'Please. I gather from Jim that you want to pick my brains about the Khazar conviction?'

'I am unhappy about it,' I said.

'I'm not surprised,' he said.

'I mean, because I don't trust the verdict,' I said.

'I mean that too,' he said. With his elbows on the arms of his chair he brought the tips of his fingers together and rested them against his lips. 'Tell me why.'

I didn't know how much detail I needed to go into but it transpired he had been following the trial closely and already had his own ideas about it. Occasionally he interrupted, asking to be reminded who this or that individual was, but mostly he remained motionless, breaking his prayer-like attitude only to reach for his glass. When I had finished, he said nothing for a minute or two, but let his gaze wander about the room as if he had only just noticed the books, the paintings, the dark furniture. At last he spoke.

'You are unhappy with the outcome,' he said. 'But what is it you are looking for? Justice? The truth?'

'Either of those would be a start,' I said. 'Both would be good.'

'It is naive of you to think –' Braithwaite began, then broke off. 'Maybe I should finish that sentence right there. No, I apologise, I'm being facetious.' He stopped again. 'The thing people always do — people who are not lawyers — is confuse the law with justice, evidence with truth. What goes on in a courtroom is not a search for truth. It really isn't, although the mythology suggests otherwise. A courtroom is a venue for a fight between two sides, each trying to persuade a jury, or in this case the Bench, that an accused person did or did not do something. That's all it is, a fight. As in a boxing match, points are scored by delivering punches on target. It may even be that a knockout punch is landed. And when it is all over, one side wins. But the outcome of any trial is not that justice has been done, or that the truth has come out, any more than the outcome of a boxing match is that the better, nobler, finer man has triumphed. Justice *may* have been done. The truth *may* have come out. But neither of these things is necessary in the application of the law. They are actually irrelevant. Yes, I'd go as far as to say that. Irrelevant. We might wish it were not so, but that is the nature of the law. And why is that? It's because truth and justice are only ever principles at best, and more often mere aspirations. They are what we aim for, what we hope for in ideal circumstances. But we never get ideal circumstances because none of us — solicitors, advocates, judges, jury, witnesses, the accused — none of us, in the end, I am *not* sorry to say, is perfect. We are all only human.'

'That word "irrelevant",' I said. 'Lately I've been wanting to strip out everything to do with this whole affair that is irrelevant, all the speculation and confusion and emotion. Concentrate on the hard facts. I feel then, despite what you say, that what would be left would be the truth.'

'You might feel it but you'd be wrong.' He stood up, lifted the decanter and refilled our glasses. 'You're missing the point. What *are* the hard facts? What you say is irrelevant in this affair is not irrelevant in life. What is irrelevant is what *makes* life. If you strip out the irrelevant, the truth won't be standing there like a gleaming sword. There won't just be no truth, there'll be nothing.'

'You mean, there *is* no truth?'

'I mean it is not pure and separate. It is dirty and decayed and has frayed edges, and holes and tears in it. The last thing the truth does is gleam.'

'You suggested that image, not me. But I'm glad I'm not a lawyer, if this is how you end up thinking.'

'Without idealism? It's the only way to think, if you want to stay sane. The lives that come before lawyers in the course of their work, the lives that are paraded in front of magistrates every day of the week, all over the world, are scruffy and soiled and stupid, and a million miles from idealism. And I'm not just talking about criminal law, I mean civil law too, buying and selling houses, legacies and divorces, commercial law, the whole kitbag. Do you think anybody involved in those processes could go home and eat his dinner, or go to the theatre, or enjoy a game of golf or a drink or a joke with friends, or even the quiet of a room like this with its books and pictures, if he took the – well, you might call it the nobler view, but I call it the naive view? It just wouldn't be possible.'

It was early spring. The evening light had dulled, and the room was murky. Braithwaite's face had become indistinct, and I was not even sure if his eyes were still open. Then he spoke again.

'I did once know someone in the law, a sheriff, who tried going down the road you're on, the noble road. He too decided that justice and the law must be one and the same, despite all the evidence' – he cleared his throat – 'to the contrary, or what was the point? And what happened to him? I'll tell you. First he took to drink, then he went mad, and finally he threw himself off a bridge.'

I had no recollection of such an event. 'Really?' I asked.

'Really,' Braithwaite said. 'Many years ago. We had our disagreements, but I was very fond of him.'

Something, I wasn't sure what, had been revealed in the half-dark. We both drank. Braithwaite cleared his throat again, reached for a table-lamp and switched it on, then walked round the room switching on other lamps strategically placed to illuminate but not glare. He refilled the glasses.

'In a way,' he said, 'he thought he was above the law, or immune to it. But of course he was not immune.'

'Nobody should be above the law,' I said.

'We're all above it, or think we are from time to time,' he said, 'whether for noble reasons or base ones. Every one of us. Some of us fiddle our expenses, or don't declare all our earnings. Drivers break the speed limit, just a little, or a lot.' He tut-tutted, like a man going at 75 mph being overtaken by another going at 90. 'We all think we're above the law, and most of the time it doesn't matter. Then there are times when it might. The Catholic Church thinks it's above the law with its sanctity of the confessional. Journalists protecting their sources say that if they named them, even under oath, it would destroy the freedom of the press. And then there are the times when it definitely does matter: when an institution like the Church protects its priests just because they're priests, for example. Or when an organisation – the police, say, or a powerful company – becomes corrupt in order to get business done. Or when a man takes the law into his own hands. For example.' He leaned forward. 'If *I* had a daughter who was abused, or raped, or killed, and I knew who'd done it, I'd kill the bastard if I could, not wait for the law to catch him and lock him up. We're all above the law, but mostly it doesn't show.'

The sudden ferocity that had surged in his voice was alarming. I felt almost as if *I* were being accused of something.

'You're sure that's what you would do?' I said.

'No,' he said, and smiled, apparently calm again. 'But I'm sure that's what I would feel.'

'I could never kill anybody,' I said.

'You've never been in a room with whoever murdered your wife and daughter,' Braithwaite said. 'Or you tell me you haven't. So how can *you* be sure?'

'Even when I thought Khazar was guilty,' I said, 'when the trial began, when I was in that courtroom and he was sitting there behind the bulletproof glass, even then I didn't want to kill him.'

'What did you want?'

I had thought about this. The answer was quite simple, really. I said, 'I wanted it to be over, and not to have to think about it any more.'

He nodded.

'I wanted to be able to go to sleep,' I said, 'and not dream, and not wake up till morning.'

He said, 'I'm afraid even justice and truth can't give you that.'

'Are you saying I'm wasting my time looking for them?'

He shook his head. 'No, not at all. If I were you that's what I'd do. All I'm saying is, be prepared to be disappointed if you ever find them.'

Jim Collins stopped me outside the department office a few days later. 'George said you'd been to see him,' he said. 'Was he helpful?'

'I don't know,' I said. 'I think so. I'm still digesting what he said.'

'What did you make of him?'

'Cool, as you said. I can't say I exactly liked him. Quite cynical. Although he got very impassioned at one point.'

'George is all right,' Jim said. 'The cynicism's a front. He got pretty bruised when he was a solicitor. He told me he saw a lot of lawyers who couldn't cope, whose lives fell apart under the pressure.'

'He mentioned a friend who jumped off a bridge,' I said. 'I wondered . . .'

'That was his brother. It was one of the things that prompted him to change direction.'

'His brother? I thought maybe a partner, a companion.'

'You think George is gay? Well, I suppose anything's possible. But he was married back then. As we all were. George was one of the ones who fell apart. He's very self-contained these days. Doesn't reveal anything he doesn't want to.'

'That,' I said, 'makes a lot of sense.'

'Do you know how I found out that Parroulet was paid for his evidence?' I said. 'Did you ever work that out?'

'You dug a lot of holes in a lot of different places.' Again, Nilsen was neither denying nor acknowledging anything.

'A policeman told me. Do you know why he told me? Because he thought the whole investigation had been wrecked, undermined by what you call the "rethink". He said it was a classic example of making evidence fit the crime rather than the crime fit the evidence. He said he was very worried by the way outside agencies were interfering with the investigation. He wasn't the only one, he told me.'

'I don't recall anyone in the police being too worried,' Nilsen said. 'I don't recall anyone raising objections.'

'He was overruled. They all wanted a result, just as you described. When Khazar and Mahmed became suspects, the police made it absolutely clear to your people that Ali's evidence wouldn't stand up in court because it was known he'd been in your pay. If Parroulet was to have any credibility it was essential that the same charge couldn't be levelled at him. Your people said the money was on the table and the police said it had to be off the table or under it. No money could change hands till a trial had taken place. So when Parroulet asked about payment the police kept it low-key and off the record, but he knew if he said the right things there'd eventually be a pay-off, he'd just have to wait for it.'

'An offer of a reward for information leading to a conviction is nothing new,' Nilsen said. 'What did your policeman find so offensive about that?'

'The amount. Your people were talking about two million dollars. You can buy a lot of narrative for that kind of money.'

'There was no guarantee he'd get anything. The police were clear with him about that. Every time he raised the subject of a reward they shut him down.'

'He knew the money was there for him if it ever came to a trial and he gave the right evidence. Whatever the police said or didn't say, he knew the offer was there. But nobody else did. The judges didn't know. Khazar's defence team were never told. If they had been they'd have gone to town on Parroulet. And without Parroulet, there was no case against Khazar.'

'But you have no proof.'

'As you said, I dug a lot of holes. I'm still digging. I've seen enough and heard enough to know what happened.'

'To change anything, you still need proof.'

I said, 'That's why you're here, though, isn't it? To set the record straight.'

'There is no record,' he said. 'Not that you or anyone else will ever see.'

'But still, that is why you're here,' I said.

He nodded beyond me, towards the window.

'Look at that snow,' he said. 'Where does it all come from?'

10

Is it fair to suggest that Carol invited herself into my life? No. Fairer to say that she invited me into *her* life, quietly but repeatedly, and that at last, without much grace, I went. I have never been sure why I did, nor have I ever had the will, or the grace, to leave again.

She was in my life, of course, before the bombing, but only as an academic colleague, my senior by a couple of years. I liked her well enough then, but always felt a little sorry for her, and a little guilty in her presence. Sorry, because she was (as I thought) competent but dull, besides being married to Harold Pritchley. Guilty, because I was so much luckier in my marriage than she was.

She had married Professor Pritchley when still one of his under-graduate students, had done a PhD — on women's poetry of the 1930s — under somebody else's supervision, and then been appointed as a lecturer. When I first arrived Harold and Carol (the cheery rhyme of their union seemed self-mocking) had been together for six or seven years, but by that stage everybody knew it was a marriage of unremitting misery. Harold was, as the Dean of Faculty and every-body else acknowledged, brilliant. He was also cruel and — by the time I knew him — a drunkard. When Carol married him he was not yet in thrall to the bottle, the brilliance must have had a certain charm, and the cruelty, which she could hardly have missed, she was deluded enough (so she later told me) to think would never be directed at her. Presumably they had both had their reasons for marrying, but all I could see in his eyes when he looked at her was how much he despised her. His malice was not discreet: all of us within the department saw it. He would humiliate her in front of us by first seeking her opinion and then exposing her ignorance of this or that subject. In private (again, I learned later) his favourite sport was to taunt her failure to get pregnant – a failure caused as much by his drinking as by any biological problem of hers. His emotional abuse was extreme, but he was, she said, too much of a coward ever to hit her. Most of the rest of us were also cowards, adherents to the middle-class religion of Nonconfrontism, and we watched, cringing, as he ground her down. On one occasion I, who was at least fifteen years younger than Harold, could not bear his rudeness, and tried to defend Carol's argument if not Carol herself. He turned on me and I was demolished too. When this happened a second time, a few weeks later, I told him he should be ashamed of himself. He said shame was the prerogative of third-raters and children, and suggested that I was only in the job I was because he had thought – wrongly, but he was *not* ashamed to admit his mistake – that I showed promise and would, given time, grow up. I reminded him that there had been an interview panel of five. He said that that only underlined the failings of management by committee. I never spoke to him again. Two months later he left us for a prestigious Fellowship at Cambridge. Nobody, as far as I know, warned Cambridge what they were really getting.

Years later Carol told me that though it must have looked as if he had left her too – the final humiliation – in fact she had refused to go with him. That decision, she said, marked the beginning of her independence, a state for which she would always be grateful. She said this with a vehemence that I thought suspect, but I did not challenge it. I had no wish to do so.

She certainly bloomed after Harold's departure – took more care of her appearance, became more animated and engaging and shed the skin of dullness she had previously worn. Perhaps even then – between her liberation from Harold and the bombing – she wanted something from me. An affair? If she flirted with me, I was oblivious. I was more than content with Emily, and by then we had Alice. The idea of a relationship on the side never so much as occurred to me.

Afterwards she was solicitous and kind, as everybody was, but somehow her sympathy did not irritate me as that of others did. Perhaps this was because I soon recognised that there was self-interest in it. Philosophy tells us that there is self-interest in all sympathy, but hers had the virtue of being neither blatant nor much disguised. She was practical too, covering for me at work on bad days, encouraging me on good ones. I knew what she wanted, but could not reciprocate. She was very patient. She probably thought I wasn't 'ready', whereas I was certain I never would be.

Several times in those first years, after an evening function of one kind or another, she offered me a lift home. She lived on the other side of town in a district that had, until the early twentieth century, been a village in its own right – the birthplace in fact of David Dibald (not that there was a plaque or street name anywhere to commemorate him) – and usually drove to work. 'It's taking you miles out of your way,' I protested, the first time. 'I'll just get a bus.' 'It'll only be fifteen minutes at this time of day,' she said. 'And it's raining.' So I accepted.

After a while I had to give directions – she didn't know my part of town, she said. But as we turned into my street a recognition stirred in her: she and Harold had looked at a house here.

'Harold thought it was too middle class,' she said.

'What did he expect? It's a middle-class area,' I said.

'He was an idiot,' she said, puncturing the generally accepted view of Professor Pritchley's intellect. She slowed the car. 'That one there. It looks all right, doesn't it? But Harold wanted to live in a mansion, although he professed to despise all social ambition. What a snob he was.'

We arrived at my house and she switched off the engine. 'It's so quiet,' she said, and we sat listening to the quietness until I felt oppressed by it.

'Thanks for the lift,' I said.

'You're welcome, Alan,' she said, and quickly asked my opinion of a student she was finding difficult, and that led on to something else, and it was all fine and unthreatening but at the same time I was thinking, *she wants to come in*, and I didn't want her to come in.

'Well,' I said, opening the passenger door, 'thanks again,' and again she said, 'You're welcome,' like a polite waitress. I got out of the car.

'See you tomorrow,' she said, and I smiled at her and closed the car door, and she drove off, and I entered my silent, empty, familiar house.

Over time these lifts and conversations became, almost, a habit we shared. We'd get to my house, sit in the car and chat about the function we'd just attended, about department politics, about books and writers. I still didn't invite her in, but gradually she became bolder, till at last she was asking questions that I wouldn't have tolerated from anyone else. She had hardly known Emily, having met her only two or three times, and had spoken to Alice just once when we bumped into her at a garden centre, and so she didn't have a claim on them, a proprietary interest, in the way that I felt my family, Emily's family, did. She did not think they *belonged* to her, and for this I was grateful.

She asked on one occasion if I'd been alone when the news came through, or if anyone had come to be with me. I told her of Jim Collins's role, how he had fielded calls and fed me drink and sat with me through most of the night. Eventually he'd had to go, back to his own family, still alive even if not together under one roof. My neighbours Brian and Pam Hewat were on a winter break in Madeira or Tenerife or some such place and weren't due back for a few days. The next morning I went to the railway station and headed south, and when I came home days later – was it seven, was it eight? – my sister, Karen, and my parents had installed themselves, having been given a key by Brian and Pam. They stayed for a week until I asked them to leave, because there was nothing they could do. 'We'd stopped hugging and started arguing, actually. It wasn't good.'

'You were in shock,' Carol said.

'Yes. Sometimes I think I still am.'

'All of you,' she said. And then: 'I wish I could have helped.'

'You had your own troubles.'

'They were nothing by comparison. And anyway that was all over by then. But obviously I couldn't have helped. What help could anyone have been?'

'People did help,' I said. 'They were incredibly helpful. You were, I remember. But really, if I am truthful, none of it even scratched the surface.'

'And now?' We had been looking straight ahead, out through the windscreen, but she turned her face to me and I met her gaze, and it was so full of hope that I could not disappoint her.

'Now you scratch the surface,' I said.

She touched my wrist lightly. It was enough to be going on with.

The next time I felt I could not simply let her drive away. I asked if she wanted a coffee. She did, of course.

I knew that she wanted me too, but I didn't understand why. I've never understood it. I am irritable, moody, antisocial, obsessive, irreparably damaged. I am not to be depended on. Why would she or anyone want me? It cannot just be pity. I would see that at once and not stand for it. But there she was, week after week, an open though never desperate invitation, and week after week I edged closer to not rejecting it. Not just weeks but years went by. Slowly she coaxed me out into some kind of light. Then the trial happened and I was back in darkness, and still she waited. Till one night – I don't know what configuration of circumstances caused it other than the coffee being supplemented by a glass of wine – I brought things to a head with a sudden, bald statement of fact.

'I'll never marry again,' I said. 'I absolutely know that.'

'Nor me,' Carol said, 'but for different reasons. There are negative ones and positive ones, don't you think?'

'Yours being?'

'Negative. I could never trust a man enough to marry him, not after Harold. There'd always be the niggling fear that anyone I liked that much would turn out to be another shit after all, and I couldn't go through that again. I don't really trust anybody any more, that's the thing. Your reasons, I imagine, are more positive.'

'I'll never meet someone who can match Emily, you mean?'

'Yes. And you won't. But that doesn't mean you can't marry again.'

'Nevertheless,' I said, 'I won't.'

We were in the living room, in two armchairs, separated by a low table. It was a summer evening, still light outside, and silhouetted against the French window Carol's head might almost have been Emily's, except that she was in the wrong place. Emily almost always sat, legs tucked up, on the sofa. I tried to picture her sitting where Carol was, and myself watching her from where I was. The picture didn't come. This made the situation easier than it might have been.

'It's not true what I said about not trusting anybody,' Carol said. 'I trust you.'

'You don't know me.'

'I've known you for years.'

I nodded, deferring to the fact.

'You're not exactly a stranger, Alan. Anyway, I trust you. Why is that? Maybe it's because you're so loyal to Emily. You won't let go. I respect that. I trust *that*.'

There was more to come, I knew. I waited.

'But you know, I think by now she would want you to let go.'

'Don't,' I said.

Don't start, I meant. But, having started, she couldn't or wouldn't stop.

'When I saw the two of you together it was obvious that you were happy and secure in each other. Even when I saw you at work, on your own. If her name was mentioned. I was jealous of what you had.'

'Don't,' I said again.

'But I was. I was jealous of you both. And you had Alice, too. I was jealous of you for having her.'

I shook my head. I wasn't going to tell her a third time.

'I was jealous of Emily.'

My surprise wasn't total, but Carol must have caught something of it in my look. She flinched, held her ground.

'I'm being very forward, aren't I?' she said.

I could have closed it down then. I could have agreed with her, made it clear that she had overstepped a mark, was pushing too much into private territory, but that wasn't really what she was doing. She was confessing something about herself. What did surprise me was that I didn't mind.

'It's fine,' I said.

'I guess what I'm saying is . . . Well, you know what I'm saying.'

We were too far apart for any touch that didn't involve one of us making an irrecoverable movement. I saw that the whole thing could easily end in awkwardness, even in tears, but again Carol impressed me. She said, 'If you want to come back to mine and stay the night it would be nice. No complications.'

She had given me my cue to retreat. 'There are always complications,' I answered at once.

'Don't fight when there's nothing to fight,' she said. 'I'm telling you, *no* complications.'

I tried to work out the consequences of going to bed with her. I tried to think of a way out if I did, a way out if I didn't. I wondered about falling asleep, waking up.

I said, 'I don't think I could.'

She breathed out, sat back. 'Okay. Sorry I asked. No I'm not.'

'I mean,' I said, 'I don't think I could stay the night. Not all night. I get restless. I'd have to come back here. But I could get a taxi. Or walk.'

'It's four miles.'

'As I said, I get restless.'

'We can stay here, if you'd rather.'

'No,' I said firmly. 'Let's go to yours.'

11

'The Case' is my name for the work I do around the bombing – the gathering and sifting of information, the analysis of so-called facts and challenging of so-called evidence. I didn't deliberately christen it, but when the doubts started, followed in due succession by the suspicions, the theories and the certainties, 'the Case' became code for all of that. I had been here before, I realised, as I created files – paper ones and electronic ones – in order to keep myself on top of the accumulating mass of information. My apprenticeship had been writing my doctoral thesis. And now I was doing it again, only this time it was, as the PhD never had been, for real. Documents piled up: the fatal accident inquiry report, medical reports, cuttings from newspapers and magazines, police reports, airline reports, insurance reports, government statements, all the paperwork relating to and leading up to the trial, the trial records and the published judgment of the court. The dining room became the dumping-ground for it all. First the piles took over the table, then the floor right round the room. I acquired one, then a second, then a third filing cabinet to contain it all. Whenever I made a space by filing something away, it was quickly filled. I recorded news items, documentaries, interviews with politicians, on cassettes and videos from radio and television, and I labelled and stored them, stacking them in chronological order in a cupboard. Into the filing cabinets went copies of my own letters to the press, to the police, to the court, to governments across the world, the replies I received, the transcripts of my public statements voicing concerns about the trial, statements made in response from individuals and institutions. My redundant dining room became a reference library with only one subject.

I made paper copies of everything I could, because I was distrustful of technology, not because of the technology itself but because of the way I came to depend on it. I hated this dependency. The years of work that could be wiped out through loss of power or computer failure – I thought of that sometimes when I couldn't sleep and it made me get up and recheck that I'd backed everything up on the external hard drive, that I had it all banked and secure. I was mindful of the fact that my emails could be intercepted and my internet use monitored. When I went to work I checked front and back doors and all the windows. I had a burglar alarm fitted. If I went away I hid the external hard drive. I was not being paranoid. So much of what I researched was about security, protection of information. My precautions were disproportionate only in the sense that they were probably inadequate.

I was increasingly a public figure, a man who rejected the official version. I was not just a dissenter but a dissenter whose dissent had added validity, because of what had happened to my loved ones. I was invited to speak on *Newsnight* and *World Report* and *Today*, and I never turned down an opportunity to voice my concerns. I went to Khazar's country, to London, New York, Washington, Brussels, Berlin. I went to the island, spoke to politicians and policemen across Europe and North Africa and the Middle East. I published articles in which I wrote not just of the failure of the law in this particular case – *the* Case – but of what that meant for our society. If the justice system could get things so spectacularly wrong, if it could then apparently turn a blind eye to error, negligence and suppression of evidence, if it could drag its heels and seem to want to avoid shining a light on any aspect of a case that might reflect badly on its own processes, if it could condone such attitudes in this most important of criminal proceedings – then what *was* justice, and whom did it serve? I asked such questions again and again, and the silence that greeted them spoke volumes, and so did the worldly shaking of heads and the muttered sympathies, which I sensed rather than heard, or heard at third-hand: 'Poor Alan Tealing. Desperately sad. Quite obsessed, poor chap. There's a word for it, isn't there?' And yes it was obsessive, I was obsessive, but for a reason and the reason was that something was badly wrong and this needed to be said and I needed to say it and *me* saying it and *me* asking more questions and *me* not being satisfied with the answers had an effect and a purpose. Yes, that way round: an effect and a purpose. It was what I was for. With Emily and Alice gone, this was my purpose, to keep the Case alive, to look for answers, to seek the truth.

There was one weekend when I'd been working on the Case all Saturday, had fallen asleep at the table then crawled into bed, woken again early on the Sunday and got up, pulled on a jumper and jeans and got back into it. Piles of paper everywhere, periodic cups of coffee, a bowl of cereal munched in front of the computer halfway through the morning – it would have seemed like a kind of madness if you'd been looking in from the outside, but I wasn't, I was inside it and it was inside me. This was when I was becoming an expert on timers. I'd done my research, read the manufacturers' manuals, plodded through long and complex papers by experts in the field, then read up on those experts, who they were, what else they knew about, what reasons they might have for saying this thing or that thing. Then I had to go back to the transcripts of the trial, picking over the evidence of the police and the forensics people. I took their sentences apart, their hesitations and supposed certainties, their inability to explain certain procedural lapses, their incompetence if it was incompetence, their defensiveness if it was that, their prickliness under oath. I made notes, remade them, revised and revised as if I were going to sit an exam. I *could* have sat an exam. This was what I was engaged in over that weekend.

At some point the doorbell rang. I was going to ignore it but I'd forgotten what day it was, thought it was still Saturday morning and that it might be the postman with something too big for the letter box, and I went to the door and opened it to bright sunshine, and Carol standing in front of me. She had a cycling helmet in one hand. Beyond her, leaning against the gatepost, was a bicycle.

Since that night when we'd gone to hers, a little stone-built cottage that had once housed a weaver's extended family, she'd never been back to mine. This was better, easier, for both of us. When we were together, we were together in her cottage. She had moved there after her divorce. Whatever its overcrowded history, it contained no ghosts for either of us.

But now she was on my doorstep.

'I hadn't heard from you,' she said. 'I thought I'd check if you were all right.'

'I'm fine,' I said.

She looked me up and down. 'Sure?'

'Yes. Why wouldn't I be?'

She stood there with her neat brown bobbed hair that she had begun to dye — to keep the grey at bay, she said, as if she were in a TV ad, or she might have been quoting *from* a TV ad — and I waited for her to say something else, to explain why she was there. She said, 'You were going to call me.'

'I was?'

'Yes, that's what we arranged on Friday. Lunchtime, don't you remember?'

I shook my head. 'I'm sorry, what exactly did we arrange?'

'We were going to meet last night, or you were going to come over for dinner. We hadn't decided. It depended how you were feeling. How we were both feeling.'

There was no point disputing that this was what had been agreed. Clearly I had let her down.

'And I know sometimes you get wrapped up in stuff,' she said, 'and I didn't want to interrupt, I didn't want to nag, so I left it last night, but then when you didn't phone today either . . .'

'Why didn't you phone me?'

'It's a lovely day. I got the bike out. I wanted to see you, Alan.'

'I'm sorry,' I said. 'It went completely out of my head.'

'Can I come in? You look like you're on guard duty.'

I stepped back and in she came. I was conscious of not having washed, of my sweaty, musty clothes. I felt suddenly ancient, shambling, an old man not long out of my bed or not long for this world, one or the other. 'Do you want something?' I said. 'Tea or coffee? I'm sorry, the place is a mess.'

Carol was ahead of me. She stopped and turned. 'Alan, do you know who I am? This is me, the woman you share a bed with from time to time. You're making me feel like you've let me in to sell you raffle tickets or something.'

'I'm sorry,' I said for the third time.

'Where do you want me to go?' she said.

'First right,' I said, on an impulse. 'That's where I've been all weekend.'

So this was Carol's first time in that room, her first view of the Case. It was in full flow, spilling off the table and pooling on chairs and other low surfaces, forming slow, fat stalagmites on the floor. She put her hand to her mouth, as if to hush a cry. She said, 'No wonder you didn't call.'

I picked up a couple of mugs and a bowl. 'I'll put the kettle on,' I said. 'Coffee?'

'Wait,' she said.

I put the things down again. 'What?'

'I've disturbed you, but since I have don't let's leave this. I'm here now. Tell me about it.'

'What? This? You know what this is.'

'The coffee can wait,' she said. 'Talk me through this.'

I suppose that was what I wanted to do, or I would never have directed her into the room. But where do you start? I couldn't tell her everything – I couldn't have talked *anyone* through *all* of it – but I told her a lot. I told her why I thought Khalil Khazar was innocent. I discoursed on the principles of justice and the admissibility of certain kinds of evidence, then I presented the case for and the case against and then I demolished the case for, which had been presented as the truth and was not the truth but the opposite. I remembered, as I always did, the jaundiced views of George Braithwaite, I gave due weight and consideration to them, yet I did not abandon my belief in truth and justice. It was a great performance, like one of my best lectures in front of a hundred undergraduates. Carol sat on a dining chair with a batch of papers on her knees and though she said nothing I could see she was enthralled. At the end I stood before her and gave a little bow and we both laughed.

'This is you, isn't it?' she said. 'This is what you do, what you really do. The rest of us go to work and we're Chaucerians or Romanticists or Modernists or whatever. We have our specialities. We're doctors of this or professors of that or readers in something else. You come home and go to work on this. It's your area of expertise.'

'Not by choice,' I said.

'That's *why* you're an expert,' she said. 'Because you had no choice. You have to get to the truth. That's what you are: you're a professor of truth.'

I liked that. In my head I capitalised it: Professor of Truth. Aloud I made a joke of it, stroked an imaginary long beard, said in a quavery voice, 'Of course, my dear, there are not many still working in the field. Few think it has any great value nowadays.'

'Professor Alan Tealing, of the Department of Truth,' Carol said.

We went through to the kitchen and I made coffee. Carol asked me subtle, intelligent questions, most but not all of which I was able to answer. She was alert and engaged in a way I had not expected, and

I managed to relax a little – was even quite pleased – about having let her into this domain, this secret, overgrown garden of mine. Yet simultaneously I resented her being there, because someone else was also there – Emily, my ghost wife, of whom no material trace remained. I felt her presence, saw her moving among the foliage. I was grateful that Carol had taken the trouble to come round, to make sure I was okay, but – if only she had not come, if only she would go away, I could get back to the Case, be uninterrupted for what was left of the day.

It was not to be. I owed Carol more than ejection. After the coffee I left her downstairs while I had a shower and put on some clean clothes. Perhaps she returned to the dining room and riffled through the Case like a spy or a psychologist, I don't know, but when I came down she was in the living room, leafing through a book she had picked off a shelf there. I saved and switched everything down, set the alarm and locked the door.

We walked into town together, Carol pushing her bike. The sunshine and the light breeze seemed to lift my spirits. We stopped for a drink and a bite to eat, then wandered on, arriving at her cottage in the early evening. We sat out on her patio with a bottle of wine, and it was relaxed and easy and nothing more was said about my having let her down, if indeed I had done so. Carol's seemingly endless patience enabled me not to worry too much about that. The worrying came later, after we'd gone to bed and she'd fallen asleep. At three o'clock I was wide awake, trying to fit everything together, scraping away at the prison walls again. I eased myself out of bed and got dressed. Carol stirred but did not wake. When she did, she would not be surprised to find me gone. It was part of how we worked. I crept down the hall and out into the street, and made my way back to the Case through the last of the night.

12

'I went to see him in prison,' I said. 'Khalil Khazar.'

'Yes,' Nilsen said. 'You didn't make a secret of it.'

'That was *my* attempt at setting the record straight,' I said. 'I needed Khazar to understand I didn't think he'd done it. And I needed to hear him tell me what he knew.'

'You could have done that and kept it to yourself, but you chose not to. You went to a Sunday paper and gave them the story.'

'I wanted the world to know I'd been face to face with him.'

'Then why didn't you tell the world what he'd said?'

'Because he was putting his second appeal together. I promised him I wouldn't say anything that might prejudice that.'

'A lot of people were very angry with you. They said you were naive.'

'That was the kindest comment. They also said I was being selective, putting out propaganda, keeping back anything that didn't fit my interpretation of events.'

'And were you?'

'I'd given him my word.'

'So it was okay for you to withhold information, but not anybody else?'

'The difference was, my reasons were entirely honourable,' I said.

'Now there's a word,' Nilsen said.

'Those people who criticised me for going, that was their right. It was my right to go. They didn't have my motivation. They believed he was guilty. I believed he was innocent.'

'Some people will believe anything.'

We were going round in circles again. I thought, why is he here, still testing me, still not giving me whatever it is he says he has to give?

'I went twice,' I said. 'That first time, and then again, near the end.'

'When he was dying.'

'Yes. People said he wasn't dying. They said it was a ploy to get himself released early. They said he was faking it.'

'But he wasn't,' Nilsen said, and he gave me a challenging look.

'No,' I said, 'but he'd changed, and not just because he was so ill. It was as if part of him had already gone on somewhere, been released.' And now when I looked back at Nilsen I thought, I may not have seen your face before but I've seen the light in your eyes, or something like it. 'He was a very religious man,' I said. 'Very devout.'

'A martyr,' Nilsen said.

'It wasn't like that,' I said. 'He didn't have the self-regard of a martyr, or the fanaticism. He just trusted his God.'

Nilsen's eyes narrowed. I wondered if he thought he shared his deity with Muslims and Jews and all the other religions of the world and they simply had the wrong description, the wrong name. Or did he think they were worshipping nothing? He couldn't, surely, think there was more than one God out there, competing for votes. And could a man really *think* any of that stuff, or did he just *feel* it?

'He didn't have a deal going, a contract,' I said. 'There were no guarantees, just his faith. I prefer that kind of religion to yours. It makes more sense, as much as any of it does.'

I suppose I was trying to goad him again, but Nilsen was not to be goaded, or at least nothing showed in his haggard face. He said, 'When he died, I saw you on TV, saying how sorry you were.'

'I was.'

'They filmed you in front of that castle,' he said. 'It looked pretty good. It was summer of course. You looked tired but they didn't keep the camera on you all the time. I remember thinking, that's a good old country. It'll be here long after we're all gone.'

'Is that what you thought?' I said.

He nodded. 'I saved that clip. I've watched it I don't know how many times. You want to know why?'

'Tell me.'

'Because I wanted to be sorry too. I wanted to feel what you felt about him. I wanted to understand what it was like.'

'Just watching me wouldn't do that,' I said.

'No,' he said, 'it didn't. But it started something. I waited to see what would happen now that he was dead. You know what happened: nothing. Just like you said in that clip.'

'So what did it start, watching me?'

'This,' he said.

His being there in my house. That was what he meant. The journey he'd made began when Khazar died, when he saw me saying what I said.

'And now?' I said.

'And now we're almost done,' he said.

He made a movement, unstiffening himself. Surely this was when I would find out what it was he had for me.

But all he said was, 'I need to use your bathroom before I go.'

13

I got on reasonably well with Alfred and Rachel when Emily first introduced me to them: they were hospitable and generous, although they were not wealthy. I think they looked on me as a kind of curiosity from the old world, amusing for a while and then to be discarded. When they realised that Emily and I were serious, that we meant to marry and that I was going to take her thousands of miles away from them, the warmth diminished. For the first three summers after the wedding we made a point of spending a month with them and Emily's brothers and their families, and once we went for Christmas too. Then Alice was born, and we had less money and less energy to make the trip. We did go, when Alice was two, or rather Emily and Alice went for a month and I joined them for ten days, but it was a stressful experience. Alfred and Rachel made uneasy grandparents, always fretful that Alice would hurt herself or break their possessions, shifting suddenly between petting and scolding her. As for me, I had ceased to be of interest. Emily tried to persuade them to come to Scotland, but they never did – the mere thought of flying made Rachel ill – and although I was relieved I also held their refusal against them. They were everything that Emily was not – insular, unadventurous, querulous – and it was only for her sake that I remained polite and superficially friendly on the phone.

After the bombing I took them some of Emily's things, an album of photographs of Emily and Alice, some of their clothes, whatever I could bear to part with that I thought they might like to have. I hoped, too, that we could make some new and better alliance from our grief, but what connected us had been taken from us. We could not even share the burial of them, here or there, because the annihilation had been so complete. Alfred and Rachel arranged a memorial service in their church, and many people came. Some I had met at our wedding, but only one or two of them since then. Most were complete strangers to me. I probably did not show much grace in receiving their sympathies. To be frank, I did not care how sorry they were. Their sorrow was genuine, I'm sure, but I did not care, any more than I cared about the genuine grief of Emily's brothers and their wives, and of Alfred and Rachel. I just wanted the day and the whole ghastly process to be over.

The obligations of bereavement are not so simply dispensed with, however. For the first few months after I returned home Rachel felt a duty to phone me every so often, and expected me to do the same, turn and turn about, even though we had nothing to give each other but painful reminders. 'I'm going to hand you on to Alfred,' Rachel would say after ten minutes, and Alfred's tired, flat voice would come down the line, asking the same questions about how I was and what was new before we concluded by saying we would speak again soon. The intervals between these calls grew longer but they continued, and sometimes, when there were developments in the police investigation, they were more animated and prolonged, but what sustained them was not love but loss. When we spoke I pictured the ocean rolling between us, vast and grey and cold.

The years passed, and then came the charges against Khalil Khazar and Waleed Mahmed and the long process of bringing them to trial, and then the trial itself. Alfred and Rachel were both in their mid-seventies by then, and Rachel had heart problems and was not keeping well. They did not attend, but asked me to keep them informed. I did, before and during, and they listened with what I felt was a kind of numb gratitude; but afterwards, when it was over, when with a sinking dread I began to articulate to them my scepticism about Khazar's guilt, our relationship grew strained, even hostile. They had greeted his conviction with satisfaction, tempered only by disappointment that the trial had not taken place in the United States where the death penalty might have been a serious possibility. To hear me say that I did not think Khazar had murdered their daughter and granddaughter was more than just hurtful to them; it was a betrayal. I had revealed my true colours at last, the limp, fluttering flag (I am sure they saw it thus) of European liberalism. We did not so much argue down the wires as make statements from one side of the Atlantic to the other, and each statement was answered by a longer silence, or a deeper breath, or a terser remark. 'I'm sorry, I cannot accept that.' 'Well, that's not how we feel.' 'That is untrue.' At the end of one such conversation I said, 'Should we go on doing this? Being in touch like this. I don't want to keep calling you if all I do is cause you distress.' 'You are the husband of our daughter,' Alfred said. 'I'm putting Rachel back on.' There was a pause, the soft rasp of a hand placed over the mouthpiece. 'Of course we must keep in touch,' Rachel said. 'You are all we have left of her. We'll talk again soon, Alan.' And she hung up.

But as the divide grew between what they believed or wanted to believe and what I couldn't, and as my profile as one of the principal sceptics grew, so whatever dialogue took place between us became more stilted. Not just with them either: I had never had much contact with her brothers; now, that ceased entirely. Eventually, five years or so after Khazar's imprisonment, everything came to a head. I had issued a long and detailed criticism of all that I felt was wrong with his conviction and this had been picked up by news agencies around the world. I had also, following my visit to him in prison, given that interview to the Sunday paper, in which I described him as a man of profound faith. This had unleashed a storm of abuse from politicians on both sides of the Atlantic, who accused me of naivety, calculation, stupidity and mendacity. One autumn night, at about ten o'clock, the telephone rang and it was not a journalist making a late-night chance bid for a story, it was Alfred.

'Alan,' he said. I recognised his voice at once.

They were five hours behind us. I pictured him, now long retired, in their gloomy house on a damp Pennsylvania evening, with thick layers of orange and red leaves going to brown in the garden at dusk, waiting to be gathered – one more thing that Alfred would be less able to cope with.

'Hello, Alfred,' I said.

'This has to stop,' he said. 'You have to stop.'

'Stop what?'

'You know. This endless . . . this endless torture. Rachel can't take it any more. She can't speak to you if you keep on with it.'

'We don't speak much now, Alfred,' I said.

'What good is it doing?' he said. There was a tremulousness in his voice, but behind that something steelier.

'It's better than doing nothing,' I said.

'There is nothing to do,' he said, and the rising emphasis on the last two words betrayed his irritation. 'It's over. Why can't you leave it? Why can't you let us have some peace?'

'I wish I could,' I said, 'but I can't. Don't you think I would leave it if it were possible?'

'Rachel is very unwell,' he said.

'I'm sorry to hear that,' I said.

'I fear for her,' he said. 'She's never been able to mourn properly. None of us have, you included, but sometimes you forget that this isn't just about you. We have all been in pain. We still are. We thought some kind of healing might begin when the trial was over, and maybe it could have, but then you started this' – he broke off, and I could almost see him searching, reaching for the right words – 'this incessant gnawing, like a dog at a bone. But there is nothing left on the bone, Alan. And now this latest madness.'

'What madness, Alfred?'

'Going to see that bastard.' I had never heard Alfred curse before. It gave him an uncharacteristic vehemence. 'What could have possessed you to do that?'

'I wasn't getting answers to my questions elsewhere. I thought, why not ask the man who's supposed to know?'

'And you expected what? Anything but a pack of lies?' The tremble in his voice was quite gone now.

'That's all I've been getting anywhere else.'

'Nonsense,' he said. 'Total nonsense. You just don't like what you've been told, what was clearly established at the trial, and so you keep on with your madcap theories about what *might* have happened instead. Well, none of us liked what we were told, but we had to get used to it. And so ought you.'

'We've been through all this,' I said. 'You know we don't agree.'

He either didn't hear me or chose not to. 'Rachel wants you to stop,' he said. 'We all want you to stop.'

'I'm sorry,' I said, 'but Khalil Khazar should not be in prison.'

'He's lucky he is,' Alfred said. 'If he hadn't have been somebody would have hunted him down and killed him by now. He's lucky to be alive.'

'He did not bomb that aircraft,' I said. 'He did not kill Emily and Alice and all those other people.'

'He told you that, did he?'

'I asked him.'

'You looked into his eyes. That's what that newspaper article said.'

'I did,' I said. 'I looked at him for I don't know how long. And yes, that's what he told me.'

'You looked into his eyes and he said he didn't do it and so you believed him. Am I right?'

'It's the closest I've got to the truth so far. Yes, I believe him.'

'What kind of an idiot are you, Alan?' Alfred said. 'I can't even bring myself to say his name, he disgusts me so much. And if you want to know, you disgust me too. I'm sorry to say that, but the fact that you went to commiserate with that animal, that bastard, after what he did to us – to you too, for God's sake – it's beyond comprehension.'

'You're not listening to me,' I said. 'He didn't do it.'

'No, I am not listening to you. He did it.'

'He did not.'

Maybe we would have gone on saying that back and forth like two kids disputing some sporting infringement, but suddenly it seemed Alfred had had enough. 'Well, I don't give a damn whether he did or didn't!' he shouted. 'I'm just asking you to stop what you are doing and give us some peace. Do you think you could have the decency to do that?'

'You are asking me to switch myself off,' I said. 'To stop thinking.'

'And let Rachel be a little easier in her mind,' he said. As quickly as it had risen, his voice had gone flat again. He said, so quietly that I almost didn't catch it, 'It is too cruel.' He was, I calculated, seventy-nine or maybe even eighty, stuck between Rachel and me, trying to mediate, and that was an impossible place to be. I imagined him replacing the receiver after we'd finished, and going back to her, and telling her that it would be all right, that I had agreed not to go on any more, or telling her that I had not agreed, that I was going to carry on. He would either have to lie or he would be hurting her. I felt sorry for him, but not so much that I myself could lie to him.

'Alfred,' I said, 'this goes beyond you and me and Rachel. I have to do this for Emily and Alice.'

There followed one of the prolonged silences that marked these exchanges. I almost thought he had quietly put the receiver down and walked away. But then he spoke one last time.

'No, I don't think so,' he said. 'It is not for them. It is for you.' And he hung up.

That was three years ago. I have not spoken to either of them since. I do not know if they are alive or dead. It is almost possible for me to say that I do not care.

I stand by what I said that night. This goes beyond all of us. It even goes beyond Emily and Alice and the other people on that flight. Beyond us all there is something else worth reaching for, greater than any of us.

I had had the same from my own family: shared grief, sympathy, fatigue, and eventually accusation. My mother got there long before Alfred did. The last time she and my father came to stay with me, they were appalled at the state of the house generally, and the state of the dining room in particular. 'You could at least have cleared the table,' my mother said. 'What is all this?' And as I explained, or tried to explain, I saw horror filling their faces. 'I thought it was your university work,' my father said. 'I had no idea . . .' My mother said briskly, 'Well, we can't eat in here.' 'No, we eat in the kitchen,' I said, 'or we can go out if you don't want to do that.' 'We'll go out,' she said.

This set the tone for a stressful, unhappy few days. When they got home she phoned me. 'It upsets me to say it, Alan, but you were never difficult like this. You were always so accommodating. You've become selfish.'

'I never used to be a bereaved husband and father,' I said.

'We're all bereaved,' she said.

'I'm sorry if you think I'm being selfish.'

'You have to let it go,' she said. 'Move on.'

'I can't let it go,' I said. 'I can't let *them* go. Can you?'

'You have to,' she said. 'You *have* to.' And she started to sob, and then apologised, and we said we'd speak again soon, and we did, but something had changed between us. And my father, quiet and stoical and sad, was there in the background. I felt I had never really known them.

Not long after that came the prison visit to Khazar, and the attendant publicity, and the gulf widened. My sister, Karen, called and said she was coming to see me. We hadn't seen each other for a couple of years. She was forty-seven then, had been married for twenty-five years to her childhood sweetheart, Geoff, and had two grown-up sons, Ben and Daniel. She still worked for the same supermarket chain but as a customer services manager. In most respects she didn't appear to me to have changed much over the decades.

I met her off the train a week later, and we went back to the house in a taxi. She'd brought a bottle of gin, her favourite tipple, and we opened it and talked.

'I take it you've been sent as an envoy,' I said.

'A what?'

'Mum and Dad asked you to come and talk some sanity into me. Am I right?'

'Actually, no. It was my own idea. They agree with me, though.'

'About what? That I'm insane?'

'Don't be silly. We love you, Alan.' As if love and madness couldn't go together.

'I know you do.'

'You can't spend the rest of your life like this. That's what we agree about. Or one day you're going to wake up and it'll be over.'

'Karen, this *is* the rest of my life. I didn't will it to be like this, but it is. And you're right, one day it will be over.'

'I don't just mean over, I mean used up, finished, gone, but you'll still be breathing. You'll be a crumbling old man and you still won't have Emily and Alice. You won't have had them all those years and years and some day soon you'll be dead. What good will that be? What good will it have done you? Or them?'

'What exactly do you mean by "that"? What good will I have done staying alive? Trying to find out who killed them? I don't know, Karen. Are you offering me something better?'

'You owe it to them to live differently.'

'You have no idea what I owe them. I am tired of having these conversations with everyone. You, Mum and Dad, Emily's family. Why do I have to justify myself to you all?'

'Alan, you know your trouble? You think too much. You always have. If you stopped thinking you had to justify yourself and just *were* yourself, you'd be a lot happier.'

'Like you, you mean.'

'Yes, like me. I know I don't have your brains and nothing that's ever happened to me is remotely as terrible as what happened to you and I've got Geoff and Ben and Daniel and so I'm lucky, but if I woke up one morning and my luck had changed, I know I'd get up and get on with it. I'd have to. And I'm not saying you should ever forget Emily and Alice and I'm not saying I've forgotten them or that I don't think about losing Geoff or the boys and how awful that would be. I'm not saying that.'

'So what are you saying?'

'I'm saying it was eighteen years ago.'

I was silent.

'Hasn't there been anybody else, not even a possibility, in eighteen years?'

'No.'

I had not, would not, mention Carol to Karen or my parents. I still never have. She is none of their business. They would load such expectations on the relationship it would destroy it. It may be as much as I can manage, but it certainly would not be enough for them.

Karen was with me for only a weekend, and we survived it. She gave up her probing and lecturing after the third gin and we talked of other, safer things, mostly Ben, Daniel and Geoff. On the Saturday we went to Edinburgh and were tourists for a day. On the Sunday we took a long walk in the country. On the Monday she went home, back to her family four hundred miles away. Not only did I not mention Carol, I kept to a minimum any possibility of Karen meeting her.

Different things woke me in the middle of the night, or would not let me go to sleep in the first place. Dreams of Alice; sudden memories jabbing like knives; complex puzzles from different filing cabinets of the Case, endlessly rearranging themselves. But worst of all was the gripping, sweat-inducing fear which hissed that I had made a terrible mistake, that for all the years in which I had argued and campaigned against the verdict of the court I had been in error. This insidious whisper said that Khalil Khazar was indeed guilty of the crime. He it was who had placed the bomb in the suitcase, who had gone in Parroulet's taxi to the airport, who had somehow managed to get the suitcase through security, on to the connecting flight to Germany and on to London. Then he had flown out on another flight, back to his own country, with a smile under his blank face, knowing he had done his job in the service of whatever his cause was. And I had refused to accept his guilt. I had looked into his eyes and he had coolly and earnestly looked back into mine and taken me for a fool. I had lost my wife and daughter to this man and then I had lost years of my life convincing myself that he was as innocent as they. I had argued with the families of other victims about it, I had clawed at the wounds of Emily's family till I had lost them as well, and I had all but lost my own relatives. This fear was with me always, and when it loomed large in the hours of darkness it tortured me, left me broken by the awfulness of what I might have done. It was as if, had I been a driver, I had run over a child not because of a momentary lapse of concentration or because the child had suddenly stepped out in front of me but through some arrogant, wilful conviction that I was in control and incapable of making a mistake. No matter how rationally I argued against the fear, reminding myself of all the piles of evidence in the

Case that spoke against it, still it persisted. It condemned me again to my ancient prison, to scraping at the mouldy walls, but this time there was no hope of release and it was my own fault that I was incarcerated. What had I done wrong? I had created my own false religion, without which I could not function, could not wake and work every day, could not *be*. I had locked myself in a cell of delusion, of total, blinkered faith in Khalil Khazar's innocence.

14

I led Nilsen into the hallway and pointed to the downstairs toilet. He moved slowly across the space, as if still treading through snow, and closed the door firmly behind him. It was the first time that he'd been out of my sight since his arrival.

I didn't want to stand sentry until he reappeared but on the other hand I didn't want him roaming the house unattended. Next to the toilet was the dining room, its door ajar. Least of all did I want him in there. I went in myself and waited, surrounded by the Case. I could hear nothing through the wall. What was he doing? Getting rid of the coffee, I assumed, but everything was quiet. Was he staring in the mirror and if so what did he see? A weakened, dying man? Or a man still in control, ticking off items on his 'to do' list? Maybe both. Then the toilet flushed, and I heard a tap running.

I was about to step back into the hallway but changed my mind. If Nilsen came into the dining room what might he see that I didn't want him to? It was inconceivable that he would not have worked out that my house must contain the Case, or something approaching it in scale. He would already have a feel for the weight of its paper, the way it made the very walls of the room bulge. The Case – his version of it, my version – was, after all, why he had come. 'Nilsen,' I called out. 'In here.' And I pulled the door wide.

He seemed to have aged by some years. He came in and there it was for him. He looked at the shelves, the table, the chairs, the floor, all covered with the live workings and the exhausted seams of my research. His gaze lingered on the filing cabinets, then came back to me.

'What?' he said.

'There's nothing you can give me that I don't already have, some-where,' I said.

'You think so?'

'Yes.'

'But I can,' he said.

He had something, I realised, clutched in his left hand, and now he stretched out his arm and opened his fingers. A tightly folded square of paper fell on the table among the other papers. He con-tinued to look at me, as if he were a conjurer expecting me to gasp or cheer. I reached for the paper, unfolded it. An address was printed on it in typed block capitals: a house number, a road, a town, a country. The town was called Sheildston. The country was Australia.

'What is this?' I asked.

'It's where he is.'

'Who?'

'Parroulet.'

I looked again at the paper. Who had typed the address? Nilsen? He appeared not to want to leave a trace of himself, not so much as a specimen of handwriting.

'This is what you came here for?'

'I came to talk to you. Yes, and to give you that.'

'This scrap of paper?'

'It's all I have. What do you want, a phone number?' He spoke as if I'd asked him a favour. 'He isn't going to talk to you across twelve thousand miles. You have to go visit him.'

'I don't want to visit Parroulet. I want to know who killed my wife and daughter. *He* doesn't know.'

'That's not why you'd go.'

'Why don't you give me the address of the bomber? The real bomber. That would be a visit worth making.'

'I can't do that. I don't know where that is. Or who that is.'

'If you did, would you tell me?'

'If I did, we'd have paid a visit ourselves.'

'Maybe you already have. Maybe you've erased them, but you still can't afford to admit it wasn't Khalil Khazar. The perpetrator is dead, and so is Khazar, but only Khazar stays guilty.'

'Not if you get Parroulet to talk.'

'If he's not going to talk to me on the phone, why would he talk to me face to face? There's nothing in it for him. Unless he's dying with a guilty conscience too.'

'You won't know till you get there.'

I dropped the paper back on the table. 'All I want is the truth and you offer me this? The address of a bought witness? Am I supposed to feel grateful?'

'I don't know what you're supposed to feel. I have nothing else to offer. But if you can get Parroulet to talk, you could force them to reopen the whole case.'

I felt faint at the thought of starting again, had a brief vision of one hole in one wall leading to another, and another, a new succession of holes in walls.

I said, 'Why not you? You're on a mission. You go to him.'

'I don't have time. Anyway, we talked to him already. That conversation is over. This is between him and you.'

I picked up the paper again, turned it over. The reverse was blank. I hadn't really expected anything else.

'I wish I'd never let you in the door,' I said.

'No you don't.'

I tried again. 'How do you know this is where he is? If you've been retired as long as you say you have.'

'You never retire. They don't let you. Or you don't let yourself. I still have contacts.'

'And they would give you this information for what reason?'

'Officially, no reason,' Nilsen said. 'Unofficially, let's say a favour, from one man to another. A guy who knows what's happening to me. Who understands the time imperative.'

Again I felt a surge of anger, at the implication that time had only started ticking when *he* learned he was dying.

'And you told him what? "God says I have to tell Tealing where Parroulet is so he can go and have a chat with him, and then all our consciences will be clear and I can die happy." Is that what you said?'

'No, but if that's what does it for you, so be it. What you think of me or my faith is of no consequence. You can mock all you like. I'm just giving you an option. But it isn't really an option, is it? You won't be able to not go. You're still in the game.'

'This place might not even exist,' I said. 'I've never heard of it.'

'The first thing you'll do after I leave,' Nilsen replied, 'is look it up.'

'I want you to leave now,' I told him.

'I'm on my way.'

I ushered him from the room. Deliberately, I left the piece of paper on the table, as if I didn't care about it, but he was right, of course, about what I would do when he was gone.

Back in the kitchen he began the laborious process of putting on his coat and fastening its buttons. Outside, the last of the light was leaking from the day. I wanted rid of him but still I found I had questions for him.

'Why should I believe you, this getting-ready-to-meet-your-maker nonsense? And even if I do believe you, why did you come to me like this, like a thief in the night? Why not just go public on everything you've told me?'

His fingers stopped their fumbling. 'Why should *you* believe me?' He gave that short, croaking laugh. 'Who else is going to? I go to the media with this, I'm just another conspiracy crank. I can't prove who I am. I might get a few minutes of someone's attention, sure, because it sounds like a story, but then they check me out at the office. "What about this guy?" they ask. "He says he worked for you." And they say, "Well, a lot of guys say that. We never heard of him. He's just another fantasist." I know how they operate. They'd deny everything. And in a few weeks or months I'll be dead. But you won't be.'

'And what makes you think I'll act on this?'

'It's like I said, I admire you.' He waved a hand in the direction of the dining room. 'You've stuck at it so far. You'll see this through too.'

I shook my head.

'Yes you will. We're alike,' he said. 'In other circumstances, we could have worked together.'

'I don't think so,' I said.

'In another life, sure we could have. You're the one I needed to reach. The other relatives got a version they believed because they wanted to. You wanted to believe it too, but you couldn't. You're the one we lied to. You're the one that can get to Parroulet. You're the one that can change everything. You're a good citizen.'

'You're full of crap,' I said.

'I don't expect you to like me,' he said. 'That doesn't matter. What matters is there's a bottom line, a calculation at the end of everything. Do we do good or do we do evil? All these details, these things we grapple with, they're part of the calculation. We get some of them wrong, I've been trying to tell you that. But the bottom line: what is it we work towards? Good or evil?'

I had no answer. He pulled his hat slowly down over his ears. It looked as if it hurt to do so. He said, 'There's nothing more I can do here.'

'So who's next?' I asked. 'You said you had other debts to settle.'

'I guess I'm clear now,' he said.

'You'd better be sure,' I said. 'If you turn up and find one thing on the sheet that hasn't been ticked off, one detail, wouldn't that make all this a waste of time?'

The doglike smile flickered. 'Time's up. And I've been pretty thorough.'

'But if you've made a mistake,' I insisted, 'if you've missed something, just one thing, and your contract is null and void, what then? The angels will be thorough too. Won't they put you on the fiery escalator down to hell?'

He did not like my flippancy.

'You don't understand, do you? The thing I have with God. I'm not some salesman with merchandise. Do you think I could sneak in somehow if he didn't want me?'

'Maybe there's a back entrance with a broken padlock. Do you believe in hell, by the way?'

His look said it was a stupid question. 'Yes, I do.'

'So do I,' I said, 'but my hell is John Milton's: "The mind is its own place, and in itself can make a heaven of hell, a hell of heaven." I don't suppose you've read Milton, have you?'

'Not lately.'

His face gave nothing away, but his mouth held the vaguest hint of amusement, or tolerance. Maybe he'd never heard of Milton.

'He believed in everything you do, but with a depth and intellect you can't even imagine. You know why?'

The faint smile was gone again. 'Tell me.'

'Because he lived four hundred years ago, when that kind of belief was still possible.'

Nilsen shook his head. He started towards the back door, and I got ahead of him and opened it.

In a moment, I thought, that paper with the Australian address on it will be the only sign that he's ever been here.

No, not quite. It was snowing again, hard. Nilsen stepped out and his boots left their marks in the snow. He'd leave a trail round the house and down the street, for a while at least. But eventually only the paper would remain.

Nilsen said, 'Goodbye, Dr Tealing. Good luck.'

Already, with the flakes settling on him, he looked like a man in a film about to perform some heroic act. Did he expect me to wish him luck back? I said nothing. He turned and began his walk along the already filled-in path. He went round the corner of the house. I looked at my boots. Coatless and hatless, not knowing why I went, I hurried after him.

Nilsen had moved with more speed than I'd thought him capable of. He was clear of the house, of the driveway. The street lights had come on, so that near them the snow fell as a pale-yellow substance, stains on the general blanket of white. I stood out in the middle of the road and glimpsed the retreating figure, slumped yet marching somehow, going into the snowstorm between the two lines of sickly torches. I felt an urge to call out, but what would I say? Goodbye? Come back? There was nothing to say. I said nothing.

And then Ted Nilsen was gone, on his way to paradise.

I went back to the house. The snow was coming down in heavy clumps, a great latticework of flakes. I kicked my boots against the wall, stepped inside, removed them. I certainly wasn't going anywhere and I didn't think Nilsen would have much luck getting out of town. I took the coffee mugs and cafetière and washed them. I thought, is there a wife? Are there children? Grandchildren? Maybe Nilsen is divorced, maybe he has a girlfriend much younger than himself, maybe he doesn't. For some reason I couldn't imagine him having a boyfriend. I thought, does anybody care about him? I thought, why do I even ask?

I went into the study and to the computer there. Who was David Dibald now? He was no one. I closed the documents I'd been working on, retrieved the Australian address, and started searching the internet for information on Sheildston. There wasn't much. It was up in the hills, almost but not quite joined to a coastal town called Turner's Strand, which lay a couple of hundred miles south of Sydney. Once Sheildston had been quite isolated – at first not much more than a logging camp, then a village with a school and a church, the place named after John Sheild, the logger whose wealth built it – but an improved road had brought it closer to Turner's Strand. It was, though, according to one website, still 'discreet and secluded'. Another applied the words 'desirable' and 'wealthy'. The area on the coast seemed busy, crowded with housing and tourist developments. 'Popular with retirees and family holidaymakers from Canberra and the south Sydney suburbs,' the second website reported of Turner's Strand. I searched in vain for images of Sheildston or an indication of the size of its population: it seemed to be a backwater of somewhere that itself was pretty unremarkable.

What were the chances that a man on a witness protection scheme, or just a man with a lot of money wanting to retire from the world, would end up in a place like that?

And what were the chances that I would go all that way to see if he had?

15

I worked late, revisiting those parts of the Case centring on Parroulet's evidence. At some point I dragged myself upstairs and went to bed. I slept fitfully, then overslept, and woke to the sound of scraping and banging outside. I pulled back the curtain and was dazzled by the sun shining from a clear blue sky on to a world of whiteness. Brian Hewat was hard at work with his snow shovel. He looked up and waved at me. I dressed and went down.

'Some storm, eh?' Brian said cheerily. 'It's a long time since I've seen so much snow. Did you hear the news?'

I hadn't, obviously. He was eager to tell me.

'They've found a body,' he said with glee. 'Just over on Woodside Road. A snowplough driver spotted him first thing this morning. It was on the radio.'

'Him?' I said.

'Middle-aged man, no details as yet,' Brian said. 'I took a walk over there, just to check if the main roads are driveable – which they are, by the way, not that you'll care.' It was typical of him that he would want to inspect the scene of the incident, that he would need an excuse to do so, and that he would take the opportunity to refer to my weird inability to drive. He is a good neighbour, Brian, but a man of small and constant calculation.

'And?' I said.

'Nothing much to see. Ambulance had been and gone. A couple of policemen were still there. The plough nearly hit him, apparently, but he was dead already, so they said. No ID on him. I asked if they'd be making door-to-door inquiries, to find out who it is.' I pictured Brian hurrying home in order to be in when they came. 'They didn't say. Well, they might have to.'

I just managed to stop myself asking what the victim had been wearing, what he looked like. It was perfectly possible that Brian had extracted this information from the police, but I wanted to keep my distance.

'I expect they'll track him down. Dental records or something. Or someone will report a missing person.'

'You're probably right,' Brian said. 'But that's assuming he's local. Poor beggar. Must have just got caught out.'

I changed the subject. 'I should get my shovel and give you a hand,' I said. 'All that work we put in yesterday was a bit of a waste of time, wasn't it?'

'We weren't to know that,' Brian said. 'Appreciate your effort, by the way.' He pointed at my grey bin, which had a perfect cube of snow on its lid. 'Don't think we'll be seeing *those* idlers today. Don't you bother yourself. I'll clear your bit of pavement too. I'm enjoying the exercise.' He made a little show of expanding his chest. 'Good for the heart. Isn't that your phone?'

I excused myself and went back in. I made it on the seventh ring.

It was Carol. We hadn't spoken for weeks, but she didn't mess about with preliminaries. She wanted to know if I was all right.

'I'm fine.'

'I just heard a report on the local radio. It said they found a body in the snow over your way.'

'So I gather,' I said.

'They said a middle-aged man. I thought I'd check it wasn't you.'

'Why would it be me?'

'I don't know, Alan, but it might have been.'

'Well, it wasn't.'

'I was worried, that's all.'

'You don't need to worry about me, Carol.'

'Well, I do. I'd like to see you. Can I come over?'

'Not going to work?'

'Campus is closed,' she said. 'But the roads aren't too bad around here, so I can get the car out. What are they like with you?'

I was about to put her off, but changed my mind. I needed to tell someone I trusted about Nilsen. I trusted Carol.

'Driveable, according to Brian next door,' I said. 'But don't try coming into the street or you might not get back out.'

'I'll be over in a while,' she said. 'Do you want me to pick anything up for you?'

'No, thanks. It'll be nice to see you.'

While I waited for her I wondered what I should do. Should I contact the police, go to the hospital, identify Nilsen's body? (Of course, it might not be his, but I had little doubt that it was.) But how *could* I identify him? All I had was a name, which was probably not his real name, and a nationality based on his accent. And how would I even begin to explain our relationship? I could see myself being dragged into a long and tedious process, in which I would have to divulge information I had no wish to divulge to anybody, least of all to the police. Nothing was to be gained from it.

There was an odd irony about the situation. I had never been able to identify Emily and Alice because nothing of them was left to be identified. Nilsen had left his physical shell, but I – the last person, presumably, to see him alive – could not and would not identify him. I wondered if he'd meant to die in the snow, if it was by accident or by choice that he'd been overwhelmed. He came, he delivered what he had to deliver, he left, he died anonymously. Perhaps it was all part of his journey plan.

I chided myself. A man is dead. Where is your sense of humanity, whoever he was and whatever he did?

But I did not feel very charitable towards Ted Nilsen.

Sooner or later, they would discover who he was. And once they had, they would inform the American Consulate in Edinburgh, and wheels would start to turn. They would know or work out who Nilsen really was, and then they would know or work out why he had been where he was and that he must have been on his way to or from me, the troublesome Dr Tealing. Why would he have wanted to see me? Might he have given me sensitive information such as the whereabouts of a protected witness? Whoever had given Nilsen Parroulet's address would realise that he might have passed it on. They would try to stop me reaching Parroulet, or warn him or the Australian authorities that I was on my way. At this moment, though – if I could believe Nilsen – nobody knew that I had the address. Nobody *would* know so long as the body remained unidentified. I had this window, perhaps several days, perhaps even a week or two. If I was going to go I had to go now.

By the time Carol arrived I had made up my mind. I told her everything. I told her about Nilsen and what he had given me and what I intended to do. I thought she would try to dissuade me, tell me I was embarking on yet another voyage to disappointment. But she didn't. 'You have to go,' she said. 'He's handed you this thing, whatever it is, and you can't pretend it doesn't exist. It's like he's pointed at a stone and told you to lift it. Of course you must lift it.'

'Even if there's nothing underneath?'

'Even if. You can afford to go, can't you?'

I think if I had said no she would have offered to help. 'I can't afford not to,' I said.

We switched on the computer. Finding and booking a flight took twenty minutes. Applying for an electronic visa took another twenty. There was some disruption at the Scottish airports because of the weather but delays were expected to be only temporary. London was clear. Carol said she would drive me to Edinburgh. I could be in Australia in two days' time.

'I'll keep an eye on the house while you're away,' Carol said.

I had visions of men turning up to look for me, getting into the house, finding Carol here alone. 'No, stay away. And let's go back to yours tonight.'

I packed the small pilot's case I used for short trips. I didn't take much in the way of clothes. What I didn't have I could buy when I arrived.

I closed down the computer, took a last look round the Case. 'There's stuff here I might need,' I said.

'You don't need any of it,' Carol replied. 'All you need is to find him.'

I picked up the external hard drive, asked if she would keep it for me. 'Of course.' I locked the house, set the alarm. We set off for her car, parked on a road that had been cleared, a few hundred yards away. As we trudged I thanked her. I said thank you to her so many times in the course of the next few hours that she told me to stop. I said she might be questioned by the police, by the Americans. They would want to know where I had gone. 'I won't tell them anything,' she said. 'It might hold things up for a day or two. What are they going to do, torture me?'

'I don't think it will come to that,' I said.

In the end, it wasn't about chance. It wasn't even about choice. I went because if I didn't . . . But I had no idea what would or wouldn't happen if I didn't. The same fear or hope that drove me always to pick up the phone when I was at home would make me get on the plane to Australia. I knew it would. Nilsen knew it would. That was why he had come to me.

As the years after the bombing had passed without a trial, and then after the trial more years had passed without Khalil Khazar's conviction being overturned, I had begun to think the unthinkable: that I might die before the truth was known about who had killed Emily and Alice. I hadn't ever doubted that the truth would come out eventually, but if it came out when I was dead what use would it be to me? Or if it came out long after all of us – all the fathers and mothers and sisters and lovers of the dead – were gone? By then, it wouldn't really be the truth at all. It would be information, of historical interest only, provided to people untouched by the event. It would be like news of some atrocity in a foreign, distant land, unreal and therefore, in a way, untrue. They would want to feel it, those people, but they wouldn't be able to, or the feeling would not be sustainable. Human sympathy can only travel so far.

Powerful forces – of governments and other organisations and some individuals – were ranged against the truth being revealed. They would not want the accepted narrative found to be in tatters. This much I did know. But it might still be possible to prove that Khazar had not planted the bomb. And if that could be proved – *only* if that could be proved – then Nilsen's precious narrative *would* be destroyed and they would have to build another to put in its place. Would that be the true narrative? I could not know, but it could not be more unacceptable to me than the present one.

But Nilsen had said it was good enough, believable enough, for others. It satisfied, insofar as anything could, their need to believe. If I destroyed the present narrative, what would that do to those people? My mother's words came back to me: 'You've become selfish.' Perhaps she was right. Perhaps Karen was right: I thought too much. Perhaps I had made more of it than I should have. Perhaps none of it mattered. I was certain – as certain as I could be – that there was no God. Perhaps George Braithwaite was right and there was also no unblemished truth, no untainted justice. And if these things did not exist, pure and whole, then neither could there be an end to my search for them. And if there could be no end, then let there be an end to it. Let me live the rest of my life without this ceaseless search for something unattainable. Let me not waste what was left to me.

That was what my mother, my sister, Emily's parents, argued. Yet it could not be done. *I* could not do it. I had to go looking for Martin Parroulet. It was beyond who I was *not* to do this. Nilsen had given me a key and I had to see if there was a lock it would turn.

At the airport check-in desk, after Carol and I had embraced and said our goodbyes, a woman in a blue uniform took my passport and scanned it, took the ticket printout and tapped the details into her computer. She said, 'Is it just hand luggage?' 'Yes,' I said, and she remarked that I was travelling light for such a long journey. 'Yes,' I said again. 'Did you pack the bag yourself?' she asked. 'Yes.' 'Could anyone have interfered with it at any time?' 'No.' 'Does it contain any sharp objects, any liquids? You won't be able to take them through security.' 'Yes, I know. Nothing like that.' On the wall behind her was a poster displaying representations of guns, knives, gas canisters and other dangerous objects. I said, 'Does anyone ever admit to having any of that stuff in their luggage?' The woman swivelled in her chair, swivelled back, looked at me more intently, as if suspicious of the purpose of my question. 'You'd be surprised,' she said. She handed me my boarding pass. 'Have a nice trip.' I thanked her and made my way to the barrier where it said PASSENGERS ONLY BEYOND THIS POINT, and joined the queue of people waiting to take off their coats, empty their pockets of coins and keys, remove their belts and subject themselves to the inspection of men and women who were trained to believe that everyone was a possible terrorist, and that none of us was safe.

2

FIRE

I

The hotel room would have been unbearable without air conditioning. It was small and comfortless, the en-suite shower needed to be ripped out and replaced, the tiles were cracked and the paintwork scuffed. The air-conditioning unit rattled and roared but the cool air it pumped round the room was merciful. I lay in the centre of the double bed in my underwear, head propped on two inadequate foam pillows, and flicked through the TV channels. I had the volume up loud to contend with the air conditioning and with the bass notes of some live band playing a street or two away. It was ten in the evening. Any minute I expected someone to bang on the door and complain, but no one did. I was on the far side of the world, my body was jumping with exhaustion, but I hoped that if I could force myself to stay awake just a little longer I might sleep right through till morning, oblivious to all noise.

The journey had passed without incident. The flight from London to Singapore and on to Sydney had been tedious but uneventful, and no difficulties had arisen at immigration or passport control – which meant, I presumed, either that Nilsen's body hadn't yet been identified or that it wasn't Nilsen's or that Parroulet wasn't here or that nobody cared that I had touched down. Occasionally I'd looked over my shoulder. I had not seen anyone remotely suspicious, but that of course meant nothing.

I'd spent a night in Sydney and the next day had boarded a coach south out of the city, through mile after mile of suburbs, past shopping

malls, technology parks, fast-food restaurants and, occasionally, sur-
prisingly old-looking industrial buildings. I'd always thought of
Australia as being a new, clean country, not one with a past of factor-
ies, grime and toil. White beaches and blue sea appeared for a few
minutes on my left, then the highway turned inland again, and a haze
of green hills rose beyond the houses on my right. The coach was only
half-full. No one was sitting next to me. What were another four
hours of travel, of staring, thinking, stretching my cramped muscles,
on top of two days I'd already spent travelling? In the last hour or so
the settlements became smaller, the stretches of farmland or scrub
between them greater. I had a sense, simultaneously, of arrival and
anti-climax. I could hardly persuade myself that Parroulet would be
at the end of the journey. And yet I had to believe that he was, or what
was my purpose in making it?

At last the coach pulled in to Turner's Strand. I had reached, perhaps, the punchline of Nilsen's final earthly joke. Had he sent me on
the longest, most pointless excursion of all, to an unremarkable little
town in search of a man who wasn't there? Well, *I* was there. I would
see it through – I heard Nilsen's voice, saw his doglike smile again –
to the end.

I'd not reckoned on the numbers of holidaymakers in the town.
When I stepped off the bus it was late afternoon and there was a
throng of people in shorts and swimwear on the main shopping street
that led to the seafront. The schools were still on holiday, of course.
There were families and young couples, bronzed gods and goddesses
and leathery old turtles all apparently in their natural habitat. In my
long trousers, shirt and jacket, I was not dressed for these crowds,
nor for the heat.

I sought out the town's tourist information office and inquired
about accommodation. The assistant said it would be difficult to find
me a single room, especially as I didn't know exactly how long I'd be
staying. She suggested I go for a coffee or a drink for half an hour

while she phoned around. 'Come back before six, though,' she warned. 'That's when we close.' All I wanted was to go to sleep, but I did as I was told, bought a coffee and a slice of cake in a cheerful little diner and wondered if an Australian Mrs Hastie might turn up out of nowhere and take me home. But no Mrs Hastie was forthcoming.

Somebody had left a copy of the local paper at my table. The front-page story was about the prolonged spell of dry weather – two months without rain – and the perilous condition of the bush. Fires were breaking out inland, and a few remote properties had had to be evacuated. The coastal zone was unaffected so far, but the authorities were asking all communities and individual citizens to exercise due vigilance. So far, the story concluded, it seemed that all the fires had started naturally, but human carelessness could not be ruled out and nor could the possibility of arson.

When I returned to the tourist office the woman said she had booked me into a hotel called the Pelican, for four nights. After that I'd have the option of extending my stay by three nights at a time. 'I'll be honest,' she said, 'it's not the best hotel around, but the staff are friendly and it hasn't got a noisy bar or anything.'

I obviously gave the impression of someone who didn't want to spend time in a noisy bar. She was more a girl than a woman. I must have looked like an old man to her.

I asked for a street map of the town. She gave me a brochure, divided into 'what to do and see' and 'where to eat, drink and shop' sections, that folded out into a reasonably detailed map. I made sure it extended as far as Sheildston. 'Can you walk to Sheildston?' I asked.

She looked surprised. 'You *can*,' she said.

'Good.'

'It's more fun down here.'

I almost laughed at the conviction with which she said this. It seemed a strange remark after what she'd said about the hotel.

Perhaps it was part of her job to stress the fun element of Turner's Strand.

'I'm not really here for fun,' I said.

'Business, is it?'

'Pretty much.'

'That's all right, then. It's just, they can be a bit snooty in Sheildston.'

'I'll bear that in mind,' I said. 'Thank you for all your help.'

'No worries,' she said. She followed me to the door and locked it behind me.

The Pelican was a short walk away, in a quiet street set back from the main downtown district. The building was old enough to need work but not so old that its shabbiness had charm. I signed in. The young man behind the reception desk said, 'If you're going out, best take your room key with you. There isn't somebody here all the time. The front door's always open though.' I said I wouldn't be going out again that evening. I climbed two flights of stairs and felt the energy draining from me with each step. I'd been lying on the bed trying to cool down ever since.

On one TV channel there was a documentary, which seemed to be about anarchism or anti-capitalism or revolution but I couldn't hear the voice-over clearly and the picture was poor. I hovered on the edge of sleep, but the twitchiness in my legs kept bringing me back. I tried to focus on the screen. Masked protestors in a city I didn't recognise surged against riot police who looked like Chinese terracotta warriors. A car was rocked and overturned, the word SCUM in red paint dribbled down the cracked window of a department store. A bloody-headed boy was dragged off by a group of angry policemen. You poor kid, I thought, you have no idea what you are up against, the sheer weight and immovability of it. I switched channels to a chat show, a game show, a chef race. A news update briefly mentioned the threat of bush fires again, but spent more time reporting a big lottery win for a couple in Wollongong. The ticket belonged to their dog, apparently. Television was the same the world over, utter trash only with different commercials. I killed the TV and let the remote drop on the sheet beside me.

In the morning, before it grew too hot, I would go looking for Parroulet's house.

I did not wake until nine o'clock. Annoyed, I got up at once and stood under the rickety shower. Searching for my razor, I realised I must have left it in the hotel in Sydney. Further irritated, I dried myself and put on clean clothes. A vague memory came of having been briefly disturbed by drunken exchanges outside my door during the night, but generally, and despite my edginess, I felt as if I'd slept better than I had for years. I went downstairs and ate breakfast – the universal self-service fare of budget hotels: cereals and fruit juices, processed bread, processed ham and cheese, jam impregnated with fruity flavours, undrinkable coffee from a machine. For the rest of my stay, I decided, I would eat elsewhere.

The other guests were mostly young and foreign – backpackers from Brazil, Ireland, Korea, Sweden. I tried to spot the ones nursing hangovers, but probably they were still in bed. I too, I reminded myself, was a foreigner. I did not linger. I collected my sunglasses and the street map from my room, and with the room key in my pocket headed back to the middle of Turner's Strand, and from there started off for Sheildston.

Whatever excitement there was in Turner's Strand seemed to be confined to the shopping and seafront zone. The further from the beach you walked, the quieter everything became. The only people I saw were a woman hanging out washing and a man weeding his garden. Had it not been for the different vegetation, the absence of snow and the bone-dry heat, I could almost have imagined myself to be at home. The heat really was intense, and seemed more so away from the sea. I considered turning back to buy a hat, but decided that the longer I delayed the hotter it would get. According to the map it was only three miles to Sheildston. I'd be there in less than an hour.

Beyond the last houses of Turner's Strand were a couple of hard, dusty football pitches and a barren-looking field, then the road began to climb, and the bush took over. The incline was gentle, but I found it hard work. The flight had taken more out of me than I'd realised. The atmosphere seemed – not heavy, because it was not humid – but thick, like the blast of air from an opened oven door. I began to sweat, and had to use first my handkerchief and then the front of my shirt to wipe my face. I regretted not having gone back for a hat.

The road – it was called Glen Road, and I wondered if John Sheild had been a Scot – turned back on itself often as it worked its way up into the hills, and where it turned it became steep, then levelled out again. I began to dread these turns. My calf muscles ached as I pushed myself round them, and my shirt was now completely drenched. I cursed my stupidity. This was supposed to be a reconnoitring exped- ition in which I did not draw attention to myself, but the way I was beginning to feel I might have to be taken back to Turner's Strand in an ambulance.

On one side the ground fell away from the road, and split into rocky gullies, dense with tangled vegetation, which presumably became watercourses when it rained. On the other side eucalyptus trees, and others I did not recognise, stretched to the sky, rising from a similarly thick bed of undergrowth. Grasshoppers kept up their tedious scraping, and there were the sounds, too, of stones or leaves disturbed by birds or insects or perhaps snakes. I knew that Australia had numerous venomous creatures: I kept to the middle of the road. Not a car had passed me in either direction in half an hour.

The trees grew taller and thicker, and occasionally shielded me from the blaze of the sun. The road, though partially striped by shadow, nevertheless beat waves of heat up through the soles of my shoes. I hadn't seen a house since leaving the town. Could I have taken a wrong turn? I consulted the map. No, there was only one road to and from Sheildston, and I was on it. I kept going. A few minutes later I rounded another bend and the road flattened out completely. I had reached the higher ground above the narrow coastal plain.

I looked back down on Turner's Strand. Most of it was hidden by the trees, but part of the beach was visible, and the sea beyond it. I'd been wondering why anyone would choose to live up on the hill, and here was one reason: the view was magnificent. The coast with its sandy bays and rocky inlets stretched north and south into the hazy distance, and a vast expanse of glittering turquoise ocean, dotted with sailboats and larger vessels, rolled to the horizon. To look out on that every day – well, you would never tire of it.

And now the houses of Sheildston started to appear. 'Discreet and secluded', 'desirable' and 'wealthy', the websites had said, and they were not wrong. The properties were mostly set away from the road, guarded by high walls or fences. Shady drives led from the gates towards half-hidden mansions in pink or white. I glimpsed grass, trimmed hedges, a tennis court, a statue or two. Almost every house, I thought, would have its own pool. From somewhere not too far away I heard children's cries, the sound of splashing. From another direction came the drone of a mower, the sit-upon kind required for big lawns.

The road meandered between these properties like a tired, depleted river, and my walk along it was laboured. I had not brought Nilsen's slip of paper with me. I knew the address by heart, knew the number of the house on Glen Road that was supposedly Parroulet's, but not all the houses had names or numbers displayed. I went on, and came to what was, or had once been, the village centre. A stone-built church, Presbyterian according to the board outside, was the most prominent building, but it didn't look as though it saw much use. Close by was another stone building, the old school, which a second noticeboard indicated was now a community hall. One poster warned that door-to-door selling was prohibited. Another advertised a few forthcoming events but when I inspected it I saw that they had all happened months before, if they had happened at all. Half a dozen houses, built mainly of wood and much smaller than the ones I had already passed, stood within a hundred-yard radius of the church, and then the earlier pattern of large, secluded properties resumed. I spotted a number in blue-and-white tiles stuck on a gatepost of one of these, and deduced from it that I would reach the house I was looking for after six more properties. Glen Road continued on its way. And so did I.

I was counting down, and knew it was Parroulet's place before I saw the number painted on one gatepost, and before I realised that it was the last house on Glen Road. It didn't look like the other properties. They, from what I could see, were well maintained and cared for. This one was separated from the road by a steel fence and, beyond that, by an expanse of tarmac cracked and swollen by the sun and dotted with tall weeds. The white paint on the cast-iron gates was peeling. Attached to the other gatepost was a mailbox with a couple of flyers hanging from its mouth, and next to it an electric buzzer and a small loudspeaker. These things had been stuck on with no aesthetic consideration. There was no sign of a vehicle, nothing left lying outside to indicate that anyone was at home. I thought I was probably looking at the back of the building. It looked as if it might not be occupied.

Nevertheless, I had arrived.

I walked as far as I could along the perimeter. Shrubs and bushes behind the high steel fence obscured most of my view whenever I stopped to peer in. At a little distance from the house I could make out another building, a garage in all likelihood. After another fifty yards the road ended at a dusty turning-area. A thin hiking track disappeared into the bush, which stretched beyond to the horizon. A permanent metal sign next to it bore the words TOTAL FIRE BAN – NO FIRES, and its arrow was pointed to the red EXTREME position. I wondered if it ever indicated any other level of risk, and who was responsible for moving the arrow.

There was no shade at all in the turning-area. The sun was pitiless. I retraced my footsteps, pausing whenever an overhanging branch provided a little relief. When I reached the gates I looked again for any sign of occupation. Well, I thought, I am here now, and I pressed the buzzer.

No response. I pressed again. Nothing. The gatepost was made of some composite material meant to resemble marble. I lowered myself to the ground, put my back against the post and closed my eyes. I knew this wasn't sensible, but I needed to think, and I needed to rest for a minute before the walk back to Turner's Strand. At least I would be going downhill.

I must have dozed for a few moments. A voice – hard, Australian, male – cut through a drowsy confusion of thoughts in my brain.

'You needn't bother nodding off,' it said. 'And you needn't think you can hang around here any longer either.'

I opened my eyes. My sunglasses seemed hardly to darken the day at all. My head ached. I struggled to my feet.

The man who had spoken was wearing khaki shorts, white socks to his knees, sandals, and a Tooheys Beer T-shirt over his big chest. He had a small pair of binoculars hanging round his neck, a wide-brimmed hat on his head, and a red, angry face.

'Don't think I haven't been watching you snooping around. What's your game?'

I had no idea where the man had come from. His clothes were clean and well pressed, as if he'd just put them on. I was conscious of my own dishevelled, unshaven, dirty and probably disreputable appearance.

'My game?'

'Yeah, what are you up to? I've had my eye on you for a while.'

'I'm not up to anything. I'm trying to make contact with the person who lives here.'

'Make contact? What do you mean, "make contact"?' He made it sound like the prelude to a criminal act.

'I've come to visit.'

'Well, it looks like you came on the wrong day, mister.'

'I'm trying to speak to the occupant.'

'We're all owners here.'

'Owner, then.'

'Well, nobody wants to speak to you, do they? I saw you ringing the bell. I've been watching you.'

His tone was unrelentingly aggressive. I said, 'Do you know him? Do you know who lives here?'

The man's rage notched up a tone. 'Don't *you*? You said "visit". Are you selling something? Is that what's going on, you're selling something? There's a sign back along the way, maybe you didn't see it, it says "no hawkers or canvassers". That applies here. So you can move on.'

'If I was selling,' I said, 'don't you think I'd have a case of samples with me? Or leaflets or something? Don't you think I'd have been at your door too?'

This seemed only to infuriate the man more.

'So what is your game, then, snooping around for no good reason? Eh?'

'I already explained. I'm trying to speak to the owner of this house. Do you know who lives here?'

'One of my neighbours lives here,' the man said. He leaned in close, inhaling noisily through his nostrils as if trying to sniff out my 'game'. 'But that's as much as you need to know. We like our privacy round here and, you know what, we mind our own business. So you can ask as many questions as you like and the only answer you'll get from me is "Move on." You understand me? Move on. Or do you want me to get the police to move you on?'

He produced a mobile phone, held it threateningly, returned it to his shorts pocket. Folding his arms he took up a stance that suggested he could wait all day until either I got the message or a patrol car rolled up.

'All right,' I said. I couldn't hang around indefinitely. It was far too hot, and the last thing I wanted was the attention of the local police. 'All right, I'm going. But I've done nothing wrong.'

'Loitering,' the man said. 'That's what you're doing.'

He stood in the middle of the road, chest projecting, with a satisfied sneer on his face. 'You should get out more,' I said, and started off, back towards Turner's Strand. If the oaf told Parroulet someone had been looking for him, that would be the end of it. But I doubted this would happen. For one thing, it didn't appear that Parroulet was at home. For another, even if he was I couldn't imagine there would be much communication between a man like that and a man like Parroulet.

'And don't come back,' was the man's parting shot, and when I turned he tapped his binoculars significantly. 'We like our privacy here.'

Perhaps they did, but I hadn't come all that way to be thwarted by a big ugly brute like him.

3

After I'd struggled back to the Pelican Hotel I collapsed for a few hours. When I came to, my head was less sore, but I felt slightly nauseous. I showered again, changed my clothes, and ventured out to buy a hat and a razor. I needed to refresh my wardrobe too. In this weather, some shorts, some loose, light shirts and a pair of deck shoes were called for. I'd known when I packed my case that what I was taking would be neither appropriate nor adequate. At the time this had seemed a trivial matter, but not now.

I decided I did not much care for Turner's Strand, or at least not for 'the Strand', which the brochure informed me was the informal name for the seafront area. The principal street was a jumble of fast-food outlets, minimarkets, ice-cream stalls, cafés, and shops bursting with beach umbrellas, snorkels, flippers, frisbees, Boogie Boards, buckets, spades and brightly coloured balls. The smell of cheap, hot fat was in the air. Along the seafront were more expensive boutiques, some restaurants, a gallery or two. The order of the day, it really did appear, was to have fun. Everybody was stripped down or dressed up for it. I found a shop that sold a few relatively sober-looking men's clothes, and got what I needed, including a hat not unlike that worn by the bully of Sheildston. I was probably highly conspicuous, a middle-aged man on his own, not here to have fun. That said, nobody seemed to pay me the slightest attention.

I bought a newspaper and sat at a café table under a sunshade, and a girl who could have been the sister or best friend of the girl in the tourist office brought me a sandwich and a beer. The other customers, all in couples or groups, were laughing and chatting but nothing I heard them say was of any importance. I looked at the paper. It was a different title from the one I'd seen the day before, but it carried a similar front-page story about the threat of bush fires. A major fire had broken out near a town twenty miles to the north, and was believed to have been started deliberately. Fire crews had fought it through the night and brought it under control, but there were worries about a westerly breeze getting up, which would drive any flames towards more populated areas. As if to emphasise the point, a sudden gust came out of nowhere and almost blew the paper, and my beer with it, off the table.

I couldn't see anybody else reading a newspaper. Everybody but me was here for fun. News was not fun. Bush fires were not fun. Here by the beach, with its perfect curve of white sand washed by the brilliant blue ocean, it was hard to imagine any danger, any sudden or utter destruction. I'd read in an in-flight magazine between Singapore and Sydney that the average Australian life expectancy was one of the highest in the world. You lived a long time, you had fun, as much of it as you could get, you died. I watched the other people. I did not want their lives to be shallow and inconsequential. I had no right to presume that they were. I wished them well. And yet I could not help thinking about the question Nilsen had asked that had so angered me: *were you even alive before the bomb went off?*

Were these people alive?

Was *I* alive?

Something flickered at the corner of my vision. I raised my sunglasses to see what it was. The glare of the low white wall, of the beach, of the sea, blinded me, and I had to lower the brim of my hat.

What was I to do? I couldn't keep returning to Sheildston every day in the vague hope of catching Parroulet at home. That would be ridiculous. But what else? I simply didn't have a plan.

And something else: Parroulet would surely have another name here. I couldn't even ask around to see if anyone knew of him.

A sudden, fantastical idea came to me, that I would break into the empty house and find some incontrovertible proof of the falseness of Parroulet's testimony. This really was madness. Perhaps I had a touch of sunstroke.

The flicker happened again, and this time I saw where it was coming from. Not from a distance, as I'd thought – a surfboard or dinghy in the waves. It was just a few feet away, at the foot of the white wall. A pale, almost translucent gecko, now as motionless as a model of itself.

What were we doing here? What was I doing here?

I thought of Nilsen again, disappearing into the snowstorm. Was he really dead? Was he in a mortuary now, in cold storage? Or had he flown back to the USA, to die or to live? How would I be, how would I act, if I had to contend with what Nilsen had said he had? A slow, terminal disease. But in a way that was what I did have.

Maybe a fast, terminal disease would be better. Maybe anything would be better – a step in front of a bus, a dive off a cliff, a walk in the sea, a walk in the snow. I had thought of these things before. In the depths of my grief I had considered ending it. Something stronger than grief had always prevented the thought from growing into action.

What did it take, to take your own life? When I'd told George Braithwaite I could never kill another person I'd meant – I believed that I'd meant – that my sense of a shared humanity was too strong to do such a thing, even under the most terrible provocation. But humanity might not be the real reason, and the same might be true of my aversion to suicide. The real reason, in both cases, might be that I was a coward.

Nilsen, now, was he a coward? He had seemed to face his own death with confidence, but that wasn't the same thing as bravery. If you were convinced that God would save you, that there *was* life after death, what need was there to be brave? Was it not braver to knock at a door, not knowing if anyone would answer? Braver to go through the door, fearful of what might or might not be on the other side? For what is it, to face death? What does it mean? Is it a braver thing to do than to face life? Is there even a difference? If you are not afraid, then to be brave is nothing. To be afraid and go forward, to meet life or death shaking but to go anyway, to walk terrified into the snowstorm or the wall of fire, that surely is the mark of bravery. To be a coward and yet still to act, that is the thing.

I thought of Carol. I had never possessed a mobile phone. This had made some aspects of my research, of my quest, difficult in the past, but still I'd always resisted getting one. I'd always felt a need to be reachable through my landline, but I also wanted sometimes *not* to be reached. People said it was up to you, you could switch a mobile off anytime, but I knew if I had one I never would. I'd always be waiting for it to ring. So Carol and I had made no arrangements about being in touch. She did not expect to hear from me, I did not expect to call her. And yet suddenly I felt as though I would like to do that.

But if I did, and anyone else was listening in, they would then know where I was.

The gecko darted forward suddenly. Stopped. It was flat against the wall, head tilted towards me. It and I exchanged views.

I thought, what advantage, for all my supposed superiority, do I have over you?

I thought, either they know already where I am, or they don't because they don't care.

The gecko had five splayed toes on each foot. From head to tail it was no more than three or four inches long. There was something fabulous and beautiful about its prehistoric ugliness.

It ran again, stopped again.

Around us both, everybody was laughing, talking. What was that to the gecko but meaningless, irrelevant noise?

What was relevant to the gecko?

I reached for my beer. The movement was slight, but it seemed to be enough to trigger the creature – if indeed it had been watching me at all – into making a dash across the floor of the café and down a crevice in one corner.

I sat back. I was alone again amid the sound and colour of the Strand.

Tomorrow, early, I would go back to Sheildston.

4

I started walking at seven and was in Sheildston by eight. I'd thought of getting a taxi from the middle of town but realised it wouldn't be necessary. The earlier start made all the difference in terms of the heat. The sky was as cloudless and the atmosphere as dry as ever. But not as still, I noticed. The breeze that was worrying the authorities was on the rise.

Glen Road didn't seem to have much in the way of commuter traffic: I counted only three cars going in the other direction. I reached the last house and was pleased not to have encountered the man in the khaki shorts and white socks. I pressed the buzzer, but as before there was no answer. The junk mail had gone from the mailbox. This was a hopeful sign – unless the vigilante, as I now thought of him, had removed it to reduce the impression that the house was unoccupied. But I saw something else. The day before, the leaflets had hung down, obscuring part of the front of the box just below its mouth. There were four letters stencilled on it that I had previously missed.

PARR

Had I been given to whooping, I would have whooped. It was such an obvious, simple reduction, and yet it seemed to prove that Nilsen had told the truth. The fact that nobody appeared to be at home was for a moment unimportant. I felt justified in having made the journey. I pressed the buzzer again, and put my ear to the loudspeaker, but there was no response, not even a crackle to suggest that someone was listening to me listening. Still, elated, I started to walk along the fence. I would go to the road-end, come back, try the buzzer once more, then return to the town and think about what to do next. I had the name Parr to work with. That was something.

When I reached the turning-area, someone else was already there, a woman. She was standing at the entrance to the bush path, looking westward. I did not want to alarm her, so deliberately scuffed the soles of my new deck shoes on the ground as I approached. She heard me and turned. At the same time a dog emerged from the under-growth and came towards me, wagging its tail.

'Good morning,' I said.

'Good day.' Her skin was so burned and wrinkled she could have been anywhere between fifty and eighty, but I reckoned nearer the latter. She had on a faded pink singlet, baggy multi-coloured shorts and stout walking-shoes, and was leaning on a long staff with a Y-shape at the top, a kind of primitive hayfork. She was solid, with fat upper arms and a large bosom. A bright red plastic band held her grey hair back from her forehead. She looked a mess and as if she were past caring.

'It's going to be another hot one,' she said.

I bent down to greet the dog, a short-coated, black-and-white, medium-sized amalgamation. 'Yes it is.'

'Rufus!' the woman called. 'Come here.'

'It's all right,' I said, but the dog wasn't interested in me, and went snuffling round the edge of the open space.

'I wish it would bloody rain,' the woman said. 'Look, there's a fire over there.'

She pointed with the prongs of her stick. I walked over to stand beside her. Far away, almost on the horizon, a thin screen of smoke hung in the blue sky.

'That's started since yesterday,' she said. 'I come twice a day to check. I get on the blower if I see anything, but they usually have it covered already.'

'It seems a long way off,' I said.

'It is, but the wind's picking up. If they don't put it out, that could be here in a couple of days, maybe less. You wouldn't believe how quickly it can move when it gets going. I wish it would bloody rain.'

'Do you live here, in Sheildston?'

'Yeah, back up the road.'

'Near the church?'

'Yeah, one of the old houses.' She laughed. 'The normal-sized ones. We're not so bad there, there's clear ground around us, but it's so dry the whole lot could go up.' She jerked her thumb in the direction of the Parroulet house. 'I wouldn't want that to be mine,' she said.

'It doesn't look like anybody's at home,' I said. 'Maybe someone should let the owners know. If there's a risk, I mean.'

'Oh, there's a risk all right. And they are at home, they just keep themselves to themselves. Listen.' Back along the road there was a brief, high-pitched buzzing sound, fading rapidly into the distance. 'That's her off on her scooter.'

'Who?'

'Mrs Parr.' She saw me start. 'You're too late if you wanted to see her. She'll have gone to Turner's Strand.'

'You mean she's been there all along?'

'Hard to tell, isn't it?' She seemed to enjoy my evident frustration. 'Are you on holiday?'

'Yes, in a way, but –'

Before I could ask more about Mrs Parr, she went on, 'We were talking about fires. We've had a few, I can tell you. The worst was long before I was around. About a hundred years ago. I've seen the photographs. All of this in front of us, as far as you can see, was completely wiped out, just a black desert, but you wouldn't know that looking at it now. Blue gums love fire. They grow back very fast. When they built old Sheildston they put a break between the houses

and the bush, and when that big fire came through the houses survived, including mine, although it did get a little scorched. You can
still see the marks. But then people forget, or they think they know
better. They don't dream it'll ever happen to them. But it will. All of
these new houses went up in the last forty years. The bush practically
grows on their doorsteps.'

The dog came back and sat panting at the woman's feet.

'All right, boy,' she said, and thumped the ground with her staff,
readying herself to move on but also, it seemed, in no great hurry to
do so.

'You've been here a long time?' I asked.

'A long time,' she said. 'Me and my husband came here in the '50s.
He passed on last year. Raised our kids here, and it was a good place
to do that, but it's changed a lot. All this money changed it. School
closed, church closed, nobody speaks to their neighbours. I don't
know who half the people are. Never see them. My son's in Sydney,
my daughter's in Melbourne. She keeps saying I should move down
and be with them, but I don't want to. I'm not a city-dweller. But
Sheildston's not the same as it was. All *right*, Rufus,' she said again,
as the dog whined with impatience.

She stood looking out at the bush a few moments longer, then
turned to go. I went with her. I sensed that she did not object to my
company, and I needed hers. I saw that, strong though her build was,
she found walking difficult and would have struggled without the
stick.

'You said Mrs Parr is actually living in this house,' I said, as we
walked back along the fence.

'That's right.'

'And then you said something about her going off on a scooter.'

'Yep.'

'What about Mr Parr?'

'What about him?'

'Do you think he's there too?'

'Oh, yeah.'

'Well, I've been pressing that buzzer for two days but they don't answer.'

'No, they don't, do they?' she said, laughing. 'It was you, was it? Roger Dinning told me there'd been a dodgy customer hanging around. You don't look like a dodgy customer.'

'I probably did yesterday. Is he the one with the binoculars?'

'That's him. His wife irons him before she lets him out. Don't worry about Roger, he's all bark. He picks up groceries for me if he's down at the Strand. Him and Betty, that's his wife, are a pain in the butt but they're the only ones that speak to me. Can't be too choosy in those circumstances, can you?'

'So you don't speak to the Parrs? I once knew Mr Parr, you see, years ago. I had the address from somebody and thought I'd look him up.'

'I don't speak to *him*,' she said. 'Nobody does. I would if I ever saw him. A bit of a recluse is Mr Parr. He's French, or Moroccan or something. I see *her* sometimes. They're not short of a dollar. Kim, her name is. Don't know his – his first name, I mean. Don't actually think Parr's his real name either, not that that's any of my business, but Parr's an English name. Always makes me think of Catherine Parr, she was Henry VIII's last wife. Kept her head and outlived him too, the old tyrant. Sorry, shut me up. Can't stop once I get going.'

'No, you're fine,' I said.

'You sound like you're English too,' she said.

'I am.'

We were almost at the gate.

'And you're on holiday?'

'Yes.'

'You knew him from before, did you? You know him better than any of us, then.'

'It was through business,' I said. 'We weren't friends. But, since I was in the area . . .'

I wouldn't have believed me for a second. Whether she did or not, she nodded.

'She's all right, Kim. I don't see much of her. She's Malaysian or Thai, I think. A lot younger than him. When they first came and you saw him and then her, well, you thought – or *I* thought – mail-order bride, you know? Derek, my late husband, he said I shouldn't judge and he was right but I wasn't judging, I was just thinking. Anyway, there's plenty of money, however he got it. What kind of business was he in?'

I hesitated, but only for a second. 'IT. Computers and suchlike.'

'Well, I guess there *is* a lot of money in that. Is that what you do too?'

'No, I'm an academic. He was doing some work for the university where I teach. That's how we met.'

'I see.' She sounded doubtful. 'Maybe you are a dodgy customer after all. I reckon *he* must be. It's like he's hiding. It's sad. The house looks sad. What's the point of being rich if you don't enjoy it?'

'Don't you think he enjoys it?'

'Well, he never looks happy, on the odd occasions I see him. I wouldn't enjoy being stuck in there all the time. What's the point? *She* has to get out, I reckon. You'd go mad otherwise.'

'How long have they been here?'

'Well, you should know. Six, seven years, something like that?'

'Yes, that would be about right.' Khazar's failed appeal had been eight years earlier. By that stage whoever authorised the reward pay-out would be confident that the conviction was going to stick, permanently. I said, 'When did you last see him?'

She shook her head. 'You ask a lot of a questions, don't you? I'll ask you one. What's your name?'

'Alan.'

She cocked her head but I didn't give her any more.

'Well, *Alan*,' she said, 'as to when I last saw him, it was months ago. I've hardly seen *her* lately as a matter of fact. I hear her going past on the scooter. Rufus barks at it. If I see her I give her a wave and she waves back. She's nice enough. She needs company, though. She must do. That's why she goes out, I'm sure. That's why she has her little shop.'

'Oh, what shop's that? In Turner's Strand? I've never met her, you see.'

'Well, it's more of a workplace than a shop. It's not open all the time, just when it suits her. She's a seamstress, a very good one. She does alterations – takes in skirts, lets out trousers, buttons and zips, all that kind of thing. She did a beautiful job on a suit of Derek's when it got too big for him towards the end. That was the one we buried him in. She's done a few of my own things in the past. I felt a bit funny, I mean she's a neighbour, it didn't feel right somehow, paying her to mend my clothes. It was all right with Derek's suit, though. He looked good in it, even when he was dead. I always went to the shop, never to the house. That's how she liked it. Me too. Kept it businesslike. Anyway, I've not been in for a long time. Can't be bothered with clothes now. Would you listen to me? I told you, I don't stop once I start. All right, boy.'

We had been standing by the Parroulet gates and Rufus was getting impatient again. She made as if to move on, but, whether out of concern or suspicion, it seemed she didn't want to leave me alone there.

'What are you going to do? Hang around in the heat again? You'll be wasting your time.'

'No,' I said, 'I'll go back into town. Maybe I'll introduce myself to Mrs Parr, ask if there's any chance of seeing – of seeing him. Is her shop easy to find? I'm staying at the Pelican.'

'Oh, the Pelican? She's just round the corner. One street further back from the shore. That's the oldest hotel in the Strand, the Pelican. It used to be good. They had dances there every weekend. It's not like that now, I bet.'

'No,' I said. 'It's not at all like that.'

'That's a shame. Derek and me used to go there a lot. Old-time dancing. Do you dance?'

'No,' I said.

'A lot of men don't. Derek did. He was a wonderful dancer. Other women would be dancing with each other but I always danced with Derek. There's nothing like it, when you've got a good dancing partner, nothing like it. I couldn't dance now, more's the pity, even if I still had Derek. Maybe I shouldn't have told you about Kim's shop, but it's not like it's a secret or anything. Anyway, if you're going back to the Strand, you can walk me and Rufus home. It's on your way. Do you mind?'

'I don't mind at all,' I said.

'What did you say your name was?'

'Alan.'

'I'm Maisie,' she said, putting her free hand on my forearm. 'Maisie Miller. Off we go, then. I won't expect you to dance.'

5

In my hotel room I pulled three buttons off one of my new shirts. With some difficulty I tore the pocket on a pair of trousers I had brought from home. I was surprised at how robust the stitching was. Then I went looking for Kim Parr's shop.

It was, as Maisie had said, very close to the Pelican. The back of the hotel, a couple of apartment blocks and a little row of storage units formed one side of the short, narrow street. On the other side were the backs of more apartments, and under them at ground level two shuttered, apparently empty shops and KIM TAILORING. In gold lettering on the glass door was the information, ALL TYPES OF TAILORING UNDERTAKEN RESIZING RESTYLING REPAIRS ALTERATIONS COATS DRESSES SHIRTS SKIRTS SUITS ZIPS HEMS COLLARS CUFFS ALSO CUSHIONS AND UPHOLSTERY. A venetian blind was lowered behind the big window, so that it was impossible to see inside. Parked against the kerb outside was a rather battered red scooter. The place looked dingy and uninviting, in a run-down street that was more like a back alley and not likely to get much passing trade. I tried the door. It opened, and a bell jangled above my head as I entered.

The contrast with the outside of the shop was remarkable. Inside, everything was neat and ordered. Perhaps it had to be this way, because there wasn't much space. Deep shelves laden with different fabrics ran along the back wall; three dummies stood in different states of undress in one corner; next to them was a rail of hangers on which various items of clothing in polythene covers awaited collection. An electric fan on a pedestal was sending waves of cool air across the room. Somewhere out of sight a radio or music system was playing classical music. The centre of the shop was taken up by a large, low table for laying out and cutting. Behind it, squeezed in at a smaller table and operating a sewing machine, was a little, neat woman, with short black hair and black-rimmed glasses. She looked up as I entered.

'Yes, can I help you?'

'I have some things to be mended.' I held out the items. 'The tourist office said you might be able to do them for me.'

The woman stood, eased herself out from behind the two tables, and came over to me.

'Please, let me see.'

'The shirt needs some buttons sewn on,' I said. 'And the trousers have a tear, just here.'

I put the clothes down on the larger table and she picked them up and inspected them.

'Yes, I can do these,' she said.

'Very good.' I reached into the pocket of my shorts. 'I have the shirt buttons here.'

She frowned. 'This is a new shirt.'

'Yes, but the buttons came off.'

She shook her head. 'Not good. You should take it back to the shop.' Then she inspected the garment more closely and made a rough, pulling gesture. 'They have been torn off.'

I laughed, embarrassed at having been so easily found out. 'Well, yes. It was me, I'm afraid. I don't know what I was thinking of. I was trying it on in my hotel and I pulled instead of undoing them. Like Superman. Can you put them back on?'

'Yes, I already said.' She picked up the trousers and looked closely at the pocket. 'This also is an accident?'

'Yes.' She does not believe me, I thought.

'Okay. The price is fifteen dollars, all right?'

'That's fine. Do you want me to pay now?'

'No, when you collect.'

She reached for a book of tickets and a pen, and began to write.

'What name, please?'

'Smith. Alan Smith.'

'You have address, telephone?'

'No, I'm a visitor here. I'm staying at the Pelican Hotel.'

I saw the pen hesitate, then write again.

'Okay. You can collect tomorrow.'

'Tomorrow morning?'

'Say, after twelve, to be sure.'

'I'll come in the afternoon,' I said.

'Yes. If not tomorrow, Monday. I'm closed Fridays and weekend.'

'I'll be back tomorrow.'

She nodded, tore a ticket from the book, and gave it to me. 'Okay, thank you.'

The business was done. She folded the shirt and trousers deftly, pinned another ticket to them and left them at a corner of the big table. Then she returned to the sewing machine. I had started towards the door but now paused, and as soon as I did so did she.

'Yes?'

I felt a need to draw her out further. 'I'm glad the tourist office people were able to send me to you,' I said.

'They don't know me,' she said, shaking her head.

'But they know of the shop,' I said. 'It's not a big town. I imagine you must often have to do emergency repairs for visitors like me.'

'No,' she said. 'Not often. Mostly local people.'

'Well, I'm lucky I found you.'

'You said they sent you,' she said.

I found the literal way she took things, her direct manner, both unsettling and refreshing. The way she spoke too – clipped, precise, almost perfect, not quite naturally imperfect, English as a foreign language – was at once harsh and attractive. I tried to judge her age, and thought she might be about thirty-five. She had sallow, smooth, beautiful skin, and her hair was sheer black and thick, yet somehow it also appeared light of weight. She looked cool and self-possessed, whereas I felt damp and sticky and in the wrong climate.

'That fan must be essential in this heat,' I said.

She frowned again. 'Yes, it is why I have it.'

'I find it very hot,' I said. 'They say there's a real danger of bush fires.'

'There is always danger.'

'But especially inland. Close to here, but inland. Places like Sheildston.'

Now she raised her chin to look at me more carefully.

'Not especially,' she said.

'That's what I heard. Ah well. I will be back tomorrow. Goodbye.'

'Goodbye,' she said, and I heard the sewing machine begin its clatter as I closed the door.

6

That night the claustrophobia of the hotel room, the awfulness of the television and the rattle of the air conditioning were all too much. I had brought some books with me – small, handy editions of obscure novels by Trollope and Galsworthy, which I'd thought I might usefully reread, and David Dibald's last novel, *The Mists of Summer* – but I couldn't bear even a page of any of them. I changed into a pair of trousers and another of my new shirts and ventured out into the beating warmth of the evening, looking for an unobtrusive place with a decent menu where I could spend an hour or two with a bottle of wine, chat to a waitress or a barman, and watch other people enjoying themselves. I found myself thinking almost enviously of the fun-lovers I had observed and thought foolish the day before. It was strange what coming to a place like this did to you. I felt – almost – not myself. It really was a bit like being on holiday.

The Strand at seven o'clock was loud and busy. Music thudded from open-air bars, crowds of young men and women swayed and yelled and squealed, the smell of frying food was everywhere in the gusty air. I walked through all this to the shore to look at the sky and the sea, both of which seemed to swarm with stars and starlight. A few shadowy figures were still down on the beach but what they were doing I could not tell. I went another fifty yards and reached the more upmarket run of boutiques and galleries, where I had previously identified a couple of restaurants too expensive to attract the masses. The prices were on the steep side for me too, but I didn't care. I had my credit card. There was a fish restaurant that looked inviting, but they wouldn't have a table free for another half-hour. I made the reservation and wandered back along the seafront.

All the shops were closed, but one of the galleries was not. There, some kind of party was in progress. A new exhibition. The door was wide open and a clutch of elegant women drinking from huge wine glasses had come outside to smoke. I murmured my apologies as I went past them into the gallery, in which fifteen or twenty similarly well-dressed men and women were talking loudly, all at the same time. Nobody appeared to pay me any heed. I picked up a price list and a glass of wine from a white-clothed table, and moved round the walls to inspect the pictures.

The show comprised some twenty oil paintings by an artist who, I assumed, was the woman in the turban and ankle-length dress holding court in the middle of the room. A short, imperious, bald man in a cream linen suit was assiduously attentive to her, and I took him for the gallery owner. The artist wore bright shades of reds, yellows and blues and she seemed to like using the same range in her paintings. They were mostly described as still lifes but I found them distinctly unstill. They were very abstract too. The titles usually explained what fruits, flowers or other objects were being depicted, which was just as well or I would often have been struggling to guess. I had a sense that the artist started quietly and then got carried away: every painting had its dark vortex or black hole out of which – or perhaps into which – swirled or burst countless vivid splashes and blotches. The actual forms of the things depicted – an apricot, a vase, a teapot – seemed completely random and diffuse. The smaller pictures cost $1,000, the larger ones twice as much. They were repetitive, pointless, messy and disturbing. I could not see any of those small red stickers that indicate a sale. Perhaps not enough drink had as yet been consumed.

Behind my back the braying chatter continued, inane and – to my ears – incongruous when uttered in down-to-earth Australian voices.

I checked myself, as Emily would have. She would have called me reactionary. Carol might have agreed with her.

At the rear of the gallery was a second, smaller room containing other works for sale by local artists. Here were things more to my liking: more figurative works, some fine photography and a series of playful, surreal, mixed-media collages. And there were two quite beautiful seascapes, not very big yet capturing the immensity of ocean and sky that I had glimpsed from the hills. They were quite different – one of a sunset and the other of a dull, grey day – but both somehow contained a sense of vastness as well as, and not just because they were unsigned, the insignificance of the artist. I admired them, and felt consoled by that fact.

Having killed most of the half-hour and a second glass of wine, I made my way back to the fish restaurant. A waiter led me to a small table to one side. The place was not big. Five couples and a party of four were the only other diners, although several tables had been moved together in the middle, and were reserved for ten or twelve people. The menu was short and to the point. Everything was expensive. I ordered mussels followed by grilled sea bass, and a bottle of Sauvignon.

I'd been thinking a lot about Kim Parr. I was intrigued by her, and ashamed of my clumsy attempts to engage her in conversation. I'd liked her quick, imperfect but completely confident speech, with its sing-song Australian intonation that still retained the vowels of her native tongue, whatever that was. It was as if she had stitched together her own voice from whatever materials she had to hand. She was certainly a cool one. How had Parroulet got her? I thought of Parroulet as sleazy, shifty, the kind of man a woman like that would see through in a minute. Of course he had money. That would be his principal, perhaps his only, attraction. But if there was money, why did she drive around on an old scooter, and why did she spend her days sewing and mending for other people? What would a house like that, up on the heights, have cost? Maybe by the time he'd bought it, spent more doing it up, made their life comfortable – maybe there hadn't been much left of Parroulet's two million. Maybe he had had to send Mrs Parr out to work.

The waiter, young and genial, came back with the wine. He asked – seemed genuinely to want to know – if I was on holiday, if I was having a good time, how long I was in Turner's Strand for. I told a couple of lies, and said I wasn't sure when I'd be leaving.

'You may not have a choice,' the waiter said. 'Did you hear about the highway going north? Been closed since lunchtime. Big fire right across it, ten miles up the road. And it's not the only one. We're almost surrounded. A ring of fire,' he said with a laugh. 'At least here we can go and stand in the sea if it gets too hot. So long as the sharks don't get us.' He shook his head. 'It'll be all right, I'm sure. Everything's so dry, that's the thing.'

'I was up at Sheildston this morning,' I said. 'I could see a fire burning in the distance.'

'Yeah, you would do up there. Think I'll stay put, myself.' He laughed again. He didn't seem much concerned at the possible danger. Nor did anybody else in the restaurant, or for that matter anyone on the Strand.

The mussels arrived. They were delicious.

I refilled my glass. I decided it would be good to speak to Carol, and to hell with eavesdroppers. She'd be at work right now. If I phoned early in the morning I might get her at home.

The foursome had finished their meal and got up to leave. The two couples were of different generations. The younger woman looked like the older woman. Mother and daughter. The younger man was being polite and deferential, trying to impress. It wasn't hard to work out the likely scenario: boyfriend's first meeting with girlfriend's parents. Just then the boyfriend said something and everybody roared with laughter. It seemed he'd passed muster.

Mother and daughter. Emily and Alice. They'd hardly been in my mind at all since I'd arrived in the town. They were the reason for my coming, yet I'd neither dreamed nor thought about them. Were they still the reason? Or were Nilsen and Parroulet and Khalil Khazar the reason?

If the latter, what on earth was I doing there?

The sea bass came. It was beautifully cooked. The waiter returned after a few minutes to check that everything was all right, and took the opportunity to top up my glass.

'I don't think I'll manage the whole bottle,' I said.

'That's all right. I'll put the cork back in and you can take it with you.'

The party for the reserved table made their entry. It was made up of most of the people from the exhibition opening. Another waiter tried to get them settled. First there were too many seats, then not enough. My waiter said, 'I better give him a hand. I'm sorry, I think it's about to get a bit raucous.'

It did. They were still spouting the same rubbish. I fortified myself against the din with more wine, ate the rest of my meal, paid the bill and, clutching my bottle, stood up to go. I felt not unpleasantly unsteady.

As I edged my way past the gallery party, the short, bald man in the linen suit pushed his chair back and stopped me.

'What did you make of the show?'

'I'm sorry?'

'You were in earlier, taking advantage of the free wine. I don't mind, but you weren't invited. What did you make of the show?'

Half of the table was oblivious to this challenge, if it was a challenge, but those seated nearest to the gallery owner, including the turbaned artist, fell silent, waiting for my answer.

'Well . . .' I began.

'A good start,' the man interrupted. 'Diplomatic. Buys you time. I don't mind you gatecrashing, but I'd like to know what you thought. That's only fair, isn't it?'

'Interesting,' I said weakly. 'I thought it was interesting.'

'He didn't like your work, Maureen!' the bald man shouted, and everybody laughed. 'That's what "interesting" means.'

I made to get past, but the bald man's chair was in the way.

'Maybe you'll come back and have another look,' he said. 'You might change your opinion. You might even *have* an opinion!'

This was greeted with more laughter. Everybody was watching now, to see what would happen next.

'You might even want to buy something, instead of just taking without so much as a please or thank-you.'

All at once I felt very tired.

'Excuse me,' I said.

'Please,' the gallery owner said.

'Leave it, Johnny,' somebody said.

'Let me past,' I said.

'Please,' the man said again.

I was suddenly overwhelmed by a desire to hit him as hard as I could. I felt the weight of the wine bottle in my grip. I said, 'Get out of my way,' and pushed the man half off his chair as I went past him.

A woman's voice yelled, 'Look out, he's got a bottle!'

I had the bottle half-raised. What, if anything, I might have done with it I have no idea, but the next moment the young waiter was behind me, very smoothly and efficiently ushering me to the door. 'All right, all right, everybody cool it!' a man shouted. 'Don't be such a tit, Johnny,' said another. And a third, whose comment cut so deep that I might have turned back but for the waiter's restraining arm, called, 'On your way, Grandpa.'

It was hotter out on the pavement than it was indoors. I was confused, not sure what had happened. Had I been in a fight? I saw that the waiter had somehow got hold of the bottle, and was offer-ing it to me.

'Bloody idiots,' he said. 'I'm sorry about that. You all right?'

'I'm fine.'

'You get on home now. You know where you're going?'

'Yes. Can I have my wine?'

'Sure you can. It's hardly worth it, but there you go.'

It turned out that I had already drunk all but a last half-glass or so. I didn't remember how or when I'd done that.

'You're right,' I said, 'it's not worth it.' But I took it anyway.

'Good night,' the waiter said.

'Good night. And thank you.'

I stumbled off in the direction of the hotel. I had enough sense to decide that it might be wise to avoid the busy main street, and got lost finding a quieter route. At some point I stopped to fill my lungs with the night air, and imagined myself exhaling smoke and sparks like a dragon. I might have tried a roar or two. A little later, or possibly a little before, I drained the rest of the bottle and very carefully placed it on somebody's doorstep, as if I were doing them a favour. Then, locating the hotel key in my pocket, I made my way to the Pelican.

7

I woke like someone I did not know, a man sprawled half-undressed on the hotel bed, head pounding, dry-mouthed, and with a tight, evil knot in the stomach. Gradually the scattered parts of the previous evening – the starlit sea, the kindly waiter, the exhibition, the absurd stand-off with the man from the gallery, the wine bottle – reassembled themselves. I recalled what I'd eaten, could taste or smell or feel a fishiness in every breath I exhaled. Sickness threatened, but did not come. I looked at my watch. It was nearly eleven – too late to phone Carol even had I been fit to do so.

I couldn't understand how I had become so rapidly and thoroughly drunk. I'd only had a bottle of wine, which hadn't seemed particularly strong. Two glasses at the gallery as well – it was quite a lot, but hardly extreme. Lying there, trying to find a cool patch of sheet on which to rest my cheek, I considered the possibility that I'd not been so much drunk as out of control, out of character. To have even momentarily entertained braining the bald man with the bottle! Thank God for the waiter, or I might now be languishing in a police cell.

I remembered paying for the meal with my credit card. If they were trying to track me down, they would find me now. How little I cared!

I sat up suddenly, to check that I wasn't actually in a police cell. The movement pulled at the knot in my belly, and I went to the bathroom to try to loosen it, but without success. I collapsed back on the bed with a moan. The bowlful of mussels, and one slyly winking mussel in particular, kept swimming into view. I got up, drank some tepid water from the tap, lay down again. I told myself to try to sleep. I had to go to see Kim Parr that afternoon.

The next time I came to, my sore head had eased but the stomach cramp was worse. Slowly I got myself ready, showering gingerly, patting myself dry, easing my limbs into my clothes. Any sudden or vigorous action hurt. I was by now pretty sure that, whatever had got into me last night, I was suffering more because of that evil mussel than because of the wine.

I put on my hat, made sure I had money in my pocket, and went out into the day. The wind was as hot as a hairdryer, the sun like a grill. The short walk to KIM TAILORING was a major exertion. I paused beside the red scooter, as if to run through a plan of action, but I did not have one other than to collect the mended clothes. I had no idea what would happen when I went in.

Kim Parr was in the same seat, working away at the sewing machine, with the radio playing as before. When she saw me she immediately stopped what she was doing, fetched the things from a shelf and showed me the repairs. The shirt looked as new, and I could not detect that there had ever been a rip in the trousers.

'Thank you,' I said. I handed her twenty dollars and she went to get change. In that brief interval nausea surged in me, and my face broke out in a sweat. I fanned myself with my hat but the shop's atmosphere was already cool from the electric fan. I staggered slightly. Black shapes like mussel shells broke up my vision.

'I need to sit down,' I said, to no one in particular.

A kind of hot fog formed about me. I heard the woman's voice say, 'Here, sit here,' and felt her fingers pushing down on my shoulders – the lightest of touches but I gave way at once. Somehow a chair was under me. I put my head forward, almost between my knees, and groaned.

'I get you water,' she said.

Sweat poured from my head on to the floor, which I could dimly see was some kind of linoleum, the colour of red earth.

'I'm sorry,' I said.

'Drink,' she said, and held a plastic cup full of ice-cold water to my lips. I took a sip.

'More.'

I drank again.

'You want doctor, ambulance?'

'No, no,' I said. 'Just let me stay here a minute. I'll be all right.'

'You don't look good,' she said.

'I don't feel good.' But my vision was clearing, and the pain in my stomach was not so cruel. Perhaps the outpouring of sweat had got the poison out of me.

'You stay there,' Kim Parr said. 'You going to fall? Faint?'

'No,' I said, although I was far from certain.

She went away briefly, and returned with a roll of paper towels. She tore several off, knelt down and wiped the floor around my feet.

'I've made your floor very wet.'

'Like a swimming pool,' she said. 'Don't want you slipping.' She tore off some more towels and handed them to me. I began to wipe my head and neck. Then I felt a churning, urgent prelude in my belly.

'Is there a toilet?' I said. 'I need to go.'

'You going to be sick?'

'Maybe. No, not sick.'

She understood my predicament. 'Okay, this way. Take it easy.' In a manner not unlike that of the waiter guiding me from the restaurant, she helped me past the hangers and dummies to what looked like a cupboard but was in fact a tiny toilet.

'Don't lock the door,' she said. 'Just in case.'

She went back to the shop. I made it to the toilet and sat down heavily, holding on to the edge of the seat with both hands. Everything gushed from me. I heard the sewing machine going again, and the radio, and hoped they covered the noises I was making. I thought again that I would faint, but held on and the feeling went by like an out-of-service bus. I wiped myself, and immediately a second and then a third evacuation happened. I don't know how long I was there. I cleaned myself again, and flushed the toilet twice. Dispersing the smell was a different matter: there was a can of air freshener, which I used liberally. The sweat was cold on me now, but I no longer felt giddy. When I thought of the bad mussel it was not leering at me. The crisis, I thought, still not entirely confidently, was now past.

'You okay?' Kim Parr called.

'Yes,' I croaked.

After a little longer, having washed my hands and splashed water on my face, I went back through to the shop.

She stopped her sewing. 'You better now?'

'Yes, thank you. I ate something bad last night. A mussel. I'm sure that's what it was.'

She shook her head. 'Sometimes they don't clean the fish enough. It only takes one little bit. Very dangerous.'

'I suppose there's always a risk with seafood.'

'You don't eat anything today,' she said. 'Give your body time off.'

'Yes, that's good advice.'

'Your five dollars is there,' she said, pointing to the big table. I saw the note sitting on top of the plastic bag that contained my folded shirt and trousers.

'Keep it,' I said. 'It's the least I can do. I've put you to all this trouble.'

'No trouble,' she said. 'Someone gets ill in my shop, a customer, what am I going to do? Charge him for it?' She let out a little trill of laughter. Her smile – it was the first time I had seen it – was like an open flower.

Five dollars was such a tiny amount.

How could I say what I had come to say, after that smile, after what had just happened? What words could I lower myself to, in order to get to Parroulet?

I started for the door, then remembered the bag of clothes and the money and came back for them. I lifted them, put them down again.

Frowning, she watched my indecisiveness. She understood that I had something else to say.

She said, 'What is it? What do you want?'

'I don't know where to start,' I said.

She stood up, away from the sewing machine. She was a small, delicate-looking woman, but strong too. I could see this. She went to the door of the shop and flipped a CLOSED/OPEN sign that hung on the inside. Then she locked the door. This, it struck me, showed great self-assurance, a lack of fear. She switched off the radio.

'Why not start with your real name?' she said.

I sat on the folding chair she had brought me earlier, taking occasional sips of cold water. She was back behind the big table, defended by it, very upright, hands folded on the table surface. The kindness that had been in her smile and her earlier actions was gone.

'My name is Alan,' I said, 'but not Smith. My name is Alan Tealing.'

'Tea-ling,' she said, stretching the name out so that it sounded like two words, oriental. 'Yes.'

'Does my name mean anything to you?'

'Nothing.' But her answer was too sharp, and she tried to soften it. 'Maybe I have heard it before. I knew Smith was not your name.'

'How did you know?'

'When you came yesterday I saw you are trouble. You had torn the clothes. You didn't come to have clothes mended. So what did you come for? I don't know, but your face was like one I've seen before. And now your name, maybe I know it too.'

'You're right. It was a pretext. I came because I want to talk to your man, your husband.'

'What man? There is no man. Do you see a man?'

'Not here. In your house in Sheildston. I know that is where he is.'

Her face, when animated, was attractive – beautiful even – but now it was a mask, blank and without emotion.

'You asked me my real name and I have told you,' I said. '*His* real name is not Parr. It is Martin Parroulet.'

Her eyes conceded nothing.

'What are you, a journalist?'

'No.'

'Then what? Why do you come here to bother me? Why do you come to be ill in my shop?' Her voice quickened as her anger grew.

'That was not meant. You have been very kind. I am trying to tell you.'

'Tell me what? I don't want to know. I don't want to know you. You are trouble.'

'I lost my wife and my daughter many years ago. They were killed in a plane crash. The bombing. You know what I am talking about.'

She stared sullenly at me.

'I was a husband and a father. If my face looks familiar it's because you've seen me on television or maybe in a newspaper. Not for a while now, but after the trial at which your husband was a witness. And my name too. That's why you know my name.'

'What has this to do with me? Maybe this is why I know you. But it has nothing to do with me.'

'It is to do with your husband, Martin Parroulet. Maybe he has spoken to you about me. He has mentioned my name or shown you my picture.'

She shook her head.

'I must speak to him. Ask him some questions.'

'Are you police?'

'No. I told you. I lost my family in the bombing.'

'What questions? There are no more questions.'

'Yes there are. I need to find out the truth.'

Abruptly she stood up and came towards me. I still felt weak and wasn't sure what would happen if I got to my feet. She stopped right in front of me and brought her face, her eyes, close to mine.

'What are you doing, Alan Tealing, bringing all that here? Yes, I know your face. I know what you said about that trial. You said it was wrong. You said it was the wrong man. But that is over, all gone. It has nothing to do with me or my husband any more. Go away and leave us alone.'

'I wish I could.'

'How do you come here? Nobody knows to come here. And why do you come with this stupid story about buttons and pockets? You think *I'm* stupid? You think I don't see you have other reasons? Why not tell the truth, if you want truth?'

'I was afraid he would not see me.'

'He won't see you. I knew you were no good. I wish I never took your stupid clothes to mend.'

'Then why did you, if you knew?' I asked.

'I never turn away work.' A strange defiant pride was in the words. 'Never. Not even from you.' Then she returned to the attack. 'Why do you come? What do you want with my husband? He won't see you. He left all that behind. He came here to have a new life. Why do you come to spoil everything?'

To my amazement, she let out another trill of laughter. But then I saw it wasn't laughter. She wiped furiously at her eyes. She sat down behind the table again, but slumped this time, resting her forehead on one hand.

I said, 'I don't wish to cause you distress, but I must see your husband. He is the only one who can help me.'

She said, 'I knew this was going to happen. One day someone would come. I've waited for it all this time. Him too. This is why he never goes out. Now you are here. But he won't see you. I won't tell him about you. So you can just go away now.'

'I can wait too,' I said. 'I'm good at it. I've been waiting many years.'

She put her hands back on the table, made herself upright once more, apparently challenging me to sit it out, to see who gave up first.

'Can you imagine,' I said, 'what it is like, to lose your wife and your only child in such a way?'

She looked away, as if something else had caught her eye.

'No,' she said. 'I cannot imagine that.'

'Well, then.'

She turned on me again. '"Well, then"? What does that mean?'

'You are a humane person,' I said. 'You have already shown that. I know you are.'

'You know nothing,' she said. And once more she seemed to look at something I could not see. Then she repeated her earlier question: 'How do you know to come here?'

'Somebody gave me information,' I said.

'Somebody?'

'A man came to my house. In Scotland. An American. He told me where your husband was.'

Emotion of some kind flickered in her eyes.

'Then you are just the first. Others will come.'

'He told only me.'

'He will tell others.'

'No. He is dead.'

Again, her eyes showed something, but whether fear or courage I could not say.

'He was ill,' I explained. 'He was dying of cancer.'

She nodded, as if slightly reassured. 'But others must know.'

'Perhaps. I don't think anyone else will come.'

'You can't be sure.'

'No, I can't be.'

She pondered this for a few moments. She said, 'A man came to your house. Then you came to our house.'

'Yes. Yesterday, and the day before. I pressed the buzzer. You were there, or someone was. I am sure of that.'

All this time the big table had been between us. Now, as though she had suddenly made a decision, she re-emerged from behind it.

'Okay, that's enough,' she said. 'You are not sick now. You must go.' She bustled around me, forcing me to stand, and as soon as I did she folded the chair and put it against a wall. 'Go. Go away now.'

'Please,' I said. 'Don't do this.'

'I need to think. I can't think with you in here. Go away. Come back later.'

I could hardly believe the rush of hope that those last three words supplied. 'When?'

'One hour. Give me one hour.'

My legs felt so weak. If I returned to the hotel, surely in an hour she would have locked up and gone. I wouldn't have the strength to go back out to Sheildston, not walking. And anyway by the time I got there she'd have warned Parroulet, and they'd have left.

She seemed to read my thoughts. 'Leave the clothes. You come back for them in one hour. I will stay till you come back.'

What could I do? She was my only means of getting to Parroulet. I said, 'One hour.'

Outside, the heat was as intense as ever. It was the middle of the afternoon. I heard the shop door shut and lock. I began to walk.

Something had changed. It took me a minute to work out what it was. An odour was in the air, so faint it was hardly there, but it was, and it was different from the usual cooking smells of the Strand. A kind of perfume, medicinal, sweet and bitter at the same time: the scent of the bush burning.

The heat drove me from the street. I went to my room and lay down.

I felt drained – I was, literally – but at least the poison was out of me. I knew I'd escaped lightly. I thought of my mother. She'd have been right round to that restaurant to complain. I, on the other hand, didn't want to go near the place ever again. Did that make me a coward?

Was Kim Parr testing me? I thought so. Despite my anxiety that she would have fled, I forced myself to undergo the test. With five minutes to go before the hour was up I set out again.

Street signs, bollards, lamp posts danced in my vision. A small creature crouched in the doorway of her shop. A dog or a cat? As I drew near, it metamorphosed into the plastic bag that contained my repaired clothes. And the scooter was no longer parked against the kerb.

So this was what it had come to: another deceit. I pushed and tugged at the door, hammered on it with my fist, peered through the glass to see if she was still inside. Nothing moved.

Enraged, I pulled the trousers and shirt from the bag and shook them, turned the bag inside out, seeking a note or some other sign that she had not tricked me. But it seemed clear that she had.

Then suddenly the anger went, and was replaced by utter exhaustion. I had not the strength to rage. All struggle was beyond me. I was up against yet another prison wall, and this one felt too thick, too hard for me to dig through.

I slid to the ground, my back against the glass door. It seemed all I was fit for now was to collapse. One collapse after another. My hands clawed at the clothes, drew them into my chest. I wanted, desperately, somebody to hold, to be held by somebody. But the street was deserted, and I was alone. In twenty-one years I had never felt so alone. Was this what I had come for? To be, finally, here in this empty alley, defeated?

I put my face into the shirt. Once I had started to weep I found I could not stop.

8

'It is no good running away,' the woman's voice said. Her shadow fell on me as she spoke. I was blindly stuffing the clothes back in the bag and gathering myself to get back to the Pelican, the first stage of my total retreat.

'Not you,' Kim Parr said. 'Me. I got three hundred metres and found I had a flat tyre.' She smiled briefly but the smile became a frown. 'You have been crying.'

There was no point in denying it. I moved aside and she unlocked the door.

'You better come in. The garage is mending the tyre but it will take an hour. I could have waited there but I came back.'

'Why did you?' I said.

'Like I said, running away is no good. We have not finished talking.'

'You appeared to have.'

She held the door for me. 'Go in. Sit down.' She switched on lights and the fan, and unfolded the chair I'd sat on before. This time she did not go behind the table, but brought out another chair and sat opposite me. Our knees were almost touching.

She stared at me.

'What?' I said.

'You asked me that question,' she answered. 'You said, can I imagine your loss? You thought I could not.'

'You said so yourself.'

'And that was true. But you assumed it. "Well, then," you said. As if that settled something. As if you had scored a point against me.'

'I don't know what you are talking about,' I said.

'No, you don't. This is what I am telling you. I have my own loss, it is with me every day. You are not the only one.'

'I have never been so stupid as to think that,' I said.

'Well, then.'

I rubbed my eyes. Everything in the room was flickering, strange and unreal to me.

'Tell me,' I said.

'My family were Chinese people, from Vietnam,' Kim Parr said. 'My father's father came to Saigon from the north. He was a farmer but he came to the city for a better life. Not easier, but better. More chance to prosper. He bought and sold rice and other food in the market. This was in the 1930s. There were many Chinese in Saigon then, with good jobs. They helped each other make money. The Vietnamese did not like them much, but the French liked them because Chinese people worked hard for their money. My father worked in the market too, but then he became apprentice to a tailor and later he started his own business. He did well. He married my mother, who was Vietnamese. This is another thing Vietnamese people did not like much, and my father's family did not like it at all because they looked down on local people, but my parents did it anyway. They had three children, a son and two daughters. I was the youngest.

'When they got married it was the '60s. Vietnam was divided, north and south. The French had gone but the Americans came instead. The war was bad, but not bad for business. Lots of American soldiers wanted suits, shirts, things to take home to their families, cheap but high quality. Then the Americans lost the war and the Communists took over. Time to settle old scores. You suffered if you didn't know the right people. My father knew only wrong people. We got by for a few years, but the Communist government squeezed us Chinese because we were good business people, knew how to make money, and they took what they liked and we let them because we knew they could take it all. Life was very tough. Lots of people, not only Chinese but anyone against the Communists, left on boats, but my father said this was too dangerous. Other Chinese people made the long journey north to China, but he said why go there, another Communist country only bigger? Then there was war with China and things got even worse. My father said one day, it is time to leave. I was eight years old, my sister was eleven and my brother was thirteen. My father paid most of the money he had left to Communist officials to let us go, then more money to get on a boat. It was a hard time but we were together and we thought it couldn't get worse. We were wrong.

'The boat was very small and it had too many people in it. More than a hundred, crowded on deck under the sun. After three days we had no water. The crew made us pay for water, which they kept from us with guns. They were supposed to take us to the Philippines or Hong Kong but we just drifted in the sea. Then another boat came with more men with guns and machetes. We had heard that there were many pirates from Thailand attacking people like us so we hid the little money we had left, some gold and precious things. The men in our boat argued with the pirates. I thought they were trying to protect us but now I know they were bartering for us. They had been waiting for the pirates to come. I saw money go between them. The pirates ordered all men, young and old, to go to their boat. They shot in the air so we knew they must be obeyed. My father told my brother, who was small for his age, to stay with us. He hugged my mother and kissed us, it felt bad, like he was saying goodbye. When all the men had gone some of the pirates came on to our boat and took everything we had, gold, rings, earrings, money, they were very rough and hurt anyone who resisted. They found my brother and pulled him from us and when he fought back one of them held him out in his hands like a dog and another one shot him in the head and they threw his body in the water. I saw this thing done. Then they left us and took the men and boys away. I did not see my father again. Never. We never knew what happened to those men and boys, but I think when the pirates had taken all their possessions they threw them in the sea.

'So now we were only women and girls on this boat, terrified, thirsty, hungry. We did not know where the crew was taking us. After two more days we reached a small island, and the crew put us ashore with some food and sailed away. We were glad to be on that island but we soon found we were not alone. There were others there already, miserable people like us, betrayed, abandoned. The world did not know about us. No government cared about us. Pirates came and went from that place and when they came they did terrible things. They stole any valuable thing anyone still had. When there was nothing left to steal worse things happened. They took my mother away, they took my sister. When they came back they were not the same people. I hid and I was small so they did not find me. We had left Vietnam because it was a very bad place for us but we went to hell instead.

'I don't remember all the things that happened there. I don't want to remember them. Many people died. My sister died. Then one day a big ship came, an American ship, and took the survivors away from that island. They took us to Hong Kong. In Hong Kong at that time there was hope. In Hong Kong they said you were a refugee. This was before so many thousands came there and they put them in the camps. When we arrived you could work. My mother and I worked night and day to earn a few dollars. She taught me everything I know about sewing and making clothes. And in Hong Kong you could apply to go somewhere else, anywhere that would take you. My mother wanted to go to America but there was confusion with the papers and after many months we heard that we could go but not to America, to Australia. One woman and her child. So we came.

'We lived in Melbourne. We had nothing. All we had was a single room and what we could do. We could sew and cut and make clothes. We did these things till our hands were stiff and our fingers bled. In the day I went to school and at night I worked with her. My mother was very ill. I mean in her mind, not her body. She had lost everything and everyone except me. She tried to look after me but she couldn't. All she could do was work. One day I came home from school and she wasn't there. Neighbours were waiting for me. A woman in uniform was there too. They told me my mother had fallen under a bus. I don't know if it was an accident or if she meant to fall, if she could not go on living any more, but anyway she was gone. I cried because I was on my own. One after another I had lost everyone I ever loved. The neighbours were kind but they did not want me. So I went to a home where they were meant to take care of me, but mostly I took care of myself. I have always taken care of myself.'

I had been sitting hunched forward, sipping water, staring at the earth-coloured linoleum, while she told her story. Only now did I look up at her.

'Can you imagine *my* loss?' she said. 'No, you can't. So don't ask me to imagine yours.'

'It is terrible, what you have endured,' I said.

'What else is there to do? I do not intend to fall under a bus. Do you?'

'No. I am a coward.'

'I don't know what that word means. You are afraid and so you don't do something? Or you are not afraid but you still don't do it? I am not a coward. I am me. Even when I run away, I don't get far. You can't run from your own life. When I come here to work, I am me.'

'You're a strong woman.'

'No. I am a lucky woman, that's all.'

'Not many would say so.'

'Not many survived. I did. I found a safe place to be.'

'You found a rich husband.'

'Do you accuse me?' The sharpness was back in her voice.

'I mean that there is safety in money. You don't need to work, do you?' I indicated the room, packed with its materials and tools and equipment. 'Not for money?'

'For money, no. For me, yes. This is how I got here, through work. I don't want to spoil a good habit. Maybe sometime again I'll need to work for money. Who can tell?' She jabbed a finger at me. 'You have a job?'

'Yes. I teach.'

She seized upon this with a kind of glee. 'Why do you teach? You teach for money?'

'Yes, but also . . .' I hesitated because I had never before faced this question, or at least it had never been asked of me so bluntly. 'But also because it is what I do.'

'Yes,' she said. 'You do what you do. I do what I do. We have no choice. All our lives are chance. I think this is true. My father talked to us about destiny. Things happen because of destiny. So when life was good, that was destiny, and when it was bad, that was destiny too. When those pirates took him, that was destiny. But I don't think so. It was luck, chance. Sometimes good luck, sometimes bad. But what's the difference? Either a thing is destiny or it is chance but it happens anyway. Nothing you can do about it.'

She stood, and put away the chair she'd been sitting on. She made a few busy, tidying movements around the room, although there was nothing to tidy. Then she was back in front of me.

'I did not *find* my husband, like you said. I was not looking for him, he was not looking for me, but we end up here together. Now you come. Is this chance or destiny? I think chance but then I always knew you would come, or someone like you, so . . . I don't know.'

'Not chance,' I said. 'I came because I knew to come.'

'It is chance your family is on that plane. It is chance my husband drives a taxi on that island. It is chance I come to Australia. It is chance I meet him in Melbourne. It is all chance.'

'Not all,' I said.

'Yes. It is even chance I get a flat tyre just now. Something happens by chance and then you deal with it.'

She gestured at me to get up. I saw once more how small she was, how determined.

'I don't want you here but you are here,' she said. 'So I am dealing with it. You go back to your hotel now, I'm going back to the garage. Tomorrow is Friday. I don't work Fridays. You come to Sheildston tomorrow. I will ask him to speak to you. But I don't make any promise.'

'Thank you,' I said.

'It's not for you,' she said. 'It's for us. I want to make you go away. When you come, press the buzzer three times short, one long. Okay?'

'Okay. What time?'

'Afternoon. Three o'clock. Remember, three short, one long. Otherwise' – she shook her head – 'no entry.'

9

I took her advice and ate nothing that day, and drank only bottled water. The sickness – everything – had left me very weary. All that evening I dozed in my room with the television on low, tuning in periodically to the latest updates about the fires. A large area inland from Turner's Strand was now ablaze. The northern highway had reopened but many cross-country roads were deemed unsafe. A few small settlements had been abandoned and a number of houses destroyed. Several people were dead or injured. The strength of the westerly wind and a general shortage of water were making the situation worse. One particular inland town, Cobsville, was repeatedly mentioned as the place the authorities were most concerned about. Yet down on the coast people seemed unfazed and untouched by these events. Lying on my bed, I could hear the music thumping away on the Strand. I imagined a scene in a kind of satirical disaster movie: the waiter from the fish restaurant, standing up to his waist in the sea with a bottle of beer in hand, sniffs the air and, addressing another waiter a few feet away, makes some casual remark about the haze of smoke above the hills. But his colleague is being dragged beneath the surface by a shark.

I slept fitfully, and woke hungry at seven. I reached for the phone beside the bed and dialled Carol's number.

'Hi. It's me.'

'Hello.' She sounded calm, remote, not in the least surprised to hear my voice. 'Where are you?'

'Where I'm supposed to be.'

'What time is it there?'

'Seven in the morning. And with you?'

'Eight – p.m. I've just finished eating. You sound tired. Is every-thing all right?'

'Apart from a dose of food poisoning, everything is fine.'

'Oh dear. Are you sure you're okay?'

'Yes.'

'You don't sound it.'

'I've made contact.'

'Was that successful?'

'I don't know yet. I'll find out later today. What about you? Any visitors?'

'None. Nothing.'

'Anything more about our friend?'

'They gave a name in the paper. Not the one you told me.'

I liked the way she'd picked up at once on my discretion. I liked the sound of her voice. That had never occurred to me before: how easy her voice was on the ear. On my ear.

'You sound far away,' I said.

'That's because I am.'

'What's the weather like?'

'Cold but clear. Still plenty of snow on the ground. And with you?'

'Hot. No snow.'

'There are terrible fires on the news. Are you anywhere near them?' This was less discreet. 'I'm fine,' I said. 'Quite safe.'

'How long will you stay?'

'I don't know. Another day or two. It depends.'

'On what you find under the stone?'

'Absolutely.'

'You be careful.'

'I will be.'

'This is the moment,' she said. I heard a catch in her voice as she stopped herself saying my name. 'Make the most of it.'

'I will,' I said.

'Then come home.'

'Yes,' I said. 'I'd better go.'

'All right. Look after yourself.'

'I will. Goodbye.'

'Goodbye.'

I hung up. What was it I was afraid of saying? What was it I was afraid of? And I wondered what she might be thinking – of our discretion, of our reticence. What unsaid things might she have hoped for me to say? I considered calling her again, but I could not bring myself to do so.

In hat, long-sleeved shirt, shorts and deck shoes, I started my walk to Sheildston for the third time, in the glare of the afternoon sun. That morning I had bought a small woven jute bag with a strap long enough to go over my shoulder, and in this I had a large bottle of cold water, a pen and notebook, and a digital voice recorder. This last item I'd also acquired that morning, almost on a whim, from a store selling cameras, phones and other electronic gadgets. I envisaged two scenarios: one in which Parroulet would consent to be interviewed, and one in which he wouldn't. In the second scenario, I thought I might still make use of the recorder but leave it in the bag. On the other hand I might not use it at all. I had no definite plan because I had no notion of what was going to happen.

Turner's Strand was as busy as ever but now at last the people seemed not only conscious of but also frightened by the conflagration that was consuming the countryside just a few miles away. There was no other story on television or radio, and that day's papers carried many images of blazing forests and burned-out buildings. More people had died, in their cars or in their homes. A man described his family's narrow escape, driving in smoke so thick they were nearly overcome through lack of oxygen. A woman spoke of houses exploding, one after another. When she was asked for her opinion of the likelihood that some of the fires had been started deliberately, she shook her head in anger. 'People are dead,' she said. 'That's murder in my book.'

The atmosphere of unrestrained, obligatory fun that had greeted me on my arrival was gone now. In its place were fear and sobriety. I'd noticed a few cars and trucks weighed down with possessions parked at the seafront, and near them shocked-looking families who had clearly not come for a relaxing vacation. The outback of the Australian imagination was not so far now from the beach and the suburbs, and it was killing people.

Just beyond the football pitches, tied to a telegraph pole and blocking the pavement, was a piece of hardboard with a message crudely written on it: EMERGENCY VEHICLES ONLY GO BACK FIRES. In the increasingly strong wind the board was straining to break from its moorings. I stepped round it and carried on. I had not seen or heard any emergency vehicles all morning. On the television news they'd said there was a shortage of fire appliances, ambulances, hoses, aeroplanes with water-lifting equipment, water itself – and that efforts were being concentrated on the most serious outbreaks. The entire population of Cobsville, twenty miles away, might have to be evacuated. A little place like Sheildston, I reckoned, would not be considered a priority by the authorities.

It had not, however, been completely forgotten. Rounding one of those steep bends, which despite the time of day, my weariness and the food poisoning I was finding less taxing than before – as if I were somehow rising beyond myself to the challenge – I came across a big police 4x4 parked across the next straight bit of road. An officer was sitting in the driver's seat with the door open, making a radio call. 'Just hold it there, mister,' he called. He spoke a few more words into the radio. A length of chain, a POLICE ROAD CLOSED metal sign, and a stack of traffic cones stood on the tarmac beside the car.

The policeman was middle-aged – that is to say, probably about my age – but he was much heavier than me. He sauntered across with his thumbs stuck in his belt.

'Where do you think you're going?'

'To Sheildston,' I said, as easily and calmly as I could.

'Do you have property up there?'

'No.'

'You're not a resident, then?'

'No, I'm a visitor.'

A prolonged gust of wind hit us, and in it was the strong, semi-sweet smell of burning. The gust was fierce and loud enough to make the policeman wait until it had died down before he spoke again.

'Well, you won't be doing any visiting today,' he said. 'Not in Sheildston.'

'Are the fires so close?'

'Very close.'

'And is nothing being done about them?'

'What do you mean?'

'To contain them. To save Sheildston.'

He seemed to take offence at the implication that nothing *was* being done.

'Look, mister, the whole state's about ready to go up. Nobody can save Sheildston if the fire comes through here. Everybody's busy trying to save Cobsville.'

Everybody except you, I thought, taking in the pale-blue shirt stretched over the enormous beer-gut as if it had just trapped it.

'That's tough on Sheildston,' I said.

'Yes it is. There are two thousand people in Cobsville. And thousands of others in towns like it – right in the path of the biggest fires.'

'There are people in Sheildston too.'

'There *were*. Now listen, I'm not having a debate about this. You're not going up there.'

'You mean you won't let me past?'

'That's exactly what I mean.'

'What harm can I do?'

'What good can you do, more like? You'd better not be thinking you're going to be some kind of hero.'

'I want to . . . check if the people I know are all right.'

'Which people's that, then?'

I almost made a mistake at this point but, miraculously, names other than 'Parr' came to my lips.

'Roger and Betty Dinning. And Maisie. Maisie Miller.'

'Oh. You know Maisie, do you?' My stock, I saw, rose a little in the policeman's eyes. 'Well, I can tell you, she's all right. Pretty upset, but safe. I took her out this morning, her and the dog. Her daughter's coming to collect them, if she can get through. And the Dinnings should be here any moment. I gave them an hour to get their valuables and that was forty-five minutes ago. Once they're down that's everybody and I'm closing the road.'

'Everybody? Are you sure?'

'Sure as I can be. You ring the bells and knock on the doors and use the tannoy to warn people – what else can you do? A lot of folks are away anyway, because of the holidays. If there's anybody left, well – good luck to them.'

'It's a hard choice,' I said, 'to leave your home and everything you have.'

'Not if it's that or burn to death. You can't fight these fires, not when they're this big and with this wind. You think you've got clear space all round your place but the fire'll just jump it. I'm sorry for those people, but you can't sit there like a sausage on a grill and think you're not going to cook.'

I acknowledged the truth of this with a nod. Reassured that I wasn't going to give any trouble, the policeman became almost friendly.

'A lot of them up there have got plenty of money. They'll have insurance. If it comes down to it, they can start again somewhere else. You know what the worst thing is?'

'No, what's the worst thing?'

'Some of these fires aren't accidents. I tell you what, if they catch the bastards . . .' He left the sentence unfinished, and gave me another hard look, suspicious perhaps that I might actually be an arsonist coming back to observe my handiwork. 'How do you know Maisie anyway?'

'An old friend,' I said. 'Long time ago.'

The policeman seemed satisfied by this vague reply. 'I thought she'd take it bad but she's a tough lady. "Neil," she says to me, "you just have to play whatever hand you get dealt." I guess she's right about that. You staying in town?'

'In Turner's Strand, yes.'

'You go back down the hill, then. You'll be safe there.'

I nodded again. 'I will be,' I said. He nodded back. I raised a hand in farewell and went round the corner. I heard the scrape of traffic cones being shoved across the road. Before the next turn I stopped and got my bearings. Then I stepped off the road, scrambled up the bank, and plunged into the undergrowth.

The dense tangle of branches and roots was in places almost impenetrable. There were thorns and burrs and sharp-edged stems, and everything was steep and hot and dry and dusty. I found a concrete channel, choked with leaves and other debris, a water run-off I guessed, and fought my way up it. I made a terrible crashing, cracking noise as I went, but even if the cop heard me he'd never be able to locate me in all the vegetation. My throat was parched, sweat poured down my face and my eyes itched and streamed. I paused, got out the water and took a long drink. When the wind dropped a little

I heard rustling, creeping sounds in the undergrowth – reptiles, birds, insects and other creatures no doubt, moving away from the fire. I tried not to think about treading on a snake or being bitten by a spider, and toiled on. In a while either the going became easier or I became better at negotiating the terrain. After ten or fifteen minutes I emerged on to the road.

Almost at once I heard a vehicle approaching, and ducked back into cover. A car stuffed with luggage and with several items of furniture lashed to the roof rack came down the hill. I saw a grim-faced Roger Binning at the wheel, a woman next to him with a handkerchief to her mouth.

I was on a straight stretch of the road, almost at the top. A feeling of triumph seized me and I began to trot into the wind. A hundred yards or so brought me round the final bend and to the first of Sheildston's houses. I slowed to a walk. The smell of burning was constant now. I found it hard to believe that everybody had fled, but there was certainly no sign of life. Was I being a complete fool? This was not my country: I knew nothing about bush fires.

I passed the old part of the village, the church, the former school, Maisie Miller's closed-up house. Nothing stirred, but to the west great streamers of grey and black smoke rose into the sky. Now it was a sense of urgency that forced me into another short run and brought me to the gates of Parroulet's house for the third time.

I was going to press the buzzer, but then I ran on again, along the fence to where the road ended. I could hear something – chopping, cracking sounds, but also a deeper underlying noise, a kind of snore. I headed to the start of the trail into the bush. The snore grew louder, and curtains of smoke, like black storms rising, dimmed the sky. And then I reached the spot where I had stood with Maisie Miller, and I saw the fire.

It was hard to judge but I didn't think it was more than a mile away, a ragged wall of flame stretching itself out to both left and right. Trees popped and curled and were consumed as if made of straw. And the snore was now a growl, and even at that distance I could feel the beat of the furnace against my face.

I ran back to the gates and pressed the buzzer. Three short bursts, one long.

There was no answer.

They had fled too, from the fire if not from me. How could I have thought that they would not?

But then I saw Kim Parr hurrying across the broken, weed-strewn tarmac. In a pair of white shorts and a black singlet, she looked like a young girl.

'You shouldn't have come!' she cried. 'I didn't think you would.'

'It's what we agreed,' I said. 'And you are still here.'

'Martin won't leave. The police came but he wouldn't let me answer them. He said they would force us to go.'

'Haven't you seen the fire? It's coming this way.'

She had a remote control in her hand and used it to release the lock on the gates. 'I don't want to see it. I can hear it and smell it, that is enough.'

'There's still time to escape, if you leave now.'

'We're not leaving,' she said.

'Did you tell him I was coming?'

'Last night. He was very angry. Today he doesn't speak to me. He'll be even more angry if I let you in.'

'But you have let me in,' I said.

'You're not going to go away, are you? You're here. But that doesn't matter right now. Only the fire matters.'

I followed her to the door, solid and white and framed by a portico. Inside was a cool, white-painted hall with huge ferns and rubber plants in great terracotta pots, and a polished tiled floor that could have been marble but probably wasn't. A staircase led to both an upper and a lower level, and there were various doors around the hall. The house, I thought, was probably twenty years old, no more. Doubtless it had been considered luxurious, even opulent, when new, but to me it appeared tired, barren, a little tawdry, the kind of modern building that is not flattered by cracks when they begin to show.

'Where is he?'

'Outside. He thinks he can save the house. I don't know. Maybe it's impossible. Look.'

She had brought me to a window and from it we looked down on a swimming pool beyond which a short stretch of lawn ended at a fence. The bush grew hard up against – and in places, overreached – this fence, which ran along the south side of the property, then turned and continued on the west side, past the pool and house and up the incline to the road. Immediately below us, at one end of the pool, was a patio, on which were set out some loungers and easy chairs, a wooden table and a couple of parasols. All this I saw in a moment, but Kim Parr had not brought me there to admire the view. She was pointing to the other side of the pool. A lone figure was frantically hacking at the nearest undergrowth with an axe. The fence had been cut and pulled apart in one place so that he could get more easily at the foliage massing on the other side. He had made a lot of progress, clearing a swathe perhaps twelve feet wide along half of the western perimeter, but there was still much to do, and even if it could be done in time it seemed hopeless, the narrowest of boundaries between life and death. 'The fire'll just jump it,' the fat cop had said. From the window, the flames that I had seen a few minutes earlier were not yet visible, but I knew how fast they were approaching. I could also see the tumult being caused in the taller trees by the wind.

'I think he has gone mad,' Kim Parr said.

We hurried downstairs to the lower level of the house, into a large space that seemed to be a utility or storage room. For a moment I hesitated, putting my jute bag and its contents on the floor, and Kim moved ahead, out on to the patio. 'Martin,' she called. I saw other tools lying on the ground: wire-clippers, a bush-saw, a machete, a rake – all, surely, completely inadequate against what was coming. Parroulet turned. He was in long trousers and a loose shirt and gardening boots, and was wearing work gloves. He was completely drenched in sweat. He advanced a couple of steps towards us. Kim stopped.

'Who the hell this is?' Parroulet said, and at once I remembered his voice, his idiosyncratic English, his evidence. Parroulet looked furious, frightened, cornered. He held the long-handled axe up as if ready to swing it at us.

Kim said, 'I told you.'

'Goddamn it, Kim!' Parroulet said. 'This I don't need.'

Something took me beyond my memory of the man. I said, 'What you need is a chainsaw.'

Parroulet gave me a murderous look. 'Nobody ask you nothing.'

I said, 'Do you have one?'

'What?' Parroulet snapped.

'A chainsaw. Do you have a chainsaw?'

'No!' Parroulet shouted. 'I don't have no goddamn chainsaw. It broke. It hit metal post and the chain broke. Almost it took my foot off. See?'

There was a gash across the toe of the right boot, which had split the leather and exposed the steel cap underneath. And now I saw, discarded beside the fence, like the head of some fierce, dead, unknown beast, the broken chainsaw.

'You happy now?'

It was as if somebody else occupied my body. I walked quickly over to where the tools lay. I picked up the machete.

'What the hell he is doing?' Parroulet screamed at Kim.

I turned away and began to strike at the vegetation with the machete. I felt the heat of the day, the thickening heat of the fire on my neck. I felt rather than saw a swinging motion close to me, heard a cry from Kim, but steeled myself neither to turn nor to use the machete in defence. Whatever was coming was coming. I struck again at the trunk of a bush, severing it, and at the same moment heard the axe thud into wood a few feet away. Neither of us looked at the other. I lifted the whole bush and flung it away from the house. Something sharp tore at the palm of my left hand. I glanced at the scratch and the sudden stitching of blood that appeared.

'Gloves!' I called to Kim. 'Do you have any more?'

'Get him gloves!' Parroulet yelled, and Kim ran indoors, and returned a minute later with some. By then, Martin Parroulet and I had made a kind of unspoken pact. We were working apart, saying nothing, barely acknowledging each other, yet somehow sharing a bond or purpose as we tried to clear as much space as possible between the house and the surrounding, swaying, jostling, as yet unfired undergrowth.

10

It would not be enough. It would never be enough. So I thought as we laboured. Both Parroulet and I were on the far side of the cut fence, hacking and sawing and hauling out branches and bushes. After a while it became impossible to heap the bush back on itself, and anyway such heaps would only cause a greater conflagration if the fire reached the edge of the space we were making. So Kim came behind us, pulling away the biggest pieces of debris and piling them in the middle of the lawn, beyond the swimming pool, as far as possible from the house. The three of us worked in silence, nobody giving instructions because it was obvious what we had to do – what we were feebly, ferociously trying to do – yet there was a kind of organised frenzy in the way we kept at it. I worked like a machine, methodical and repetitive, but I felt angry and joyous and powerful in my movements. Yesterday I had been sick and weak and done, barely able to put one foot in front of the other. Today I was alive. Sweat lashed from me like rain. Every muscle and bone ached, my wrists and arms were criss-crossed with weals and cuts and I could feel, under the thickness of the gloves, the blisters rising to cover my soft, academic's fingers and palms. But I kept going, through the pain, through the conviction that what we were doing was utterly futile. I had seen what was approaching. But why did it not come? The flames had seemed so close – an hour, two hours ago? – I didn't know how long. Why had they not yet arrived?

Then I was at the end of the fence, where it joined the roadside fence. Parroulet was still hacking away behind me, and down on the lawn Kim was piling up more branches, but I had done as much as I could. My weakness had caught up with me. I was filthy, drained, shaking with exertion. Every inch of me seemed to have been bitten by insects or cut or torn or bruised by the bush. I turned to limp back towards Parroulet.

'We can do nothing more,' I said.

'Yes,' Parroulet said breathlessly, barely pausing. 'Yes, we can do more.'

Somewhere out of our sight came a crash, a huge tree falling, followed by a shout from Kim. 'Look!'

We both turned to where she was pointing. Beyond the clear passage we had made, above the highest point of the foliage that awaited the fire, a single tongue of flame was licking at the air. It leaped and fell, leaped again, and after it came a shower of sparks, deep red against the darkened sky.

Now we would see, I remember thinking. But I did not know what I thought we would see.

There was, all at once, almost no sky left, only the huge smoke clouds of destruction. And I realised that it was becoming harder to find breath, that the fire must be sucking the oxygen out of the atmosphere, and Pompeii and smothering ash suddenly came into my mind, and I wondered if we would suffocate before we were burned, and how long it would take, and whether we would feel any pain.

Parroulet signalled me to follow, and we both retreated to the patio. Kim joined us. Parroulet went into the utility room, and brought out an assortment of outdoor clothes – long trousers, fleeces, jackets, hats, more gloves, scarves, even two ski masks. 'Put on them,' he said, and began to dress himself, layer upon layer. We looked at him as if he really were insane. Then, arrayed like a cross between a scarecrow and some ghoulish figure from myth or nightmare, with a scarf wrapped round his face, he plunged into the pool, swam to the edge and pulled himself out.

'Now you, now you!' he shouted, and we saw that he was right, and we too made ourselves into scarecrows, and soaked ourselves against the heat that was now upon us and that would, if it got the chance, burn us without even touching us. And while we did this Parroulet took a pile of towels and dipped them into the pool, and left them lying where they could be easily reached.

'Help me now with this,' Parroulet said, and he beckoned us into the utility room. In one corner was a coiled hose with an adjustable nozzle at one end, and a small machine that looked to me like a vacuum cleaner. Parroulet removed a cap from it and fixed one end of the hose in its place. Then he pulled out the machine's long electric cord and plugged it into a socket beside the door. 'Wait here,' he told Kim. He handed the coil of hose to me. 'Carry it.' He picked up the machine and we went back outside. It did not occur to me to ask questions.

'This is what more we can do,' Parroulet said fiercely. 'I am right, you will see.'

The machine was a submersible pump. Parroulet lowered it on a nylon cord into the deep end of the pool until it settled on the bottom. I unwound the hose. Parroulet shouted at Kim, 'Now! Switch on!'

There was a belching, gurgling sound as the motor kicked in. The hose lay dormant in my hands, then suddenly it spluttered and a fat spout of water flopped from it. Parroulet grabbed the hose from me and screwed the nozzle until it produced a continuous thin jet of water. He began to soak the space we had cleared, making a kind of wet corridor between the fire and the house. I looked at the pool, still lapping from our dives. It was about forty feet long by twenty wide. How much water was in there I had no idea, but even the contents of an entire swimming pool seemed inconsequential against what I had seen advancing on us.

The noise of the fire increased, the smoke-filled sky turned pink and orange above the trees beyond our firebreak, and sparks and ash began to fall into the pool and on to the patio. On the lawn little explosions occurred where debris landed and ignited the grass. The fire, though it gorged on whatever new material it found, also brought food with it, carrying it high in the air and dropping it like crumbs as it moved on. I was a sodden, clumsy ogre, lumbering from one place to another, stamping out the spot fires before they could spread. Kim was doing the same on the paved area by the house, kicking burning sticks into the pool. And under the roar of the fire came another sound, a continuous sigh, a hiss, as the heat sucked the wetness from the ground where Parroulet was still spraying.

How long this strange masque lasted I do not know. Whenever I paused, breathless and parched, to see where I needed to go next, I saw the wrapped figure of the woman stamping and kicking, or working with a bucket, to the handle of which she had attached a rope and which she dropped into the pool and used to drown smouldering debris. And always there too, between the pool and the fire, was the man, stationary, or moving only slowly as he continued to play the hose, silhouetted against the smoke and flame like a blacksmith or a demon. And had those two, the man and the woman, paused to look in my direction, they would have seen a half-blind grotesque, beating at the ground with a spade, dispersing fire and killing it with plodding feet, a lurching solitary dancer. I felt almost as if I were asleep, dancing in my sleep, and in that odd half-conscious state I began to work my way back to the house, to see what I could more usefully be doing there. To save the house was surely the crucial thing. The woman saw me and screamed something, and I lumbered faster towards her, unable to hear what she was saying, until we were so close that her words came through the other noise.

'Your shoes! Your shoes!'

I looked down, and saw that the deck shoes had burst into flame. My feet were on fire and I had not felt it. I stumbled to the pool and threw myself in, and fell for a long second through air and then hit water, and realised that the level had dropped a foot or more. I kicked at my shoes to get them off but they would not leave me. Half-choking from swallowing smoke or water or both, I swam to the side, hauled myself out with the woman's help, and tried to stand. Immediately I fell over, and began to pull at the mess of shoe on one foot, and she was beside me pulling at the other. The shoes came away and I yelled. My feet were dotted with bits of melted shoe that had stuck to the skin and burned it. The woman hurried to the pile of wet towels, seized a couple and wrapped my feet in them, and I lay exhausted on the slabs and watched the man with his hose, tiny against the fiery sky. I believed that we were about to die, all three of us.

Suddenly the man dropped the hose and came in a limping, bent run towards us. Between them they lifted and carried me into the utility room, and he shut the door. The roar of destruction was above us now, godlike and terrible. It passed over us, and I felt my throat closing, and my eyes, and everything was dark, and it seemed that no light could ever shine again.

11

When I reopened my eyes, the door of the room was open again. There was air coming in – cooler, and relatively free of smoke – but the darkness remained, and this was because night had come. I was lying on my side on the hard floor, and could see through the door to the outside. Something blinked, then something else, then more in twos and threes. The stars were returning to the sky.

I had a fit of coughing and tried to get up, but the towels round my feet prevented this. Cautiously I unpeeled the towels. At the last layer I felt the pull between cotton and skin and considered whether it was wise to continue, but all I wanted was to get the towels off so I kept going. I couldn't see properly what condition my feet were in, but they didn't hurt as much as I expected. I understood I was probably in shock. I badly wanted a drink. Whisky, wine, beer, anything. And before that, water.

I crawled outside on my hands and knees. The stink of ash and smoke was everywhere. The pump had stopped working and the wind had died away. All quiet. My stinging eyes picked out the shape of Parroulet, stripped of his protective clothing down to shorts and T-shirt, walking in the grey, black, glowing aftermath like a man crossing a battlefield.

I hauled myself off the ground and into one of the chairs on the patio. I couldn't understand why none of them was damaged. The wooden table too seemed untouched by fire. Yet beyond the house and pool everything, as far as I could see, was scorched or broken or gone completely.

I heard movement behind me and saw a beam of light. Kim Parr came out from the house, guiding herself with a torch. In her other hand was a bottle of water, which she handed to me and from which I gratefully and greedily drank. She went back inside, then returned carrying something else, which she put on the table. It was a candle on a ceramic dish. She struck a match. It was almost miraculous to see the match ignite, her hand hold it to the wick, the candle flame grow. Even after what we had experienced, there was reassurance and comfort in the flame.

Kim looked as if she'd had a wash. She'd also changed into dry clothes. Mine hung on me, heavy and wet.

I said, 'How long have I been asleep?'

'A while,' she said. 'Forty minutes. An hour. I made sure you weren't dead, then left you.'

'What time is it?'

'I don't know. Maybe nine, ten.'

'What happened? Where is the fire?'

'It missed us. It has gone that way.' She pointed vaguely to the north.

'Missed us?'

'By a few metres, yes.'

'Are you all right?'

'Yes.'

'What about him?'

'He's okay.'

'What's he doing?'

'He is looking for the cat.'

'What cat?'

'We have a cat. We shut her inside before you came but now she's gone. She must have got out again.'

She spoke very quietly, as if she didn't want to disturb the search or the strange stillness. Everything was so quiet compared with how it had been before.

'The power is out,' she said. 'I think so anyway. But there is water for a shower. You want a shower?'

'I don't know if I can manage that.'

She helped me up. Between us we took off most of my clothes, leaving a sodden pile on the floor of the utility room. Then, gingerly, with her support, I made my way up the stairs. She showed me to a bedroom off the hall. There was an en suite, with a big shower cabinet, white towels, soap, shampoo – she lit more candles to illuminate the room. She said, 'Be careful.' As she was leaving she said, 'I'll find you some clothes.'

I washed myself as well as I could in cold water. The smell of smoke, the scars of all that desperate work, would take a while to fade. There was a plastic stool, which I took into the shower to take the weight off my burned feet. When I was done I looked into the bedroom, and saw a polo shirt, a pair of boxers and loose cotton trousers of some dark colour laid out on the bed. No shoes. They were Parroulet's clothes of course. I didn't want to put them on, baulking especially at the underwear, but I had little choice. What were they? They were only clothes.

I blew out the candles in the bathroom and just as I did so the overhead light came on.

There was a knock on the door. 'Come in,' I said.

'It is a miracle,' Kim said. 'We have water and electricity.'

'Yes, it's a miracle,' I said.

'Let me see your feet,' she said.

The bedroom was, I supposed from its pristine condition, a guest room for the guests they probably never had. I sat on the edge of the bed and she picked some remaining bits of shoe from my soles with tweezers, applied ointment and wrapped my feet in bandages. 'You go to hospital soon as you can,' she said. 'Tomorrow maybe.'

From a long way off Parroulet called her name. It felt conspiratorial, to be there in the bedroom with her while her husband wandered the battlefield outside.

'You come down later,' she said. 'I better go now.'

I thought about lying back on the bed but knew if I did I would instantly fall asleep. That was not what I had come for. I had to struggle to remember what I had come for. It was as if I had come to help put out a fire. I got up, hobbled to the stairs, and went down to the lower level of the house.

Parroulet had injured himself earlier. He was limping quite badly, but not apparently because of his encounter with the chainsaw. It was his other, left leg that was giving him trouble. Watching from the utility room, I saw that he could hardly put any weight on it. But I saw something else too: that this was not Parroulet's priority. In fact he seemed hardly to notice that he was hurt at all. He had called Kim because he had found the cat.

At the last possible moment, it appeared, the wind must have shifted direction, enough to drive the flames northward, along the line of the break we had made. The fire was a contrary beast, a greedy but fussy eater, chewing up some things made of steel or even concrete but leaving others made of wood or plastic. It had, with just a few stray sparks, ignited and destroyed things not in its path, but had passed almost directly over others and left them more or less untouched. So it was with Parroulet's house, and so it was with the pile of branches that Kim had made in the middle of the lawn. It had not escaped entirely: its outer covering was charred and ash-covered and it had collapsed so that it resembled some primitive dwelling with the roof fallen in. And it was from somewhere in that surviving heap in the middle of the devastated grass that Parroulet had heard the cat mewling. Now, holding in one hand the scarf that he had worn round his face during the fire, Parroulet was limping slowly and deliberately towards the sound.

I came to the outer door and found Kim, a few steps beyond on the patio, silently watching her husband. Without turning she motioned at me to be still. I leaned at the door on my bandaged feet, waiting for whatever was to happen.

With a grace at odds with his disarray and awkward gait, Parroulet moved forward. The further he went from the electric light of the house into the starlight and the shadows, the less defined and more ethereal he became. I could hear terror and pain and rage in the cat's repeated whine, and as Parroulet closed in the noise grew louder and more distressed. But Parroulet seemed quite calm. He was whispering to the cat, coaxing and reassuring it. He crouched now, just a few feet from the heap, almost lost from my sight. The cat continued to mewl, and Parroulet to talk back, till the cat quietened and it was hard to distinguish the one voice from the other. Minute after minute went by. Neither Kim nor I moved. At last Parroulet slowly raised himself from the ground, turned and started the walk back to the house. He moved into the light. He had the cat, wrapped in the scarf and held gently against his chest, and was still whispering to it. I could see only the head, the huge frightened eyes, the singed and scarred fur. Parroulet came inside. He did not so much as glance at me in passing. I might as well not have existed, and something in me resented his refusal to acknowledge me even now. Yet at the same time I could not but be impressed by his single-minded tenderness towards the cat.

Kim followed Parroulet upstairs, presumably to help care for the animal. Left alone, again I had to resist the temptation to sit and close my eyes. I shuffled out on my bandages to the far end of the pool, to look at the sky, the garden, the house.

How much of Sheildston had escaped the inferno? This would have been the first house in its path, so it was possible that, with the change of wind direction, the whole place had been missed. But other houses might not have been so fortunate: burning debris flung out by the fire might have landed on properties where no one was left to extinguish it. If the fat cop had been right, only the three of us had remained in Sheildston.

And nobody, surely, would come up the road to view the damage till morning.

I couldn't leave if I wanted to, even if Parroulet threw me out. I couldn't walk a hundred yards, let alone all the way to Turner's Strand.

The water left in the pool had a scum of ash and charred wood floating on it.

The sky was full of stars.

I am alive, I thought, really alive.

I remembered what Nilsen had said about that.

I remembered clearing snow around my house. Was that house still standing? Was Carol all right? Was there anything at all on the other side of the world?

I did not know. I knew only that I was where I was, and that I was alive.

Kim reappeared with two tins of beer.

'Sit,' she said. 'Get off those feet.'

'If I sit I'll never stand again,' I said, but I came over and we sat at the table. The coldness of the beer was so sharp it took away all other hurt.

There was a neatness, a composure about her that was remarkable given all that had occurred. Was this how she had got through everything life had thrown at her?

'How is the cat?' I asked.

'The cat will live. Her paws were burned. We put cream on them, and bandages. Like your feet. She is a good patient, but very frightened. Martin is looking after her.'

'Is he? Or is he hiding from me?'

She shook her head, but not in answer to my question. 'You are both the same. We have been through all this, we survive, and the first thing he says to me is, "I will not speak to him," and the first thing you say is, "Is he hiding from me?"'

'Then I'd say he was.'

'He says he has nothing to say to you.'

'He has everything to say to me. Does he know who I am?'

'Yes, I told him last night. He knows you and what you think of him.'

'I don't think anything of him. I want to ask him about what he said at the trial, that's all.'

'That is not true. You think that man who died went to prison because of him. You think Martin told lies for money.'

'Didn't he?'

She looked as if she might take the beer back. 'You are not very nice, Alan Tealing,' she said. 'Why do you do this? After what has happened? After I have helped you?'

'That has nothing to do with it.'

'No?' She flared up, as she had before. 'Then why don't you just leave now? Go on! He doesn't want you in this house. I don't want you. Go!'

'You know I can't.'

'No, not unless I take you. So what, then? You want to go or stay?'

'I want to speak to your husband.'

'Yes.' Her voice calmed again. 'So be a bit more polite, I think. Then maybe something can happen, okay?'

'I'm sorry,' I said.

She rubbed her eyes, shook her head again. When she caught me staring at her she said, still angry, 'Smoke.'

'I know.'

She sighed. 'He will see you,' she said. 'He says no but he will. It is coming, that talk between you. It has to happen, for both of you. But first I will tell you who he is because you don't know. You only know him from the trial, but that is not only who he is.'

I nodded.

'I said to you before, it is all chance that he was a witness. It is all chance that we are here, the three of us, still alive.'

'I understand.'

'To understand you must listen. So listen. When I first met Martin I did not think anything much about him. You know how we met? The same way I met you. He came to my shop, in Melbourne. He came with a coat to mend, a quiet, shy man. We talked. He came again, with some other things. Alterations. He had not been in Australia long and was not very confident. Because of this and the mending I never thought he was rich, even though he did not work. To me he was just lonely and wanted to have conversation. I liked him. We were good company.

'One day he asked me to go out with him. A drink, a meal. It took him a lot of courage to ask me, I could see, and because of that I said yes. And we became friends. For some weeks that was what we were, friends.

'Then another day came when he said he wanted to take me somewhere, away for the weekend. It was separate rooms, very correct, or I wouldn't have gone. I trusted him. He drove me in a big expensive car, a Mercedes, and that made me think, but it was not his, he had hired it. Maybe this was to impress me but I don't think so. He knew me by then. He said when he had his taxi it was a Mercedes because it was comfortable and never went wrong. All the taxi drivers had Mercedes. And he brought me to Turner's Strand, and then here. We stood outside the house. It was a beautiful day. The flowers, the trees, everything was beautiful. He said, "This would be a good place to live," and I agreed. Then he took out the remote and opened the gate. I said, "What are you doing?" He said, "Come, I show you round," and we went in. The house was empty but all in good condition, not run-down like now. This is six years ago. He said, "Would you like to live here with me? This is my house." Well, I saw it must be true. "We could get married," he said, "if you want."'

'He bribed you with the house.'

She made that shake of her head again. 'You don't want to think any good of him. It's true I wished he had not shown me the house before he said about getting married. But that was his way and I knew right then that it wouldn't have made any difference. I would still say yes. But I never say yes without time to think. So I told him, "I'll give you my answer when we get back to Melbourne."'

'You must have wondered where his money came from?'

'Yes, but I did not ask. He never said about the trial and I did not know anything about it. I decided to marry him because of what I knew, not because of what I didn't know. I knew he was not cruel or bad. He was not clever enough to be a big businessman. He was not clever or stupid enough to be a criminal. Maybe he had won the lottery or maybe he had inherited money from his family, but he never said. He was old-fashioned, and I liked that. To ask me to marry him when we had not been in bed, that was something. He had not even tried to get me into bed. I knew where he was from and I knew he had come to Australia for a new life. That was his chance, same as me. What business was it of mine, his money? He said I would never have to work again. I said yes I would. It was my business, not his. He accepted that. So I said yes.'

A business transaction, I thought. 'It doesn't sound like you were in love,' I said.

'What do you mean by "love"? It is not a crime to marry. What does anyone mean when they say "love"? We were right for each other. He didn't have to ask me, nobody made me say yes. We were old enough to know what we wanted.

'We got married. I closed my shop. We came here and furnished the house. This was our new life together. We swam in the pool, I grew flowers, he cut the grass. I cooked. Sometimes he cooked. I read books. He taught himself to paint. I set up my new shop. We got the cat.

'But then there was a change, after a year, not much more than that. I noticed it first because of the car. He had bought one, a Mercedes of course, and we went shopping or drove to different places on the coast or even to Sydney. But he always liked to come home, never to stay away for a night. He did all the driving. That car is too big for me even if I wanted to drive, but I don't.'

Had she, like me, been afraid of failure? I did not think so.

'He bought me my little scooter which I liked more. So anyway, we didn't go for drives so much. He would only go if I went with him, never alone, and after a while he didn't go at all. The car stayed in the garage. It is still there. He didn't even start the engine. I carried food and some small things from the town on the scooter, and every week or two weeks I went to the supermarket and did a big shopping and they delivered it. I say big but it wasn't much. We lived like poor people, ate like poor people, and that is how we live now. He never went out, not even to walk outside the gate. He watched TV or was on the computer or he painted. Or he swam up and down the pool or sat on the patio playing with the cat. He did not talk to the neighbours. He did not drink much, only smoked cigarettes, and even not many of them, not like he used to when he had the taxi. Sometimes he did not talk to me for a whole day. I asked him what was wrong. He said nothing was wrong. He looked empty, lonely, like the first time he came into the shop with his coat that needed a repair. I could not make him speak to me. So I went to work. I worked long days down there in the shop. That was why I had it. I always have to work. Like I told you before.'

'He painted,' I said.

'Yes. He liked to paint.'

'What does he paint?' But I already knew. I could see those two paintings in the gallery at Turner's Strand. I knew they were by him.

'The sea,' she said.

'You have to work,' I said. 'Maybe he has to paint.'

'When I work I feel good about myself. I don't think he feels good about himself, even when he painted. And he has given it up now. Do you know the story of King Midas? You must. Everybody knows that story. Everything he touched turned to gold but it did not make him happy. It made him like a prisoner. Martin was like Midas. I was afraid that he would touch me, like Midas touched his daughter, and I would turn to gold, I would be a prisoner too. So one day I said, you must talk to me or I will go away. I made him say where the money came from. And he told me about the trial. He told me that the Americans paid him for giving evidence.'

'Did he say how much?'

'Yes.'

'They say it was two million dollars.'

She made a face. 'If you know, you know.'

'Was it?'

'I don't know exactly. Something like that, yes.'

'And did he say why they paid him so much? Did he tell you what kind of evidence?'

'That is between him and you. If you are asking did he say he made up lies to get the money, no, of course he didn't say that. He said what he said and then he stopped. So I found out for myself. I looked on the internet. Everything was there. I don't remember the bombing when it happened. I was in the care home then, I had plenty trouble of my own. I read many web pages about it, all the different ideas about what happened. I read about the trial. I saw your name and what you said. I learned a lot, more than Martin ever told me. All he said was where the money came from, and this was why he had a new name, and why he was here, and why he had no contact with his family or friends from home. So you see the money really had made him like a prisoner. Like King Midas in his palace. It has been this way for five, six years.'

I said, 'Why have you stayed? This is not a life for someone like you.'

'Someone like me? Who is someone like me? What should someone like me do? Walk away from him? What good will that do? I didn't want to leave him. I wanted to help him. When I knew the cause I was afraid for the same reason he was – I was afraid that what had happened would come and find us and hurt us. When that man, Khazar, died, I thought maybe it was over and things would change, but nothing changed. Martin knew it was not over.'

She picked up her tin, but it was empty, as mine had been for a while. This seemed to bring her to some kind of decision, and she stood up.

'We don't have much time here, do we?' she said. 'To help each other. So we should try to help each other in the time we have. Don't you think?'

'You and me?' I asked, standing too, and feeling again my wounded feet.

'I don't mean that. I mean here, in this life. We don't have much time. We should be kind to each other.'

I didn't have any answer. She said, 'Come now. We'll get some more beer and you can take it in to Martin. Maybe now it can be over.'

She went ahead of me. As I followed, I remembered the jute bag and its contents. It seemed days ago since I had dropped it on the floor, but it was still there. I bent to retrieve it.

'You won't need that,' Kim said. She had turned and was watching me.

'I might.'

'No, you won't,' she said. She did not mean the bag, she meant the recorder. I realised this as I felt inside for it and found that it wasn't there.

I was about to protest, but her look told me that there was no point.

'Just go,' she said. 'Just talk to each other.'

13

I felt like a student outside his tutor's room, about to deliver an essay or have one returned. Kim had brought me to the upper level of the house, pointed to the door, and gone back downstairs. I held two tins of beer, cold offerings that I felt uncomfortable about bringing, yet I had not resisted when she took them from the fridge and put them into my hands.

I did not think I would be able to knock at the man's door, but then I saw that it was ajar, not shut tight. I pushed it open.

A standard lamp was switched on but it did not cast a strong light. The room occupied the south-east corner of the building, with one window facing out over the garden and another across the ridge towards the sea. They were big windows, and the southern one opened on to a balcony overlooking the swimming pool. The night sky was moonless, deep and dark and vast, and scattered with stars. There seemed even more of them from this height than from the ground. Closer to the horizon the sky was hazier, and streaked with the pink and orange of fires still burning some distance away.

Martin Parroulet was sitting in an armchair to one side of the balcony window. He was still in the shorts and T-shirt he'd stripped down to when he went looking for the cat. The lamplight seemed to separate his thin receding hair from his skull. His left leg, the one he'd been limping on, was stretched out, with the foot resting on a stool. Going towards him and looking down on the balding head, I thought that we must be about the same age. This had never occurred to me before. I had always thought of him as an older man.

Parroulet did not move but he knew I had come in and he did not seem surprised that I was there. He said, very quietly, 'Open them over there. Do not give fear to the cat.'

The cat was settled against his chest and belly. Its head was up, its eyes alert, as if it might bolt at any moment. Parroulet's right hand cradled the cat's hindquarters. The hand was huge, the hand of a peasant or of the son of a peasant. This too was something I had not previously noticed.

The tins of beer gave fierce little hisses when I opened them. The cat's ears pricked up but it stayed where it was. I approached again and Parroulet put out his left hand and took one of the tins, but did not drink from it.

Opposite Parroulet's armchair was an upright wooden chair with a loose cushion. I wondered if the chair had been placed there deliberately for me, and if so who had placed it. I sat down and took a drink.

Neither of us spoke. The meaty index finger of Parroulet's hand stroked the cat's fur. His eyes were fixed on me all the time. He seemed wary. The cat too watched me. It could have been a scene from a bad film.

A minute passed. A minute of silence in such circumstances is a very long time. At last Parroulet sipped from his tin of beer.

'You come with the fire,' he said. 'You go with the fire.'

'The fire is gone already,' I said.

'You want me to thank you? For you help save my house? I'm not sure to thank you. Maybe you bring the fire.'

'You think I started it?'

Parroulet shrugged. 'No. Not start it. But if you don't come, fire don't come. Not one without other. Maybe.'

'I'd have come anyway.'

Parroulet lapsed into silence again. He had a big, broad nose and in these moments his breathing was the loudest, almost the only, sound in the room.

'Who send you?' he asked.

'An American. He knew where you were.'

'How? Nobody know this. What is his name?'

'Ted Nilsen.'

'I don't know this name. Who is he?'

'An agent. CIA probably. That was not his real name. He knew all about you.'

'He is spy?'

'Yes, I suppose you could say he was. He is dead now.'

'Dead? Who kill him?'

'Nobody. He died of natural causes.' But as I said this I realised that I did not know it for sure. 'Bad health and bad weather,' I said.

The corners of Parroulet's already downcast mouth fell further, as if to signify scepticism.

'He died in a snowstorm,' I said.

'When?'

'A week ago. Just after he told me about you, and where to find you.'

'If he know all about me, what is it more you want?'

'I want the truth, Mr Parroulet.'

'That is not my name. My name is Parr.'

I said, 'Please don't treat me like a fool.'

He said nothing. I felt my patience fraying. Be calm, I told myself, this is what you are here for.

'My name is Alan Tealing. You are Martin Parroulet. You gave evidence against Khalil Khazar. Your evidence convicted him. If you would admit that what you said was made up, manufactured, so it could be shown that Khazar should not have been found guilty, then the police would have to reopen the case. They would have to start looking again for who really murdered my wife and daughter.'

I remembered something else about Parroulet as I said all this. Parroulet's spoken English had never been good in court, but his comprehension had been fine. There had been a simultaneous translation service available but he had not made use of it, and during cross-examination he had very seldom asked for a question to be repeated. And so I did not think that Parroulet would be easily confused by the conditional clauses and mixed tenses I had used, even if he pretended to be. I certainly did not intend to make what I had to say easier for him.

There was another thing. For nearly a week now the details of the Case had hardly been present in my consciousness. I had worried that I might not know what to say if this encounter ever took place. And now it was happening, and it was all still there, the motivation, the memories, and I did not need to worry. Kim was right. We just needed to talk.

Parroulet said, 'Khalil Khazar is dead. This spy you speak of, this Nilsen, is dead. Nothing can be done.'

'Yes it can,' I said.

'Your wife is dead. Your child is dead.' Parroulet bowed his head, and made some soft pacifying sound to the cat before he looked at me again. 'I am sorry for saying this. Nothing can be done.'

'You are not dead,' I said. 'I am not dead.'

Parroulet concentrated on stroking the cat.

'Kim is not dead,' I said.

The cat stretched, more at ease. Two white patches in the dim light showed the bandages on its front paws.

'Did you ever have a child?'

Parroulet shook his head. 'No.'

'Did you never want children?'

The thin-haired head shook again.

'What good is this? Why you are ask this questions?'

'Because I have to. Did you?'

There was another long silence. Eventually Parroulet gave a kind of groan. 'Yes. But it is not possible.'

'How not possible?'

'Kim.'

'What about Kim?'

Another groan. 'She cannot have child. Something happen when she is child herself. Very bad things happen to her in Vietnam.'

'She told me about some of them.'

Parroulet's scowl deepened.

'When I went to her shop, we talked. She talked about her family.'

'You know all about my wife? So talk to her. Why you want talk to me? I know nothing.'

'What do you think happened to her? Something physical?'

Parroulet shrugged. 'She keep some things in herself. Maybe physical, yes. Or maybe in her head. You see bad things, maybe it get in your head, change your body. She have some problem with the eggs. The doctors give her check and say she can maybe get treatment, but she don't want treatment. She always say if it happen it happen, but it never happen.'

'She told me about her father being taken by the pirates, and the pirates killing her brother on the boat. She told me about her mother. And her sister, and what happened to her.'

Parroulet said, 'What happen to who?'

'Her older sister. The one who died. Her mother and her sister were raped. She didn't say so but that's what she meant.'

Parroulet shook his head. 'There was mother and father and brother. I think there was not sister.'

I was about to contradict him, but he seemed quite definite.

'I think there was not sister,' he repeated. 'Yes, she has tell me this sometime. And the sister dies. But sometime she tell me different. It is her they rape. It is terrible time for her. Long ago, when she is child.'

He looked as if he expected me to say something, but I could not speak.

'When she say one thing or other thing, it is not lie,' he went on. 'It is very bad memory. You understand?'

I nodded. 'Yes.'

'So we never have child,' Parroulet said. 'What I am to do, leave her? Because she can't have baby? No, I don't leave her. She is my wife.'

He drank from his tin.

'You ask this questions that hurt. Why?'

'Because if you knew,' I began, but that wasn't right. 'Because if I could tell you. What it feels like, to be a father. And then not to be. To have that taken from you.'

'I am sorry,' Parroulet said. 'For you, I am sorry, okay? You lose your child. So I did also but in a different way. For me it is nothing, you say. You cannot lose child you never have. But it is not nothing. And for Kim too. She never lose child but it is not nothing. She lose all her children when she was child herself.'

'My child –' I wanted to say something about Alice losing everything, every chance and possibility of her life – but he spoke again.

'Do you believe in the God?'

Not another one, I thought. 'No,' I said. 'God *is* dead.'

To my surprise, he nodded vigorously. 'God, yes. Yes, he is dead. But for me not so long ago. For long time I do not think this. When I am little boy, even young man, I believe in him. He is alive then. On the island, he is very big, very strong, you understand? It is not possible in my family there to think God is dead. So when I think this things, I keep them in myself. I come here, after the trial, and I meet with Kim, and God goes away some place. Good, I like this. Then Kim can't have baby, and I think maybe he is still there, in the dark.

He is punish me. What for he is punish me? Because I tell lie? No, I don't tell lie. Because I take money? Yes, because I take money, like Judas.'

He drank some more beer, apparently marshalling his thoughts. Was this, I wondered, the prelude to a confession? Or did he really have nothing to confess? I thought of the recorder that Kim had confiscated. If only I had it, if only it were switched on and running. Yet if it were I thought Parroulet would somehow sense it and not speak at all. There was no logic behind this notion, but I could not dispel it.

'When I am young man,' Parroulet said, 'I want to get away from island. Always I want to leave. What life is it, driving taxi all your days? My father is driver, so I am driver. It is a job, that is all. You put down money to get a car, then you work to own it. You make some money but never enough, then you trade in for other car, and you work to own this new car, so your life goes. Round and round, you never can get off, like a machine, okay? And the island, it is small, you drive the same roads every day, always back to the same place. Round and round. You can't ever get off the island. I feel this but I can do nothing. This is my life.'

'There are worse lives,' I said.

'A man has his life, that is all. If there is worse or better, what does he know of that?' Parroulet stared at me, as if seeing me anew. 'You think I come to this trial without history,' he said. 'You think I am little actor on stage. I come on, I say lines, I go away. You think only you have history. Then if I say lines you don't like, you say no, those are wrong lines. Why? Because they don't fit your history. Well, I have history too. I bring it with me to the courtroom.'

'I know you did,' I said.

'No, you don't know it. You say it but you don't know it. One man don't know another man. You don't know me, I don't know you. It is impossible.'

'Is it?' At that moment, I did not think I could disagree.

'What is it you do to live, to eat?' he asked.

'I work in a university. I teach.'

'What you teach?'

'Literature. I teach English Literature.'

'Books?' Parroulet said. 'I don't know books. I know what is a mechanic. I know what is a priest, a baker, electrician. But books? How do you teach books? It is just so many words. Like noise on paper.'

I said nothing, because there seemed no point, but he repeated himself, 'Like noise on paper, is all a book is,' and so I said, 'Yes, you're right. That's a good description. And I teach how to pick out the words from the noise, how to make sense of particular words, or words used in a particular way by a particular writer. I try to teach my students about life through books. Is that so hard to understand?'

He shrugged. 'I don't know. What is this "particular"? Life is not in a book. Maybe you think life is like a book. Maybe you think a book is like life. You think this?'

I drew breath, to try to explain, but the breath was enough for him.

'We are different,' he said. 'That is all. Well, okay. One day, in *my* life, a change happen. The police come, the island police and your police, and they ask questions of many drivers. Me also. They take me away from others. They say I can help them.

'They tell me this story. Well, we all know about the bombing. It is big world story and this is what we do, taxi drivers, we read news, we hear news, we talk news. They say the bomb start from there, on the island. It is incredible. We never hear this before. But it is possible, why not? It must start from some place.

'You know they show me pictures, many pictures. Arabs, Africans, Turkish, French. The police come again and again. Look, they say, look, look, look. I look till I cannot see. They show me Khalil Khazar.

They do not say but I know it is him they want. They say, you can make justice, help us. They say, no pressure, no pressure.' He puffed dismissively. 'They say, we know what he did, so help us. Sometimes they come with other men, Americans. One time Americans come themselves. They say, if you help us we help you. What you want, Martin? You want to help us? What you want?'

He was becoming agitated, speaking more quickly although not loudly. His hand encased the cat but I think he had forgotten it was there.

'What did you want?' I said.

'Do you know what is pressure?' he said. 'You know about that? I say something, they catch it in their hand. They show it to me. This is the thing you give us, Martin, but last week it is different. Today you say it another way. So, this way or that way? Now say it again. So I try, and I learn what it is to say. Martin, you are hero, they tell me, you are the guy. I say no, I am not hero. Yes, they say, because you know this man, you identify him. But they have shown me many photographs and get me to tell story many times, so now I'm not so sure again. First I give them wrong man, then later they show me more pictures and I give them right man. How can I be sure what is right man? The man I see, or the man they want? It is one year ago. It is five years. How can you remember all this years ago? So they leave me alone for some time but then they come back. Always they are nice to me, they give me wine and meals. But I am afraid, because men have come from Khazar's country, very polite but they say don't talk to police, we will treat you very well. Whatever you like, you can have. I tell this to police, they say, don't worry, we will protect you. I say how? Protect me how? You pay me? You look after me? They say, we don't make promise like that but you will be okay. They tell me there is reward, a lot of dollar. The Americans, not the police. I say, what is it for, this money? To protect me? They tell me it is for tell truth about Khazar. It is him they want. I go to police again, I ask if I get reward if I testify. They say we can't promise nothing, but you will be okay if Khazar is guilty. So if he is not guilty, then what? He is guilty, they say, you just say what you know and he is guilty. Then I say, his friends, people from his country, they will see me and know it is me who send him to the prison. They will come after me. What they will do to me if I point at him and say, that is him? This is very big deal, yes? Maybe they will kill me. The police say, it is not you only, there are other witnesses, they cannot blame you only. And anyway we will keep you safe, give you change of name, new place to live if you want that. So I say, you want me to do this, and for what? To end my life as it is, to change for ever? We will protect you, they say. And if I do this, I say, then I get big money? This is my question. Because this is big deal they ask. Martin, we don't promise, they say, but there is a way of looking, you know, when you say a thing, that is the way they look. And I know, and they know, I won't do it otherwise. I am not mad.

'And now Khazar and the other man . . .' He stopped, searching for the name, and I supplied it. 'Yes, Waleed Mahmed, they are waiting for trial, they are in custody, it is going to happen, and it is ten years, twelve years ago, and I cannot remember all little things from then. Mahmed, I never see him, he is nothing to do with me, but Khazar – all I know, it is Khazar they want. The police say it's okay, we will help with your memory. Here, this is what you tell us before. All my statements they bring to me, but they say forget this, forget this, only remember this. It is this day, remember, it is this picture, it is this time, remember. My head is so full of everything, it is so long ago, I am confuse. So I think it is better to be safe and say, I don't know.

'But somehow they know this, what I am thinking, it is in my eyes maybe, and so they come back and this time they are not so nice. They are a little angry. Martin, they say, we have spend all this time with you, we have promise good things for you, but you must give us something back or we cannot help you. Why you are go back on your word? I say I do not go back on my word, I make no promise. They say, but you will be in court, you must say what you have tell us which is the truth, and if you tell a lie *you* will go to prison for a long time. This make me very afraid. I know they are threaten me even though soon after they are smiling again. They say, look, you are a special person because we need you so we can make sure Khazar is found guilty. He is part of a bigger thing but we cannot tell you about that. I say, what thing? They say, we cannot tell you about it. There are other men like him, he is not alone. They will make more bombs, we cannot arrest these men because we don't have proof against them but if we get Khazar the things they are planning will not happen. Khazar, he is the one of them all that must not get away.'

He was no longer speaking to me. He was speaking to himself. He sounded like a man running over in his head hours and hours of interviews, years of them, a man drowning in statements and corrections to statements, and always what had kept him surfacing must have been the promise of reward, the possibility of escape not just from the island and his life there but from the endless questions and answers, the evidence, the trial itself. If he could just get through to the end, it would all be over, and he could be somewhere else, a new and different man. *He* could get away. That had been his hope, I thought, watching his worried mouth and hearing his convoluted speech. That had been his hope and his plan, and it had failed.

There was something in his words — *the one of them all that must not get away* — that was like an echo coming right round the world at me. Something Nilsen had said.

'So,' Parroulet said, 'you know what happen. I am in court, in witness box. I can trust no one but I know one thing: if I do what police tell me I have something with them, a deal, a bargain. The other side? I have nothing, only fear. So I make up my mind. I have to stick to my story, tell it like it is. I can't go back now. There is the man,

Khazar. It is him they want. It is him I drive to the airport. It is him I see with the suitcase. It is him I see without the suitcase. This is the story. And you know, they never tell me it is only my word that send him to jail. They always say, before trial, there is other witnesses, there is other evidence. Hard evidence, they tell me. But this is not true. It is only . . . circumstantial. It is me against Khazar. They make me stand up and it is me alone.'

I remembered my conversation with Khazar in prison. His lawyers had advised him not to take the stand. You will not mean to, they'd said, but you may incriminate yourself. Leave it to the prosecution to prove that you are guilty. It is not for you or us to make their task any easier. And Khazar had told me, speaking of Parroulet, that when he heard him describing the taxi journey, when he saw him pointing, saying, 'That is the man,' he wanted to defend himself, to speak out, to declare his innocence, to say, 'This man who accuses me, I have never seen him before in my life,' but fighting against himself he heeded his lawyers' warnings and held his peace. And how deeply he regretted that, since the lawyers had failed to protect him as they had promised they would.

But then, Khazar had admitted, he could not altogether blame them. His solicitor had told him all along, 'Do not surrender yourself for trial. It is not possible for you to receive a fair trial.' He had listened, and been half-persuaded, because the solicitor was an honest and decent man. But everybody else had said he should go. The government of his country – and it was not to be argued with – had told him to go, to clear not only his own name but that of the country. He would be home in a year, they said, a hero of the nation. He did not want to be a hero, but he wanted to clear his name. So he went. It was out of his hands. It was not to do with the actions of men. Everything was in the hands of God – the God both Martin Parroulet and I thought was dead.

I looked at Parroulet, with his big hand clutching the now dozing

cat, and his thin hair cruelly illuminated by the lamplight, and I
thought of Khazar behind the bulletproof glass, quiet and dignified
and intent on the proceedings, sometimes donning headphones to
hear in Arabic what was being said – and I saw them as I had not seen
them then, as two men who did not wish to be heroes, who were not
heroes, forced unarmed into an arena against armoured giants. What
chance, really, had either of them had?

Parroulet had lapsed into silence, and in the space what Nilsen had
said came back to me. *If one got away . . . it wouldn't be . . . forgivable.*
And then, *we had motivation too. Everyone had motivation.* And I
understood, there in that half-lit room in Parroulet's supposed sanctuary, I understood – not for the first time because I'd been through
this so often before, but clearer than I'd ever seen it – the meaning of
Nilsen's words. Nilsen hadn't, of course, told me the whole truth. He
hadn't *levelled* with me. He'd hinted at it and then veered away
because even then, so close to his own death, he couldn't bring himself to admit what the real motivation was. He couldn't give me that
one thing, not straight into my hands, though it had been sitting there
between us. He'd made me come to Parroulet so that I'd know for
sure. One *had* got away. The agent in Germany, working undercover
in the terrorist cell, had helped to make bombs and one of them had
got away. It was constructed using a barometric timer and it was
taken from Germany, probably overland, and by ferry to England,
and then in its suitcase it got through the security system at Heathrow,
in fact it bypassed the security checks entirely because somebody had
a pass to the baggage-handling area, and there it was loaded on to the
flight. The bomb that killed Emily and Alice and all those people. No
wonder when Nilsen's people realised what had happened they did
everything possible to undo the narrative and reconstruct it. *If one
got away . . .* It wasn't a question of 'if'. It wasn't a question. It was a
statement, as much of one as I'd ever get from someone with knowledge, of what had happened.

I saw this, and I saw too that whatever I could or could not persuade Parroulet to do, to tell me something in confidence or to make a public statement of some sort, that deep, deep truth would never come out. It would never be verified because it was not verifiable. It was a truth that would only ever be in the domain of conspiracy theorists, where it could be entertained, derided, dismissed, but never proved. I saw this and I heard George Braithwaite warning me that I might be disappointed if I ever met the truth, and I thought, this is as close, now, here, as I will ever get.

I looked at Parroulet and for the first time I felt something for him that was not disdain or disappointment. I felt sympathy.

He spoke again. He seemed to have come back, more or less, to the present. 'So it is finish,' he said. 'Khazar is guilty. I go to police. Now protect me, I say. Now pay me. Ah, they say, but Khazar will appeal. I get very angry then. They see this. They say, don't worry, Martin, but I worry. How I can eat, how I can live? I cannot drive taxi now, it is too much public, too dangerous. To sit in a car with some man in back I don't know — after what I say in court how I can do that day after day? How I can look always in mirror to see what is going to happen? How I can look over my shoulder everywhere I go? They say, be calm, Martin, this will be soon over, you will be safe. And the Americans make plans for me. To find a country that will take me, a country where I want to go. They make papers for me. I will be other person. Everything is ready, they say. Another year pass. They give me some money so I can live but it is not enough. Why I am being punish for doing what they tell me?

'Then one day the appeal of Khazar happen. The judges reject it. It is the end for him. The next day Americans say, now, Martin, you can go. I do not believe them, but actually it is true. They give me air ticket, place to stay here when I come, in Melbourne, they give me bank account, plastic card, cheque book in name of Parr. Soon, they say, the money will be there. And one day it is. Incredible. It is only numbers on a screen but I try to take out some money and it works! I take out more. For a few days, a few months, I think at last yes, I can live again. All this money. And I meet Kim. Yes, for a year life is good.'

He had been taking occasional sips of beer while he spoke. Now he drained the tin, crushed it in his hand and dropped it. He lowered his foot to the floor and moved forward, and gently laid the cat in the deep part of the chair where he had been sitting. The animal made a small protest and tried to struggle up, but then, evidently exhausted, lay still. Parroulet stood, pausing for a moment to get his balance.

'But it is good only on surface. Underneath it is dark.' He tapped his chest. 'In here. I don't say this to her because already I think I make her unhappy enough. But everything is black for me. I cannot hide it. She ask me, what is it wrong with you? And I say it is God who punish me. She says, for what? I tell her about the trial. She says, if it is God, if you have done wrong in his eye, then ask him to forgive. If it is not God, then you punish yourself. Why?'

He sighed heavily. 'I don't know why. What is my crime, Dr Tealing? If I have done wrong, I am sorry.'

It was the first, the only, time that I had seen no calculation, no defence in his eyes. I took my chance.

'Then make amends,' I said. 'Don't ask for forgiveness from God. He's not there. Say something in public. Write it down and give it to me. You can still make the case against Khazar fall apart, even though he is dead. You can still help us get at the truth.'

He shook his head. 'Come. I show you something.'

He limped to the door, and I limped after him. We were like two soldiers in the First World War, made old in the trenches and limping back from them, one after the other. Into my mind came David Dibald, who was in that war but never wrote about it, never came back, whose fiction was all about life before it, before the loss of innocence.

Parroulet led me to the next room and switched on the main light. A kind of small study, barren in the glare of the light, was revealed. There was a desk, a cabinet, a computer, a printer, a TV. The walls were naked.

In the middle of the room Parroulet turned. 'You come here because you hate me,' he said.

'No, I don't hate you,' I said.

'Why you don't hate me? You lose everything, and it is not Khazar you hate, not when he is alive, not when he is dead. It is me you hate.'

'No,' I said. 'I hate what happened. The bomb. And I hate what you did, what you said in court. I hate the fact that they paid you to do it. When Khazar was convicted it put a massive barrier in the way of the truth. Without you that wouldn't have happened. That's what I hate, not you.'

'It is same thing,' he said. He went to the desk, opened a drawer and took something from it. A key. He closed that drawer and unlocked another. 'Look,' he said, and I approached and saw what lay in the otherwise empty drawer.

'That is how much I have fear,' he said. 'I am not hero. I have fear. All this time, I am afraid of someone come. I don't know who but one day maybe he come. They say to me, Martin, you are safe now, you never hear from us again, but how do I know this? And how they can be sure I am safe? And what does this "safe" mean? Safe for me, or for them? Maybe they don't come, but if someone else come, like you, then what? If I tell you I make mistake at trial? If you tell the world? Maybe it is better for them if they make sure. Better safe or sorry, yes?'

'Than,' I said. 'Better safe *than* sorry. Yes.'

'So I keep this here, always. But really I know, if they want to make sure, this won't stop them. So who do I keep it for? For you, for me?'

The drawer lay open. The gun in it was a threat or an invitation.

We were both beside it, so close our shirts were touching. It felt like looking over the edge of a cliff.

I thought of my own fear, my looking over my shoulder, my wondering who might come in pursuit of me. It seemed a long time since Nilsen had come, but it was only a week. And before that there had been years of it, of fear and wondering, but there was nothing there now. Nobody was coming, and even if they were I didn't care.

I reached out for the gun, but then I didn't. It was the last thing I wanted to touch.

'Not you, not me,' I said. 'Not either of us.'

Parroulet nodded. He seemed relieved, as if I'd declined some terrible offer.

'You go away tomorrow,' he said. 'Kim fix you bed, you can sleep here, but you go in morning. I don't want to see you again. I thank you for fighting fire with me. I don't thank you for coming.'

I said, 'I don't have what I came for.'

'We will see. What do you came for? The truth? You must know by now, I don't have it.'

'To say you made a mistake,' I said, 'to describe the pressure they put you under, as you have told me this evening, that would be something. That would be a start.'

'We will see,' he said again. He half-turned, as we both heard footsteps, then the faint mewl of the cat. With sudden swiftness Parroulet pushed the drawer shut and locked it, and put away the key.

'Now you go sleep,' he said. 'I stay here. I have plenty to do. Clear up. Take care of my cat.' He turned fully, and Kim was in the doorway. 'Take care of my wife,' he said, smiling at her.

Kim held the creature out to him. 'I heard her crying,' she said. 'You were not there.'

14

I sat in a wicker chair in a corner of the guest room where earlier Kim had tended my feet, and watched as she plumped pillows and turned down the sheet.

'In the morning I will take you to the hospital,' she said.

'Thank you,' I said. 'You are kind.'

'It's what I said before. It is not much to be kind.'

'Women are better at it than men.'

She gave one of the pillows an extra thump. 'That is stupid. Why do you say such a thing? Men can be kind.'

'By choice?' I said. 'Or by chance?'

She gave me a little, unamused smile. 'You always play word games. Why don't you stop being so clever?'

'You sound like my sister,' I said.

'You have a sister?'

'Yes.'

'Good. Be kind to her. Who else? A mother, a father?'

'Yes,' I said, and I felt ashamed. 'They are still alive.'

'And who else?'

'No one else.'

'I don't believe you. It is a long time since . . . everything. Don't you have anyone now? Not just to be kind to. More than that.'

I shook my head. 'It wouldn't be enough.'

She had finished with the bed. She said, 'I'm going to get you some water,' and she left the room. I felt so weary that the gap between the chair and the bed seemed like a chasm, not wide but too terrifyingly deep to cross. On the other side, above the bed, hung one of those seascapes that Parroulet had once painted obsessively but that now, according to Kim, he no longer did. This one looked like an evening view, in muted colours, mostly shades of blue. You could see the ocean and the sky, but you couldn't see clearly where they met, and if there were any boats out there you couldn't see them either. It was a painting of nothing, really, but I could have looked at it for a long time.

Kim returned with a bottle of water, which she put beside the bed. She also had the jute bag.

'Here are your things,' she said, and I knew that the recorder would be in it again. 'He is upstairs, at his desk. He is writing something, I don't know what. I thought I should tell you.'

She stood there, small and strong, with her arms folded, and yet I knew that she was not so strong, and it was as if she had been thinking, in the few minutes she had been away, exactly how to say what she now said.

'Alan Tealing,' she said, with that same curious elongation of the syllables, 'sometimes it happens, you love someone but you don't know why. Sometimes you love someone but you don't like them. Sometimes you love someone but they don't love you. It isn't enough, it is never enough, but it is still love.'

'I told you,' I said, 'I don't have anyone.'

'I'm not talking about you,' she said. 'The thing I know about love is you can't stop it, you can't kill it. Love can die, but it's nothing to do with you.'

A pause.

'And you can't make it either, in a bowl, like a recipe. But if it is there, what do you do? Throw it out? Leave it to go rotten?'

'I don't have anyone.'

'There is always someone,' she said, and she looked at me very long and hard before she went away.

She didn't know who she was talking about, but I did.

Somehow I made it across that chasm into the bed. I knew that I would sleep, and I did not expect to dream. But before I slept, thoughts passed like gulls across the grey sky of my mind.

I thought of Parroulet's gun, lying in its drawer, and the fear that kept it there. I thought of the little plastic clip in the wooden bowl on my desk at home.

I thought of Ted Nilsen, cold in the snow, in the mortuary. I thought of him not there.

I thought of Maisie Miller and her dog, and of Roger Dinning and his wife. 'Blue gums love fire,' Maisie had said. 'They grow back very fast.' Tomorrow I would see if their houses were still standing, and they would be back to see too. I thought of my own house, and my neighbours Brian and Pam. I thought of the fires, and how many people and houses they might have taken. I thought how cruel a place the world can be.

I thought of Khalil Khazar, and those words of Nilsen: *In other circumstances . . . In another life.* And that thing he'd said that would always haunt me: *were you even alive before the bomb went off?*

I thought of Emily, the little girl I had never known, the one Alfred and Rachel could never forget. I thought of Alfred and Rachel. I thought how long it was since I had kissed my wife goodnight.

I thought of Alice, the little girl she was, the woman she never became. I thought of whom she might have loved, if she had had the chance or the choice.

I thought of Carol. I would phone her from the hotel, say I was coming home. I'd tell her I'd call again from the airport, to let her know my flight. I'd ask her to meet me. I'd say how good it would be to see her. I would mean it.

I thought of the morning. I knew I could not walk back to Turner's Strand. Kim would have to give me a ride on her scooter or maybe she would have to call a taxi, if a taxi could get to us. But it was by neither of these methods that, lying there with sleep rushing in from all sides, I imagined myself leaving Sheildston. I imagined myself alone, going down the twisting road. I saw myself in my hat and borrowed clothes, with the jute bag over my shoulder with its contents, including whatever Parroulet had written. I saw myself moving through a charred and smoking wasteland, past animal corpses and the skeletons of trees, my shoes and ankles white with ash. I'd walk past the roadblocks and the fallen trunks, the wrecked cars and the road signs stripped of their painted words and symbols. I'd be returning from a war. I'd be limping home from the trenches. I'd be coming out of the fiery furnace. I'd be back from the dead, with news.

ACKNOWLEDGEMENTS

Thanks to my editor, Simon Prosser at Hamish Hamilton, to my agent, Natasha Fairweather at A. P. Watt, and to Anna Kelly, Sarah Coward, Donald Winchester, Alistair J. M. Duff, Gwen Enstam, Robert Forrester and others who have helped and advised me.

A version of the first half of this novel was written during my time as Writer in Residence at Edinburgh Napier University, and I am grateful to the University and the Binks Trust for the opportunities afforded by that post.

Biggest thanks, and all my love as ever, to Marianne.

JAMES ROBERTSON

THE TESTAMENT OF GIDEON MACK

LONGLISTED FOR THE MAN BOOKER PRIZE 2006

SHORTLISTED FOR THE SALTIRE SOCIETY SCOTTISH BOOK OF THE
YEAR AWARD 2006

For Gideon Mack, faithless minister, unfaithful husband and troubled soul, the
existence of God, let alone the Devil, is no more credible than that of ghosts or
fairies. Until the day he falls into a gorge and is rescued by someone who might
just be Satan himself.

Mack's testament – a compelling blend of memoir, legend, history and, quite
probably, madness – recounts one man's emotional crisis, disappearance,
resurrection and death. It also transports you into an utterly mesmerising
exploration of the very nature of belief.

'Fascinating, extraordinary, strange, rich' *Sunday Telegraph*

'Overwhelmingly compassionate and thought-provoking. Demands another read'
Irvine Welsh, *Guardian*

'Hugely enjoyable, very funny, deeply refreshing . . . its touch of devilry makes it
even more of a joy' *Herald*

JAMES ROBERTSON

AND THE LAND LAY STILL

And the Land Lay Still is nothing less than the story of a nation. James Robertson's breathtaking novel is a portrait of modern Scotland as seen through the eyes of natives and immigrants, journalists and politicians, drop-outs and spooks, all trying to make their way through a country in the throes of great and rapid change. It is a moving, sweeping story of family, friendship, struggle and hope – epic in every sense.

'Wonderful, brilliant, panoramic, illuminating. A joy to read' **Irvine Welsh**, *Guardian*

'Toweringly ambitious, virtually flawlessly realized, a masterpiece and, without a doubt, my book of the year' *Daily Mail*

'Powerful and moving. A brilliant and multifaceted saga of Scottish life in the second half of the twentieth century' *Sunday Times*

'A jam-packed, dizzying piece of fiction' *Scotland on Sunday*

JAMES ROBERTSON

365: STORIES

At the beginning of 2013, James Robertson set himself the task of creating a new short story every day of the year, the only restriction being that each one must be exactly 365 words long. Throughout this year, 2014, the stories are being published daily online, and in November 2014 they will be gathered together and published in one volume for the first time. Some draw on elements of ancient myth and legend, others are outtakes from Scottish history and folklore; there are squibs and satires on contemporary issues and insanities, songs and ballads in disguise, fairytales, stories inspired by dreams or in the form of interviews, and personal memories and observations shaped into narratives that have universal resonances.

Underpinning all of them are insistent and vital questions: who are we? What are we doing here? What happens next? And, again and again, Robertson interrogates the matter of what a story is, and why stories are crucial to humans both as individuals and as members of families and wider communities.

AVAILABLE IN PAPERBACK FROM NOVEMBER 2014

**TO READ TODAY'S STORY AND TO VIEW THE ARCHIVE, GO TO
WWW.FIVEDIALS.COM/365**

He just wanted a decent book to read ...

Not too much to ask, is it? It was in 1935 when Allen Lane, Managing Director of Bodley Head Publishers, stood on a platform at Exeter railway station looking for something good to read on his journey back to London. His choice was limited to popular magazines and poor-quality paperbacks – the same choice faced every day by the vast majority of readers, few of whom could afford hardbacks. Lane's disappointment and subsequent anger at the range of books generally available led him to found a company – and change the world.

'We believed in the existence in this country of a vast reading public for intelligent books at a low price, and staked everything on it'
Sir Allen Lane, 1902–1970, founder of Penguin Books

The quality paperback had arrived – and not just in bookshops. Lane was adamant that his Penguins should appear in chain stores and tobacconists, and should cost no more than a packet of cigarettes.

Reading habits (and cigarette prices) have changed since 1935, but Penguin still believes in publishing the best books for everybody to enjoy. We still believe that good design costs no more than bad design, and we still believe that quality books published passionately and responsibly make the world a better place.

So wherever you see the little bird – whether it's on a piece of prize-winning literary fiction or a celebrity autobiography, political tour de force or historical masterpiece, a serial-killer thriller, reference book, world classic or a piece of pure escapism – you can bet that it represents the very best that the genre has to offer.

Whatever you like to read – trust Penguin.